Get first-hand ne

updates about new releases and

and an exclusive **FREE eBook Box Set**

when you

JOIN MY VIP READER CLUB.

See back of book for details >>

ABOUT THE BOOK

"The Sappho Romance" is a standalone Alternative History spinoff novel written by me, Jacquie Lyon (Jac), of "Sealed with a Kiss" fame. "Sealed with a Kiss" is a novel by Sam Skyborne in the **Lesvos Island Collection**.

This novel has a companion text: a new, fictionalised, English translation of the controversial 1894 French publication in Paris by Pierre Louÿs of "The Songs of Bilitis". This translation includes subtle, new interpretations of some of the original poems—given the new interpretation I have revealed in here.

You can download a copy of "The Songs of Bilitis" for FREE here: (http://SamSkyborne.com/SOB/)

Lastly, for your reading convenience, at the end of this book, you will find a glossary of relevant terms and brief explanations about who's who and what's what among the mortals, gods and places featured in the story.

SYNOPSIS

The best-kept secret of antiquity—the veil has finally been lifted on the legend of Sappho and her true love, Phaon. A vivid tale of rivalry, passion, power, loss and love.

It all started on an 'unsinkable' ship, caught in the eye of a raging storm. Here, politics and passion collided and by an act of the Gods, a young slave girl is spared and given another chance at life—a life beyond even her wildest imaginings.

They said a slave could not surpass her master…

They said a wife is the property of her husband…

They said women had no place in a 'man's world'…

Three courageous women choose to break the rules… to follow their hearts, leaving a trail of mystery, myth and legend so bizarre that it has taken almost 3000 years to uncover.

THE SAPPHO ROMANCE

JACQUIE LYON & SAM SKYBORNE

DUKEBOX.LIFE

Published by DukeBox.life.
http://DukeBox.life.

To my dearest Dorothy.
Thank you for your legacy. Even in death you shall be my guide.

And to all of you who have had a Dorothy in their lives. Count yourselves blessed.

- Jacquie Lyon

PREFACE BY JACQUIE LYON

I have not written this story as a philologist or a classical scholar, simply as an author with an interest both in storytelling and in Sappho, as well as in the countless stories she has inspired. So, I would like to emphasise that I do not profess to be presenting or arguing any issues of fact, not least because there is unfortunately so little that is truly known about Sappho, her life, her peers and her society.

Instead, this novel follows the model of "The Alexander Romance" and "The Aesop Romance".[1] These are both fictional biographies about those two well-known historic characters, of whom as little is known and, in their telling, any existing facts have been used, manipulated and retold with a view to entertain and enthral.

In order to meet that end most effectively, I feel that the modern reader might possibly benefit from a little background information on the historical and political context of the times and the characters that inhabit this tale.

The story takes place a little before 600 BCE in Greece, mostly on the island of Lesvos, which is located in the north-eastern Aegean, off the west coast of Anatolia (Turkey today). Although Lesvos is the third-largest Greek island, the Strait of Mytilene that separates it from Turkey is only five and a half kilometres wide at its narrowest point. As a result, in those days, culturally the island was closer to Anatolia than the Mycenaean civilisation on mainland Greece. This meant that, among other things, on account of the Phoenician influence, and unlike elsewhere in Greece, society in Lesvos had a more liberal approach to women, affording them more freedom and leeway than almost anywhere else in the known world, with perhaps the exception of Sparta.

The island flourished largely thanks to its production and export of olives, olive oil, and wine. It was prosperous enough to be able to support a naval force which allowed it control over areas in Anatolia to the east and Thrace in the north.

Sappho was a famous poet, born on the island. She is widely regarded as one of the greatest lyric poets and she was given names such as the "Tenth Muse" or the "Mortal Muse". Not much is known definitively about her and her life on Lesvos, only what can be gleaned from the few fragments of her poetry that survive today and those few accounts by later writers who wrote about her or quoted her work.

It is believed she was from a wealthy aristocratic family and had three brothers, two of whom she mentioned in her poetry.

She was a contemporary of another well-known poet and orator, Alcaeus of Mytilene, who was the youngest brother of a warrior called Antimenidas.

Leading up to Sappho's time, the Penthelid dynasty had dominated the island as tyrants. In around 630 BCE they were ousted by a group of disgruntled aristocrats. However, this was not a swift transition. For years to follow, some of the cities continued to suffer from rivalries between the tyrants and the aristocratic clans.

It was during these clan feuds that Pittacus and Antimenidas would have fought side by side, until Pittacus eventually betrayed Antimenidas and joined the opposition—a fact for which Antimenidas could never forgive his friend and mentor. Not long afterwards, Pittacus went on to become the first elected aisymnētēs, (an official with essentially unlimited power, not unlike a tyrant) of Mytilene and was later heralded as one of the seven sages of ancient Greece for his work in restoring harmony to the region as well as his reputation for sage-like rhetoric and insights. During his reign, as Solon did in Athens, Pittacus was responsible for instigating a new legal code in

Mytilene, since he was of the belief that strong laws were the best protection a city could have.

Around the turn of the century Sappho was exiled with Alcaeus to Sicily on account of their participation in the feuds.

There has been much speculation about Sappho's personal life. Many stories describe Alcaeus as being one of Sappho's lovers. Other accounts speak of Alcaeus having numerous young male lovers, of which young Melanippus was one.

It has also been suggested that Sappho might have been married to a wealthy man named Kerkylas of Andros and had many children by him. There is an ongoing debate about whether the young girl mentioned in her poetry, called Kleïs, was her daughter or a slave girl of whom she was particularly fond.

This brings us to undoubtedly the most controversial topic surrounding Sappho: her sexuality and her liaisons with women. Some suggest that she must have been a teacher, or that she ran an academy for young girls to school them in the art of song, music and pleasing their husbands. Others contend that her poetry bears witness to far more significant emotional and physical relationships with women. As a result of this, the words 'sapphic' and 'lesbian' have come to be associated with female homosexuality.

However, it is important to note that those words did not have any such connotations at the time. We do know that the attitude towards gender and sexuality was quite different in those times. Despite the moderating influence from nearby Anatolia, on Lesvos, women and slaves were not even second-class citizens. Men who were citizens were all that really counted. Women were property. What women did for pleasure was inconsequential so long as it did not interfere with their husband's right to their property (of which their women were part). Men would not have felt threatened by their wives having other female lovers. In fact, some scholars argue that intimacy and companionship between women were encouraged, so that they would not stray into the hands of other men.

Bilitis was another lesser known poet who came to Lesvos from

Pamphylia—today southern Turkey. Very little is known about her too, other than what can be gleaned from a translated manuscript that was published in Paris towards the end of the 19th century called *The Songs of Bilitis*. This is a collection in four parts of her poetry, allegedly found in her tomb and translated into French. In her poems she talks about her liaison with Sappho, and as a result, the transcription manuscript was initially deemed to be certain proof of Sappho's lesbianism. To date, neither the location of Bilitis's tomb, nor the authenticity of the translated poems, has been verified.

Phaon was a renowned ferryman in Mytilene who carried people across the Strait from Mytilene to Anatolia. He features in a number of pivotal—if not only for the purposes of this story—ancient myths and legends:

> "There was amazement among the Lesbians about Phaon's way of life. Aphrodite wanted to thank him so she put on the appearance of an old woman and asked old Phaon about crossing the strait. He carried her across and asked nothing in return. What did the goddess do then? She transformed him from an old man—repaid him with youth and beauty. This is the Phaon Sappho loved and celebrated in song."[2] - Xanthias 605 BCE

> "Many people say Sappho fell in love with Phaon—not Sappho the poet but some other Lesbian woman—and when she did not get him, she threw herself off the cliffs of Lefkas." - Photios *Lexicon*

> "The temple of Apollo on the 'White Rock' at Lefkas is believed to be the site to put an end to desire, 'where Sappho, in pursuing a young ferryman named Phaon to Sicily, was so stung by being spurned that she threw herself from the cliffs'." - Strabo in Geography quoting Menander Fragment 258

Lastly, I would like to draw the reader's attention to the easy-read reference Notes, Glossary and Cast List of characters at the back of the novel. I have deliberately limited the notes to only those I thought essential to avoid misunderstanding or confusion, and references to the specific fragments of Sappho's poetry, as classified by Loeb, and to *The Songs of Bilitis*, all of which I have drawn into this narrative. As mentioned at the start, this book is not intended to be an academic work, but a work of fiction, so the Notes and Glossary have been included for your pleasure and convenience, should they be of interest, not as specific citations.

Jacquie Lyon

Skala Eressos 2019

LAST EPITAPH

It is here beneath the dark leaves of the laurel trees and the amorous blooms of the roses that I will lie forever. I, who could weave words into song and cause kisses to bloom.

I came of age in the land of the nymphs; I lived on the island of lovers; I died on the island of Kyprus. That is why my name is distinguished, and my tombstone well-polished with oil.

Do not weep for me, you who have tarried here: my funeral was well celebrated—the mourners scratched their cheeks as they should; my mirrors and necklaces were placed in my tomb.

And now, a ghostly shadow, I walk in pale fields of white asphodels and memories of my earthly existence bring me joy in my underworld life.

- Bilitis

PROLOGUE

People leave home for many reasons. Helen of Troy did it for love. Agamemnon did it out of loyalty to avenge his brother, Menelaus, Helen's husband's honour. Some people, like Paris, never did.

I ran from a broken heart.

I guess my life, and the lives of a few notable others, could have turned out quite differently had I not left my home, my family and my child in Pamphylia, at the age of sixteen. In fact, at the time I thought my life was over—and it very nearly was.

Instead, I swore I would never love again—a promise to myself I managed to keep for many, many moons.

My uncle was a wealthy Phoenician merchant. When I was little and he came to see us on one of his sporadic visits, he enthralled me with tales of wonder about far-flung lands. So, when he happened to be passing by in my time of need, I stowed away on his ship.

I stayed hidden for as long as I could before revealing myself to him, out of fear he would be angry and return me home. As it happened, he was a mild-mannered man and responded initially more with indifference than irritation. However, ships, in those days, were not suitable places for women. Although I kept to myself, unfortunately my mere presence seemed to cause disruption amongst his men.

So instead of seeing the world, as was my plan, my uncle dropped me off at his first port of call, Mytilene. He had a villa there and no wife or children, and he decided it would be more suitable to make that my home.

That's how I started my new life in Mytilene.

I never did find out what my mother thought about me leaving, since I didn't see her again, nor my child.

Mytilene was a big place with a lively port and I consoled my restless spirit by watching the ships come and go and soaking up the tales of the seamen's adventures.

From the beginning, I was very independent, since I didn't have a husband and my uncle was away a lot. I was able to come and go as I pleased. Some would say I lived a man's life—a very rare privilege— and I suppose they would be right.

I tended to keep to myself, mostly. At the time there was a growing undercurrent of tension because I was the niece of a Phoenician merchant and new in town, people naturally kept their distance. That suited me fine. After what I had just been through in my home town, I was not looking to form long-standing connections.

It is true however that during that time I did have many lovers, but not many loves.

This is the story of one of those loves.

The events of this tale inspire all the extremes of emotions, from great joy and ecstasy to great sorrow and shame on my part. However, despite my personal feelings, this story needs to be told. The parties concerned deserve their memory to be honoured and the truth should be known.

Until now, I have been paralysed into silence by my guilt and sadness for the lives affected by my five times eight years on life's journey. It is only now, in hindsight, through the omniscience bestowed on the dead that I finally know there is no merit or salvation in blame or retribution and therefore I am able to tell the whole story.

A life, a personal history is what it is—a journey—in which one can only ever approach each challenge, each love and each adventure with the tools, knowledge and maturity one has developed in that time. It is important to realise that no matter what life has taught you so far, you will almost never be entirely equal to what is thrown at you next.

I know I was not.

However, I ask you, dear reader, to withhold your judgement until you know the full story.

PART I

1

The whole town was buzzing with nerves and excitement. It was to be the festival of Kallisteia, a celebration of the island of Lesvos's federation under Mytilene, held in the Temple of Messon. As was tradition, part of the main festivities included the largest beauty pageant in all of Greece, to which crowds flocked from near and far. However, the highlight for me and undoubtedly countless others, was to be the performance by the much-loved poet, performer and teacher, Sappho and her female choir.

I had personally met Sappho[1], if you can call one night of intimacy that, shortly after I arrived in Mytilene. At the very least it was one memorable night for me, not that I had the least idea who I had the privilege of being in bed with at the time. But it was thanks to the Lady Sappho that I first came to sample the magnificent sensual fruits of women—a particular initiation that I suspect she might have lived to regret.

Unfortunately, my morning errand, feeding a new litter of starving kittens that I stumbled across on my walk along the coastline a few days before, had taken longer than I'd anticipated. So, I arrived late, barely in time to catch the last of Sappho's solo recitals.

He seems to me equal to gods that man
whoever he is who opposite you
sits and listens close
to your sweet speaking...[2]

Although Sappho was performing on the raised amphitheatre in the southeast corner of the temple and was addressing a large audience, I could see her attention was trained on someone in a small group sitting to the front and to the right of the stage.

...and lovely laughing—oh it
puts the heart in my chest on wings
for when I look at you, even a moment, no speaking
is left in me...

I stood up on tiptoes to see who could be the focus of the full, intensely passionate attention for which she was so well known both as a performer and privately, to those who had the good fortune of getting to know her more intimately.

...no: tongue breaks and thin
fire is racing under skin
and in eyes no sight and drumming
Fills ears
and cold sweat holds me and shaking
Grips me all, greener than grass
I am, and dead—or almost
I seem to me,
but all is to be dared
for only this, our love is real—

"Enough, enough," a gruff voice cut across her melodic refrain. "More wine!"

The rude disturbance came from the area towards which Sappho had been directing her impassioned recital. I scanned the sea of faces and at once I recognised the grisly features and portly physique of one of the most influential business men in the town—the long-time mariner, known to all as Old Phaon the ferryman. He was drunkenly holding court in the middle of the throng. I only knew him slightly because he a business associate of my uncle.

I took the opportunity offered by the break in the performance to gently push past the wall of men standing in front of me. I recognised one of them as Antimenidas, the war veteran and older brother of another rising star orator and lyric poet, Alcaeus. He caught my eye because of how awkward and out of place he looked. I could empathise. I hid it well, but crowds never pleased me, perhaps because I didn't have many friends and preferred to keep my own council. I wondered what a hardened soldier would be doing at such a thespian event.

As if on cue, I heard Alcaeus's beautifully modulated voice coming from the front row where he was sitting amidst a large crowd of doting friends and fans.

"A performance more typical of a divinity, as holy and pure from a honey-smiling Sappho," he said, loud enough for everyone to hear.[3] He stood up and started applauding. The crowd joined in, forming a large standing ovation to Sappho.

I heard a number of audience members near me tittering conspiratorially amongst themselves. They seemed overly delighted to be witnessing what they thought of as evidence supporting the long-standing rumours that the two poets were also secretly passionate lovers.

Trust Alcaeus, with his effeminate flamboyance, to milk the moment, I thought. I was sure that the two poet-performers knew exactly what they were doing—playing to the audience, ever aware that any signs of chemistry between the two friends was an immense crowd pleaser. The only reason they seemed to get away with their ostentatious flirting, and Alcaeus was not accused of blatantly mocking and cuckolding Kerkylas of Andros, Sappho's dry but influential husband, was because Alcaeus was so obviously more interested in buff young men than any woman.

Sappho took a deep, gracious bow, and made her way off the stage.

Below the stage, Alcaeus stood with open arms to welcome her. When she got to him, she leaned in and accepted his embrace and congratulations. Then she laughed and gently pushed him aside.

"My dear Alcaeus, what exalted compliments you give. You flatter me. Thank you. But perhaps you should find yourself a nice young boy to entertain you." She then looked around and frowned with affection. "Oh, I forget. You already have a few. Where is that lovely young Melanippus anyway?"

The gaggle of young men around Alcaeus giggled with exuberant mirth.

Sappho dropped herself into the empty seat next to a young, slight, strawberry blond girl. "Besides, I have a fair daughter, with a form like a golden flower, Kleïs my beloved, dearer than all of Lydia, to tend to me."[4] Sappho reached over and caressed the slave-girl's jawline. The young girl basked in the momentary show of affection. However, I noticed her face drop when, almost immediately, Sappho's attention was diverted to a nearby effusive group of admirers.

Even then, in the middle of the shower of praise from her fans, Sappho seemed distracted. She kept glancing down to the area near Old Phaon which she had been focussed on during her performance. I watched curiously and at the first lull in the conversation, Sappho politely excused herself and headed for the exit of the temple. On her way out she paused and glanced back.

A few heartbeats later I noticed a young, tall, dark haired slave-girl get up and say something to the drunken Old Phaon. He grunted and waved her off irritably. She turned and made her way towards the same exit.

Sappho slipped out from behind a column where she had been waiting. She wrapped her arms around Anactoria's tall, lean, boy-like frame, spun her round and playfully pinned her against the cool marble column.

"Stand and face me my beloved, and unveil the grace in thine eyes,"[5] Sappho recited, smiling, seeking out the deep, dark eyes she adored so much. She reached up and gently stroked a dark lock of the taller woman's hair. Then she kissed her deeply, until they were both breathless.

Anactoria used the strength of her taller frame to swing Sappho around until she was now the one pinned against the pillar. The taller woman leant in and began to kiss the soft almond skin on Sappho's neck, biting gently at her flesh, causing goose bumps to break out over Sappho's entire body.

Then, sure that Sappho was happy to remain trapped between her body and the pillar, she slowly slid one hand from Sappho's knee, up her thigh, sending shivers up Sappho's spine, eventually seeking out the edge of her undergarment.

"Oh yes! Aphrodite, have mercy!" Sappho gasped and pulled Anactoria closer. "I need you so much! I want to feel you inside me, now."

Anactoria didn't wait to be asked again. She slipped her long, cool fingers past the cloth until she found Sappho's hot, moist delta.

"Someone got themselves a little excited on stage," Anactoria teased as she plunged one, then two, then three fingers inside Sappho's warm, wet centre.

"Yes!" Sappho gasped pushing down and meeting every thrust with gusto. "Yes, take me!" She dug her fingers into Anactoria's muscular shoulders, biting into the soft flesh to stifle the roar of pleasure as it rose and eventually erupted from her centre.

Breathless and weak, Sappho rested her head on Anactoria's chest.

Anactoria held her tightly, supporting her weight, until Sappho finally regained her strength and could stand again.

Anactoria gently lifted her lover's head towards her and planted several soft kisses on her face.

"I can't wait for the day that you can be completely mine, and only mine!" Sappho said with a slightly groggy, lazy voice.

Anactoria stiffened and gently but firmly straightened up and turned away from Sappho.

The sudden change in mood disturbed Sappho. "What?"

"We've been through this. You know that isn't possible. Old Phaon will never sell me."

Sappho reached for Anactoria's hand, feeling their physical separation like an arctic chill.

"I don't believe in anything being impossible. You know I'm working on it. I have to believe, by the will of Aphrodite, we will make this happen. She would never let a pure love such as ours lie fallow."

Anactoria shook her head. "You have already tried to negotiate with Phaon for me and he has turned you down. He won't budge. I know it."

"That man seems to himself a god."[6] Sappho said in irritation. "But I will try again." She set her jaw. "That is what I wanted to tell you. I've already got Kerkylas to agree to a much higher bid—an offer Old Phaon can't refuse."

Anactoria shook her head ruefully. "I know Phaon. He'll never relent, and the more you show him how interested you are the more he will take pleasure in denying you. Believe me." There was a hardness to Anactoria's voice that bore evidence to bitter personal experience.

"I don't understand why he is so attached to you? Well, I mean, I do because I would never let you go if I was given the choice either." Sappho shook her head. "But he does not feel about you like I do."

Anactoria studied the column above Sappho's head and shrugged.

"I'm determined! I'm about to offer him almost the equivalent of half a pound of silver. I'm sure that will change his mind."

Anactoria's eyes widened. "With that you could buy a galley of slaves."

Sappho nodded, looking pleased.

Suddenly remembering the time, Anactoria glanced over at the temple "I must go back, before Phaon's good humour turns sour."

Sappho reached out and grabbed her hand again. "Please stay, just a little longer."

Anactoria shook her head. "I can't."

"Okay, well, then at least come see me tomorrow evening." Sappho stepped forward and pulled Anactoria's head down and rested her forehead on hers. "I need to feel you," she whispered. "I need to hold you and I need to ignite your pleasure, like my life depended on it, as you have just done to me."

Anactoria pulled away. "I'll see what I can do," she said as she gave an almost imperceptible nod.

Sappho's soft, full features morphed into a broad smile. "Great. Come for dinner.… I want to feast on you."

Anactoria's smile broadened. She leaned back in and kissed Sappho one last time. Then she turned and was gone.

Sappho rested back against the pillar. She took a deep breath, straightened her chiton, and tidied her long brown hair into a bun on her head with a mother-of-pearl hairpin. Then she straightened up and with a determined step headed back into the temple.

Sappho headed straight for where Old Phaon sat slouched, the rounded backrest of his klismos cutting into his fleshy ribs and the curved legs adding to the illusion of strain on the chair. He had his eyes closed and was drunkenly waving a mastos around, while his fat fingers absentmindedly assaulted the delicate female form on the cup to the rhythm of the interval music.

"Phaon of Mytilene, I have a proposition for you," Sappho said in a business-like tone as she stood before him.

He opened his tiny bloodshot eyes a little wider and peered at her. "Ugh," he grunted.

"I, and my husband, would like to make you an offer I think you'd agree would be foolish to refuse."

"What kind of offer?" he drawled.

"Twenty minae for one of your slaves," Sappho said and raised her chin in determination.

He nodded his head and held up his mastos. "That is indeed a very good offer." He prodded a skinny, mousey looking slave girl on the floor in front of him. "You can have Bina here. I was looking to sell her anyway as she is a little too timid for my liking."

"No, Phaon. It's not this one I want."

He peered at her, his beady eyes reduced to small slits. "Oh, you had a particular slave in mind?"

Sappho cleared her throat. "I... my husband and I... want that one," she pointed casually at Anactoria. "She would fit our purpose best."

"Her?" he asked evenly.

Sappho nodded.

"Hmm," he grunted. He looked Anactoria up and down as if considering the prospect. "You want Ana?"

Sappho held her breath as she nodded a small but resolute nod.

"Hmm," he said. "And you are offering me twenty minae for her?"

Sappho nodded again. "That is our final offer."

He took a deep breath and contorted his lips into a downward arc as if tasting something sour. "Well, that is a good offer." Then he lifted his mastos and wafted it dismissively. "But she is not for sale."

"Why?" she said, sounding a little too desperate. Then she caught herself and adopted a more casual air. "Come now Phaon, surely everything is for sale these days for the right price."

"If you want her..." he said slowly as if the words were treacle on his tongue.

Sappho visibly leaned forward to hear what he was about to say.

"Then you can hire her for the night for three minae."

Sappho scoffed. "What? Hire her for three minae? That is ridiculous!"

Phaon nodded sagely, looking a bit like Silenus, the fat, thick lipped and squat nosed companion to the wine-god Dionysus. "If you want her, that is my offer."

"But, good Phaon," Sappho tried a different tack, "you have so many lovely slaves. Surely, you can part with this one?"

"Do you insult my intelligence?" He burst into a loud roar so abruptly that Sappho had to take a step backwards. "I'm an astute businessman." Then he regained his composure. "Why would I part with such a prize possession?" He reached over and with his fleshy fingers cupped Anactoria's chin. "Especially one so multi-talented and who performs phallilingus so well." He stuck his grubby thumb into her mouth, nodding at her to suck. She obeyed. "And one who has such a high pain threshold." He pinched her cheek almost to the point of drawing blood.

Sappho had to dig her nails into her palms to stop herself from lashing out.

Finally, he turned his attention back to Sappho and waved his hand dismissing her. "If you have any other business deals to discuss, perhaps ask your husband to approach me—man to man. I won't have a woman meddle with me in business." He turned and addressed no-one in particular. "What is this island coming to? Women getting ahead of themselves, thinking they can participate in business and other mannish pursuits. It is unheard of anywhere else."

"But—" Sappho tried to speak.

"Don't you speak to me like that! I know your type...."[7] He spat in her direction.

"My type?" Sappho said aghast.

"Yes," he said, his bulbous nose twitching, "mannish women, who think you are a match for men."

Sappho's jaw dropped.

"The worst thing I could've done is send Ana to you for tutelage. You might have taught her well in the art of pleasuring men..." he smirked. "But you also infected her with your wayward ideas that women could be compared to men." Again, his mouth pulled into a tight sneer. "I will have none of it!" He spat again—a thick globule of spittle landed on the floor in front of Sappho. "Now be gone." He closed his little eyes and started to sway to the harp music emanating from the stage where two young girls were performing a doleful duet.

———

I am not sure exactly what drove me to get involved at the time.

Perhaps it was just a natural curiosity about Sappho and her dealings—a misguided fascination with the rich and famous.

Perhaps I felt an uncomfortable sense of recognition, of identification on seeing him sitting on his own at his empty table fondling his mastos—a lonely rock in the sea of joshing, laughing groups of people. There was a man, like Antimenidas, like me—a loner—though each of us solitary for possibly different reasons. In Old Phaon's case, although he was one of the most powerful and influential business men on Mytilene, I suspected too much power had corrupted too much.

Regardless of the cause, I found myself heading over to his table. "Hello, Old Phaon."

He looked up. His thick neck, bulbous nose and small eyes giving him the overwhelming resemblance of an overstuffed, fat, ferret. When he recognised me, surprise registered in his tiny pellet pupils and a leery grin contorted his features.

"Oh, my dear, Bilitis, how nice to see you. Sit! Sit! Sit!"

I smiled and took the offered seat. "Are you having a good festival?" I asked.

"Splendid, splendid."

I tried to not recoil at the flying drops of spittle that exploded from his thick lips.

"I saw you had a visit from Lady Sappho," I asked, deciding that he was drunk enough not to warrant excessive subtlety.

He shook his head. "Yes, yes." He pouted and puffed dismissively. "Women trying to meddle in a man's business."

I raised my eyebrows, but he did not seem to see the irony in saying that to me.

I tried to sound as disinterested as possible. "What did she want?"

"To buy one of my slaves." He huffed at the prospect.

"And, are you going to sell?"

"No," he shook his head in an uncoordinated oval, "I will not."

Then he seemed to notice me again. "But, enough about that. Tell me about you. You seem to have gone from love to love, but have never found forgetfulness or peace[8]." He took a large swig of his drink.

It occurred to me that perhaps it was that same quest that drove him to delve so deeply into the bottom of countless kraters of wine.

"Whatever happened to that pretty little thing you often had on your arm? I quite liked her myself." He swirled the air between us with a fat finger as he tried to remember. "What was her name?"

The thought of him with the delicate little flower that is Mnasidika made my stomach turn.[9] My heart creased behind my ribs every time I thought of her. To the world at large, she was nothing more than my little plaything. It was only I who knew my pain.

"One must move forward," I said.

He didn't seem to notice that I hadn't answered his question.

"Does that mean you are looking for a bit of new action?" He tried to wink at me suggestively, but it turned out more of a deliberate, uncoordinated blink.

I laughed politely. "That is a most generous offer. Sadly, you are not my type. But thank you."

"Ah yes, of course. You only have an eye for the ladies."

I smiled. "I do."

He turned stiffly in his seat to scan the crowds around him. Then, a thought struck him. "Well, then I have just the balm for you."

He beckoned to someone. "Here, how about I let you have Ana for the night. Nothing like a bit of new flesh to get over a corpse." He blinked and with his free, sweaty paw patted my arm.

I tried not to recoil.

The moment she got up I recognised her. It was the slave girl I saw follow Sappho out of the temple earlier.

"This is Ana. My prize, my beauty." He gazed up at her with a look as close to adoration as I had ever seen on a man.

A tight smile formed on her lips, then she dropped her gaze respectfully.

At this close distance I noticed how utterly gorgeous she was— how unusual, in that she looked neither feminine nor manly. She was a perfect blend. I looked her up and down. No wonder Sappho was trying to get her hands on her.

"Ana is no ordinary specimen," he said, spraying his spittle across the table once more. "She is a young slave born in Sardis.[10] She has not her equal in the world, for she *is* both man and woman," he grabbed one of her not too small breasts and squeezed it roughly, "although her breast and long hair and clear voice are most deceptive." He seemed to be momentarily distracted by the feel of her flesh in his hand. "She has known no one here excepting Sappho, who is… madly in love with her and who just offered me twenty minae." He repeated the information, in that way that drunks forget they have just told you the same thing.

"How much do you want for her?"

"For you, as the pretty niece of my esteemed colleague…" he turned and tried to focus on me, "you can have her for one minae for the night." Then he thought better of it. One of his fat, sweaty paws found their way onto my thigh and he smiled, forfeiting the little space occupied by his tiny eyes. "Or maybe you can have her… *on me* for the night." He guffawed at his own joke, displaying more of his wine stained molars as he tugged at my inner thigh.

I swallowed down the bit of bile that rose in the back of my throat.

I glanced over at the young slave again. I had to admit she really was very striking. There was something very captivating about her androgynous looks and, surprisingly for a slave, confident demeanour. Maybe she *was* just what I needed to get over Mnasidika. I couldn't deny that I also felt a little, not too insignificant thrill at the idea of having for a bed partner someone who was so coveted by Sappho herself.

My silence seemed to speak for me.

"Great, that's settled," he said and slapped my leg.

"Come, drink with me. I'm celebrating!" he announced.

"Oh, what's the occasion?" I asked.

"In less than a moon, my new ship sets sail to Anatolia," he announced.

I had heard stories of a brand-new fleet of ships that Old Phaon and a few leading merchants had commissioned. They were allegedly better than any that had come before and cost a fortune—a fortune my uncle was not willing to invest yet. He would rather wait and see if they proved as effective as promised before buying in.

"I shall have to come and see it," I said.

"Yes, and Phaon the Great has…" At that moment he spotted an empty wine kylix on the table in front of me, perhaps left there by his previous guest or perhaps placed there in hope of attracting company. Before I could stop him, he took aim and slopped half of the contents of his own mastos vaguely in the direction of the shallow wine cup, missing completely but thankfully not noticing in his zest to toast his own good fortune.

He held up his mastos.

I raised the empty kylix. "To Old Phaon the Great."

"I've been commissioned by none other than our esteemed aisymnētēs to take, shall we say, precious cargo to Anatolia." He winked. He then theatrically raised his finger to his squishy lips. "Ssh!" More spit flew in my direction. "It's all very secret." He started to lift his mastos to his lips again, but finding it empty he looked a little confused. Then as if struck by a memory he turned to me again. "I've been meaning to speak to your uncle about hiring some of his men. I need more hands on deck." He frowned slightly, "I seem to have lost a few overboard over the years."

"I'll tell him to call on you as soon as he's back."

He nodded and that seemed to conclude business. He returned his attention to tracking down a wine seller in the crowds around him.

Having over satisfied my initial curiosity to a level bordering revulsion, I grabbed the opportunity to excuse myself. After suffering another sweaty paw press, I got up and left, with Old Phaon's androgynous slave following at my elbow.

Alcaeus had been thoroughly enjoying the festivities at the Kallisteia. He was in his element, surrounded by talented, artistic performers, musicians and poets like Sappho, and others who truly appreciate that sort of thing, like Tyrrhaeus, Melanippus and his circle of friends.

Other, less appreciative mortals, like Sappho's Kerkylas and Alcaeus's brothers, didn't have much time for the arts and tended to skip these sorts of occasions if they could.

That was why he was so surprised when he felt a tap on his shoulder and turned to find his middle brother, Cicis, standing behind him. Where Cicis was, there certainly their oldest brother, Antimenidas, would be too.

Cicis was born slower than other boys and as a result was bullied a lot. Even though he was older than Alcaeus, Alcaeus and Antimenidas had to look after him. After their mother died, Antimenidas had taken that responsibility far more seriously, and since then, he hardly ever let Cicis out of his sight, dragging him around everywhere he went. This often involved Cicis in the faction-fighting between them, and first Myrsilus, and now Pittacus—situations which, in Alcaeus's view, were no place for his vulnerable brother, but Antimenidas wouldn't listen to reason.

Alcaeus excused himself from his group of friends and followed Cicis, scanning the crowds for his oldest brother's bulky frame. Finally, he saw him skulking to one side of the temple, looking decidedly out of place. He wondered what could possibly have brought Antimenidas here.

"Good to see you're brushing up on the arts," Alcaeus said.

"I'm not here for that!" Antimenidas replied gruffly.

"Now, why does that not surprise me?"

"I came to gather information."

"Of course, you did." Alcaeus nodded. "What information could you possibly get from a beauty pageant in a temple?" He tried not to laugh.

Antimenidas's reproachful stare evaporated his mirth.

"Wine is a peep-hole on a man."[11] Antimenidas said scanning the crowds around them.

Alcaeus rolled his eyes at his brother quoting him. "So, is there a reason you dragged me away from having a good time and talking with my friends?"

"Do you think I would waste our time if it was not important?" Antimenidas scowled. "Cicis and I just overheard a conversation about some precious cargo being taken to Anatolia."

"Oh?" Alcaeus still did not see how this could be so important.

"*Cargo* precious to our aisymnētēs." Antimenidas paused waiting for the information to register with his brother. "This could be the opportunity we've been looking for."

"You think Pittacus is going to Lydia?" Alcaeus asked frowning. "That seems a bit unlikely and even if so that boat will then be so well guarded, you wouldn't even be able to break wind in a storm without getting arrested."

"I think it's even better than that."

Alcaeus rarely saw Antimenidas smile. It was an incongruous and unsettling sight due to the large pale scar that ran across his cheek—a war injury—that severed the nerves on one side of his face.

Alcaeus frowned. "What?"

"What is more important to Pittacus than his own life?"

Alcaeus hated it when his brother tried to use oration tactics on him. If only his brother would accept that he was the brawn, and leave the brain work to Alcaeus. "His prized reputation for justice and wisdom?"

Antimenidas glanced at Alcaeus, momentarily thrown by his flippant response. "No, you moron!"[12]

Alcaeus laughed, then stopped when he realised Antimenidas wasn't joking. He followed Antimenidas's gaze to where it rested on the young Tyrrhaeus, son of the aisymnētēs who was laughing and chatting amongst Alcaeus's circle of friends. "You think *Tyrrhaeus* is going to Lydia?"

Antimenidas nodded.

"Are you sure?"

Antimenidas shifted his weight in that way he did when he was about to ask a favour. "Not completely. That's why I called you over. I need you to do some digging. It should be easy. You do hang out in the same crowd."

"I do not…" Alcaeus was about to object but stopped himself. He was by no means a soldier, a fact he felt always seemed to deeply disappoint his brother, but he was good at getting people to talk— almost as good as he was at writing poetry. But, could he do *this*?

A deep frown crossed his brow. "What do you want Tyrrhaeus for? You are not going to hurt him, are you? He is only a boy, and quite innocent in all this. Just because his father —"

"Alcaeus, man up and stop being such a pansy. Stop thinking with your phallus, for once."

"I do not —" Alcaeus stopped himself again. Why did his brother always seem to have the power to reduce him to a petulant child? Now was not the time to bicker and cause a scene. This was serious.

"Is this not taking the faction fight a bit too far?" Alcaeus regretted the question before it had even left his lips. He could see the blood rush to Antimenidas's face making his pale scar stand out like a bleached fold in his sun-weathered face.

"Have you forgotten what that traitor did? Have you forgotten how we all swore an oath of allegiance, united in our rise against the tyrant, Myrsilus? Do you remember how we fought side by side on the battle field with that coward, Pittacus, and then how when the wind changed, he turned on us! No, this is definitely not taking anything too far."

Alcaeus knew his brother meant every word. He also understood why Antimenidas felt so strongly. There was a time, when he was growing up, when Pittacus was like an older brother to Antimenidas. Their closeness made his betrayal even more painful for him. Alcaeus was still very young when all that happened, so a lot of that had passed him by. However, he loved and respected his brother and would always be loyal to him and, thus far, he had always stuck with the fight, even if it was often against his better judgement.

"And you are sure there isn't another way?"

"Don't you see, if we take his son hostage, we will have Pittacus exactly where we want him. He will do anything to have his beloved boy back. No harm will come to the boy, unless necessary. It will give us the perfect opportunity to get the boy to intervene and talk sense to his father."

Alcaeus always worried about what his brother might deem 'necessary' in situations like this. He swallowed hard, not wanting to explore that thought any further.

"I really hope so," Alcaeus said. Then he tried another track. "You realise Pittacus will stop at nothing if something happens to his only son and we were behind it."

Antimenidas didn't respond but Alcaeus could see his jaw set in the familiar resolve. This was going to happen one way or another whether Alcaeus liked it or not.

2

I left the Kallisteia soon after my exchange with Old Phaon. The rest of the performers were not to my liking and to be honest I was looking forward to devouring the fruits of the gorgeous slave I had just been gifted. And, although I secretly took great pleasure in knowing I was about to sample ambrosia from Sappho's cherished amphora, I didn't relish the potential confrontation with her if I were to rub it in her face. Instead, I retired home to my uncle's villa. It was still early afternoon and he was away for a few weeks on a trip to deliver silk to mainland Greece, leaving the entire house to me.

We went straight to my gynaeceum.

I poured myself a kylix of wine while I tried to decide how best to proceed with our private afternoon's festivities. I was still sipping the tart liquid when I felt a soft tickling sensation on my shoulder. My breath caught. I turned to find the slave had just kissed my neck. I was stunned and instantly felt my delta pulse between my legs. Not only had she taken it upon herself to strip entirely naked without my command, she had dared to touch me—a transgression against a freeman nothing short of a slight on Zeus himself. Rather than wanting to punish her I felt my delta flood. I wanted her to take me. I prayed to the gods she would have the fortitude to follow through.

There was a moment in which the world stood still. Neither of us moved. I don't think I even took a breath. I could have sworn I felt the earth tremble with me in those moments of anticipation. When it happened it felt so powerful, like Mount Olympus had awakened. First the rumbling, then rising, out of breath, gasping, rolling, tumbling, a growing avalanche gathering and building, hurtling, neither of us knowing where the one begins and the other ends. I could have sworn she had morphed into a Hecatoncheires—her strong hands and soft, warm mouth seeming to be everywhere on me at once. Her strength empowered me, her intuition meeting my every need and, in a manner befitting the volcano of the gods, I burst open.

I don't remember falling asleep. But, when I awoke, I found my bedchamber bathed in the late afternoon shadows and the slave curled, asleep, on the bed next to me—her strong, lean, boyish body cocooned around mine in a protective shell. I momentarily allowed myself to enjoy the comfort of her strong arms wrapped around me.

It felt so unlike anything I was used to. Mnasidika, my recent undoing, was petite and somewhat child-like. Sappho once described her as 'more finely shaped than soft Gyrinno'.[1] It is true. It was I who wrapped myself around her.

This was different.

The memory of our intimacy earlier flooded my mind and I could feel my delta react once more. But rather than take action I merely lay there admiring her from the position I was in.

I had to agree, she was breathtaking.

Her body was tall, lithe, lean and muscled, with strong, broad shoulders and narrow hips. Old Phaon was right; she was both man and woman in one. Not in genitalia, although I had heard that was possible, but in manner and the way she carried herself. It was mesmerising. She had the softest feminine skin and most shapely breasts, combined with the physique and demeanour of a virile young man. But it was her eyes that pierced straight through my indifference.

Even though I lay there very still, trying not to wake her, she must have sensed the tension in my body. She opened her deep, dark eyes and they seemed to seek out my soul.

She gave me a small smile before the reality of the situation hit.

"Oh, Mistress, I'm so sorry," she said quickly and started to scurry away, out of my bed. "I should probably go."

The moment was broken.

I felt an overpowering turmoil grip my stomach—a combination of feeling bereft and an irrational rage.

"Did I say you could leave?" I barked.

She stopped and turned with her head down. "I'm sorry, Mistress."

She looked like a different person. So submissive. So subservient. There was not a trace of her former power and the confidence with which she had taken me earlier. Oh, how I wished I could once more glimpse that Amazon who claimed me and made me hers so deftly before. I longed for her to overpower me again.

Instead, without dropping my commanding facade, I ordered her back to my bed. "I will tell you when you can leave."

She lay back down on the bed next to me. I sat up on my elbow and shifted up closer to her. Sensing my need, she stretched out her arm past my elbow, exposing her chest and shoulder so I could lie on her.

I accepted the unspoken invitation. It felt good as she wrapped her arm around my shoulders and pulled me into her. I was about to rest my hand on her chest, but hesitated, feeling like I should ask her permission. I shrugged off the thought. She is a slave. Her body belongs to Old Phaon, and for now, loaned to me, to do with whatever I please. I slowly lowered my hand onto her chest, taking long enough so she could protest, even though I knew she wouldn't. Her body felt smooth and firm under my head and hand. I made sure to avoid her more intimate areas—her dark, succulent nipples. I wondered if they were always that erect. I wondered what would pleasure her. She was a slave! I reminded myself. One had no business considering a slave's needs. If it came to doing anything to a slave, it was purely for one's own gratification.

I pictured her writhing under my touch and I imagined her muscles tense and her face change as she strained against her body's yearning and my command to resist. Another pulse clenched in my delta.

"What is your name?" I asked as tersely as I could.

"What do you want it to be?"

"No," I shook my head against her shoulder. "I mean your real name. I heard Old Phaon call you Ana. I assume that's short for something."

"I was named Anactoria at birth."

I pushed myself up onto my elbow. I couldn't help think what a lovely name it was. "Who gave it to you?"

"My master."

"So, you have been with him your whole life?"

She nodded. "Yes, for as long as I can remember."

"And your parents? Are they still part of Old Phaon's oikos?"

She shook her head. "I never knew my parents. The story is that my mother died in childbirth, and no one knows who my father is. Even if they do know, no one will tell me."

A powerful urge to protect her overcame me and I lent down and kissed her, but rather than allow me to take charge, she gently and firmly pushed me off her. Slowly but surely, I could see that confident, assertive creature she was earlier take over again.

Soon the things she was doing to my body were threatening to claim my sanity. I desperately wanted it to both stop and never end!

It was well into the night when I felt Anactoria stir. She sat up and, in the darkness, I saw her get up and start to dress.

"Where do you think you're going?" I asked, feeling both irritated and bereft.

"I need to return to my master," she said quietly as if not to disturb the night around us.

The thought of her leaving me and returning to that toad-like man and possibly engaging in his carnal pleasures made me almost sick.

I shook the thought from my head. What was I doing? How could I allow myself to care so quickly… and that for a slave, who does not even belong to me?

"Be gone with you! And tell your master I found your skills lacking and I shan't be needing your services again." The moment the words left my mouth I regretted them. Oh, how I would have loved to see her again, to have her pleasure me all night and all day every day. But I wouldn't have that. I could not allow someone to have that power over me, least of all someone else's slave, over whom I had no control.

I wouldn't turn to look at her again. I didn't want to see her expression. I needed to hurt her, but I couldn't bear seeing any pain in her eyes. Would she even show me? Or did none of this mean anything to her? Instead, I got up and busied myself at my dresser until she bid me good night and I heard her soft footsteps disappear out of my bedchamber.

When Anactoria arrived back at Old Phaon's house in the early morning, she tried to slip in, hoping that he would be sound asleep by then.

Sneaking around, without him knowing, was complicated by his insistence on having her near him almost all the time. From very early on, Old Phaon seemed to single her out over all his other household slaves. It was not that he seemed to like her better than the rest, it was more like he had selected her as his own personal pet. As soon as she was old enough, he insisted she had separate sleeping quarters, away from the other slaves, directly adjacent to his own. This meant she now had to tiptoe right past his bedroom door.

She had almost managed it, but as she reached her own room, she heard his chamber door open.

"Ana?"

Her heart sank at the tell-tale drunken slur of her name.

"Is that you?"

She took a deep breath, braced herself and turned to him.

"Yes, Master."

"You're late. Come in here and help." He stood holding onto the door for support and was brandishing a kopis, which he liked to use during his sex play with his slaves. His chiton was covered in blood and Anactoria recognised the tell-tale bulge of his leather olisbos bobbing up and down at the lower edge of the garment. If you didn't know what was really going on inside that chamber, you might actually find the sight rather comical.

As she neared the door, she could already see the carnage inside and her stomach clenched. There was blood everywhere and, Kalliope, one of her fellow slaves, was lying on the floor, either unconscious or very close to it, possibly from too much pain or a loss of blood.

"By Zeus! What have you done?" Anactoria rushed over to Kalliope. She saw that her whole body was covered in multiple crimson lacerations. One of her nipples hung by a thread.

"Can you clean it up?" Old Phaon slurred behind her. "She couldn't even last until the foreplay was finished." He topped up his copper mastos and took a big swig from it.

Anactoria clenched her fists with both sorrow and rage. She stood and squared up to Phaon. "This is going too far! You can't treat—"

The blow came fast and solid and connected squarely with her cheek, the force of it throwing her off balance.

"This is your fault. You hear me," he spat in her face. "This is your fault! How dare you answer back to me? Who do you think you are?

Ever since you were little you always thought you were better than everybody." Anactoria recognised the familiar drunken rage in his eyes. "But here," he grabbed her by the shoulders and dragged her to the bed. Although he was a portly drunkard, from his many years of hard work out at sea, he was still very strong. "Let me show you how much better you and the likes of your Spartan friend, Sappho, are.[2] Women should know their place. You are all good for one thing, and one thing only."

He forcefully bent her forward over the bed, pinning her down with his weight and clamping her head into the already blood-stained fabric, almost suffocating her. Momentarily laying down the kopis, he thrust the dildo into her. He reached for the kopis again and roughly began to thrust his hips against her driving the large dildo deep inside her. He leant in and sneered, close to her ear. "Women and slaves are nothing. Empty vessels, from which I can drink, or *fill* with whatever I desire." Then, demonstrating his power, he roughly grabbed her hair and lifted her backwards off the bed exposing her chest and breasts as he ran the cold, sharp metal of the kopis along her neck.

Yet in contrast to Kalliope, there was not a single cut on Anactoria.

Finding himself unable to follow through with his threat he shoved her back onto the bed and resumed his drunken blundering into her.

It was in moments like these that Anactoria wished with all her heart that she could put an end to Phaon. She wished she had the courage to stop this torture once and for all. She doubted that she was strong enough in her body, her mind and heart to kill another human being. If she did not succeed, she knew he would take his revenge by making her watch him vent his anger and vengeance on the other slaves.

She also knew from ample personal experience, judging by his uncoordinated movements and slurred speech, that he wouldn't last much longer before he passed out. She just had to hold on a little longer.

She squeezed her eyes shut, bit down hard on her lower lip and, like so many times before, she escaped in her mind to the safety of her inner world—a different world, where women were equals and slaves were free.[3]

"This is going to be a mistake," Alcaeus said to Antimenidas.

The two of them sat at the high table in the kitchen. Antimenidas noisily sucked at the bones of the chicken thigh, left over from the late meal that Melissa, their last remaining house slave, had cooked for them.

After their mother's death the house no longer felt like a home. It merely served as a roof over their heads and the occasional place to sleep. As the oldest and now the head of the household, Antimenidas had decided to sell on all the other slaves. However, he could not bring himself to let Melissa go. She was their mother's personal slave and the woman who had reared them during their early years.

"Why are you suddenly so worried about whether this is a mistake?" Antimenidas asked, putting down the clean bone.

"You know why. This is no ordinary faction-fighting tactic. If you do this, you will be crossing a line, to a place you cannot easily come back from. If you go after Tyrrhaeus, there is nothing stopping Pittacus deciding to come after Cicis or worse."

Antimenidas looked up.

For a moment Alcaeus hoped he had finally struck an empathetic chord.

Antimenidas shook his head. "There is nothing stopping Pittacus coming after any of us anyway." He wiped his greasy hands on a boiled cloth that was lying on the table. "This is our only chance to get Pittacus's attention."

"Why don't you just admit it?"

"Admit what?"

"You are still angry with Pittacus for changing sides and deserting you."

Antimenidas banged his hand on the table so hard the dishes jumped and made Alcaeus flinch. "This is not revenge. This is for our cause. If I wanted revenge the little scrote of a boy would have breathed his last breath a long time ago."

"That is my point," Alcaeus said. "This has nothing to do with him. Just because his father is Pittacus, he should not need to be involved. He has done nothing to you. In fact, he wants nothing more than to get away from his father and all of this."

Antimenidas shook his head, clearly not wanting to hear. "And you know this, how?"

Alcaeus swallowed. There was a long silence.

"Exactly. In my experience, the olives do not fall far from the tree, and even if they do, we cannot afford to let this opportunity go by. Maybe the disappearance of his son is the only thing that will make Pittacus stop and listen."

"But killing him will close Pittacus down for good."

"Do you think I was born under a rock? Of course, we are not going to kill Tyrrhaeus. What would we have to bargain with?"

Alcaeus thought long and hard. Antimenidas picked chicken flesh from between his teeth with a shard of chicken bone.

"Okay," Alcaeus said.

Antimenidas grunted.

"But I am coming with you."

Antimenidas almost choked on the bone. "You what?"

"I'm coming with you to make sure you do not do anything stupid."

"Stupid!"

"If one hair on that boy's head gets damaged, all our necks are on the line, and personally, I like my neck and don't want it severed in some bloody act of revenge by Pittacus."

Antimenidas looked at his brother curiously. Then, after a long moment's thought he finally nodded. "Well, if that is what it takes for you to stop whingeing at me and help, then okay."

Sappho entered her bedchamber. She had spent most of the afternoon dreaming up all the delightful things she was hoping to do with Anactoria later. Now it was time for her preparations.

She closed the chamber door behind her and went straight to her closet. She wanted to make this a special evening and she knew exactly what she was going to wear.

"I wrote you a poem," a voice said behind her.

"By Aphrodite!" She clutched at her throat in fright. Spinning round, she found Alcaeus lounging casually on her bed.

"Don't do that! You'll send me to Tartarus."

He smiled his cute, boyish smile. "Here, read it." He held out a short scroll.

Sappho grabbed it playfully. "Violet-haired, holy, sweetly-smiling Sappho…"[4] she started, then in order to avoid embarrassment, she continued to read quietly to the end.

"Other than not quite violet," she tugged at the dark red-brown lock on her shoulder, "I think you'll make a better poet than a burglar."

Alcaeus shrugged. "Why? Nobody saw me, and I came wearing a hood." He tugged at the material that now lay resting on his shoulders.

"Your timing is poor. Kerkylas is due home," she whispered. "You know he will be furious if he finds you in my chamber. He's already suspicious that there's something between us. Even though, Aphrodite knows, I keep telling him you are like my brother."

"If only there was." He clasped his chest. "You know, you have my heart."

Sappho rolled her eyes. "Yes, yes. I know it's only for safekeeping, while you pass your loins around those beautiful young boys you fraternise with."

"Oh, sweet Sappho," he slid down on his knees before her, "you know you just need to say the word and I'll pledge you my all, and you can discard that old husk of a Kerkylas. You do know he is too old for you?"

She gently rested her hand on his shoulder. "But if you love and respect us both, you would choose another, younger bed-fellow. I will not connect with you, old woman with young man."[5] She turned and carried on to her closet.

"But we're equal in years," he protested.

"Exactly my point." She said over her shoulder. "That, for a woman, is old."

Sappho selected and pulled out an expensive looking, violet, silk gown and took it over to the bed.

Alcaeus got up and headed to her now open closet. He started to inspect her array of colourful cloaks and tunics. Eventually he pulled out a yellow-gold silk himation and wrapped it around his shoulders.

"Oh, how you wound me," he said in a pouting voice, lifting the fabric up over his head to partly obscure his face in an exaggerated display of bashfulness.

Then, as if seeing a beloved old toy-box, he darted to her dressing-table and swooped down to it, in such a flurry that Sappho's himation billowed out behind him. On the small shrine-like table he picked up her mother-of-pearl hair pin and started arranging his own curly, slightly voluminous dark hair before pinning it up. When done, he got up and sashayed along the length of the room pretending to be a glamorous courtesan.

Meanwhile, Sappho was busy arranging a cluster of scented candles and incense near the bed.

Finally, bored of his own antics, Alcaeus put the himation back in the closet and then went to sprawl on Sappho's bed to watch her work.

"Sappho," he began more contemplatively than before.

"Hmm," she said not taking her attention off the candleholder she was cleaning and refilling.

"Which do you think is the highest form of love?"

"What do you mean?" she said absentmindedly.

"I mean, what do we do when various loves in our lives arrive at a point at odds with each other. Which do you think is the purest, the highest of them all? Which should take precedence? Is it the love between lovers, or familial love, or love of friendship? If pushed, whom should we choose to worship more? Eros? Pothos? Imeros? Anternos? Hymenaeus? Aphrodite? Or even Hestia guarding our family and home?"

Sappho's attention was grabbed by Alcaeus's serious tone. She took a deep breath and sat down on the bed next to him. "That is a very good question and it is why people turn to poets for answers."

"So, what is the answer?"

Sappho shook her head. "I think that is a question we each need answer for ourselves."

Alcaeus rolled his eyes. "Spoken as a true poet," he teased.

"You think that is bad. I also think the answer can differ depending on one's position or circumstance in life."

Alcaeus pulled a nearby pillow over his head. "At least I know we poets will never be out of a job."

Sappho laughed and got up as Alcaeus sat up.

Sappho noticed he still had his hair tied up with her hairpin.

"Now, put that back," she said.

"I need it," he replied with a pout.

"For what?"

"For good luck."

It was Sappho's turn to roll her eyes.

"It's true. I'm going on a big, top secret mission in the next few days and you might never see me again."

"That is all very melodramatic, even for you, my friend," Sappho teased.

Alcaeus chuckled. "It is. Don't you love it?"

Sappho took another good look at her friend. Something told her he was only half-joking.

"What is Antimenidas up to now?" Sappho asked. "And why on earth are you getting involved? I thought you'd made it clear to him you are a poet and you won't be getting involved in his political intrigues anymore."

Alcaeus nodded. "I had. But I need to, this time."

Sappho frowned. Yes, there was definitely something different about her childhood friend. Something was troubling him. She also knew he would probably not tell her the truth, at least not yet.

"I wish to tell you," Alcaeus said, "honestly, I do. But shame prevents me."[6]

"You see…. If you had a desire for what is honourable or good, and your tongue was not stirring up something evil to say, shame would not cover your eyes, but you would state your claim."

They both heard the footsteps approaching outside her chamber door.

Sappho was the first to react. She waved him towards the window. "Go!"

He was halfway out when Sappho realised that he still had her hairpin. "Look after it. It's my favourite," she hissed.

Alcaeus smiled and saluted.

"Now hurry! Before someone sees you."

Alcaeus pulled his hood over his head and climbed along the balcony ledge and disappeared down the pillar to the road below.

Anactoria arrived outside Sappho's residence. Curiously, a man was busy climbing down one of the pillars, from what she knew to be Sappho's balcony. When he saw her watching, he gave a cocky smile and put his finger to his lips suggesting she kept quiet. He looked a little familiar, but had pulled his himation over his head and Anactoria couldn't quite place him. Then he jumped down to the road and quickly headed in the opposite direction, glancing back to beam her a final cheeky grin.

Anactoria continued to the entrance way into Sappho's residence. She knocked.

Kleïs, the auburn-haired young woman who was Sappho's personal slave, opened the door.

"Lady Sappho is expecting me," Anactoria said.

Kleïs barely grunted before she turned and lead the way to Sappho's gynaeceum.

Anactoria knew that Kleïs didn't like her. She suspected that Kleïs found her a threat and was jealous of Sappho's affection towards her. But there was not much Anactoria could do about that. That was a matter for Kleïs and Sappho to work out. Instead, she resolved to always be as civil and pleasant to Kleïs as possible. After all, everyone knew, tensions between slaves could be lethal.

Kleïs had hoped to see the back of Anactoria the day her tutelage ended, all those moons ago. Sadly, she showed up like a bad odour even more often these days.

Kleïs knew it wasn't necessary to escort Anactoria to Sappho's gynaeceum, since Anactoria knew the house very well. But keeping an eye on Anactoria when she was not with Sappho was the least she could do. It was her job. No matter how intimate Sappho might currently be with Anactoria, Anactoria was *not* one of Sappho's oikos. And as a good slave, Kleïs needed to supervise all of her mistress' personal guests in and around the house.

Kleïs definitely was a good slave.

Privately, she didn't like to think of herself as a slave at all—more like a daughter, if not *the* personal companion and intimate confidant to her mistress. As a result of her tireless service, she had earned great favour and thus a very close bond with Sappho. This afforded her a number of privileges and special treatment way beyond that usually bestowed on a slave. Sappho relied on her for almost everything, hence she rarely left Sappho's side.

Worryingly though, Sappho had recently started to dismiss Kleïs whenever Anactoria called. That was unheard of. She wondered whether Master Kerkylas would approve. Not that she was inclined to tell him.

The only time she was happy to be relieved of her duties and dismissed was when Kerkylas himself requested intimate time with his wife. Thankfully that was something Sappho agreed to less and less frequently.

———

There came a loud knock at Sappho's gynaeceum. Her stomach quivered in expectation. She had been unable to concentrate on anything other than her darling Anactoria all day.

But, before she could even reach the door to the gynaeceum, it swung open and in strode Kerkylas—the last person she wanted to see right then.

"Was that Alcaeus?" he asked, clearly looking for blood.

"And a 'hello' to you too Kerkylas, my husband. Nice to see you too."

Kerkylas momentarily looked abashed.

"Alcaeus, was here, yes," Sappho continued with a suave smile. "He came to say good bye. He's going on a mission."

"Hmph," he huffed, both relieved and disgruntled. He was relieved that Alcaeus had left, hopefully for some moons, but disgruntled that he had not caught him there, to make sure it was for good. The thought of his wife and that pansy-boy together was distinctly repulsive. "That can only mean trouble."

He frowned suddenly, slightly distracted. Then he remembered what he wanted to say. "You know I don't like him hanging around here!"

"You mean in my bedchamber or my gynaeceum?" Sappho teased.

Kerkylas put his hands on his hips, ready to assert his authority.

"Relax, Kerkylas." Sappho said. "You know Alcaeus is more interested in boys and, we've been through this, to me he's like my brother." She turned and carried on adding the final touches to the little shrine of candles and ointments she had been preparing.

"Yes, well, you might be childhood friends, but still, I don't like the way he looks at you. Besides, it is not good for politics, him hanging around here. He has turned against Pittacus. I cannot be seen to be associated with his brother's faction."

"Kerkylas, he really is harmless."

"Ineffective is not the same as harmless. Really Sappho, that is my final word on the matter." Kerkylas turned on his heel making for a resolute exit. However, on seeing Kleïs accompanying a visitor, he turned back. "Are you working all evening again, tonight?"

"Yes, my dear Kerkylas. Sadly, these girls need me." Sappho looked genuinely remorseful. "Tartarus, half the men in Mytilene need me," she said jest-fully, "to help these girls, I mean," she added quickly when she realised Kerkylas could easily misinterpret her humour.

Kerkylas looked like he was about to object but then he seemed to think better of it. He nodded at Sappho and turned towards Kleïs. He looked her up and down. "You. Come to my andron when you're done here."

Kleïs looked panicked and turned to Sappho for help.

"My dear Kerkylas," Sappho said, in her best golden-honeyed voice, sashaying up to him in the way she knew he found irresistible. When she reached him, she ran her index finger along his collarbone and down his chest. "You agreed I could have one slave all to myself." She looked up and met his gaze, continuing her finger trail down to his groin, finally, not too gently, cupping his manhood through his chiton. "Not to mention, I don't want you completely spent later, when I've finished work."

Kerkylas glanced between Kleïs and Sappho weighing up his options. Finally, his eyes landed on Sappho, then he grunted, turned and left.

Once he had gone, Kleïs let out a relieved breath.

After that little display towards Kerkylas, Kleïs was pretty sure, Sappho was going to need her services for the rest of the evening. She went to take her usual seat on a mountain of soft furnishings in the corner of the room near the fireplace—ready to tend to each and every one of Sappho's personal needs. But, before she had time to cross the room, Sappho stopped her. "Thank you Kleïs. That'll be all for tonight. You can have the evening off. I'll send for you when I need you."

At first, Kleïs felt bewildered, sure she had misheard.

"Mistress?" Kleïs asked.

"And close the door behind you, please," Sappho said. "I don't want to be interrupted by anyone."

Faced with the order, Kleïs nodded, lowered her head and made for the door. She had to grit her teeth hard to suppress the tears that were threatening to spill.

Once outside in the dark, cool corridor Kleïs paused and tried to gather herself. *Dismissed! Again! Just like Kerkylas. How could Sappho do that to her?*

Once the chamber door closed behind Kleïs, Sappho rushed up to Anactoria. She grabbed her hands and squeezed them, a broad grin of happiness bunching her almond cheeks. "Oh, I'm so pleased you came."

Anactoria looked sombre, her jaw muscles clenched. "So, you still sleep with Kerkylas?"

Sappho frowned, trying to make sense of Anactoria's words and distant manner. Then it dawned on her.

"Oh that," she waved it off and went to her dresser where one of her kitchen slaves had placed the wine and delicacies she had ordered for their evening. She poured them each a kylix of wine and brought them over to Anactoria.

"To answer your question," she said with deliberation, "yes, occasionally. It is my duty. He is desperate for another child. I am ever hopeful for a girl. But believe me, it is purely in body." She handed Anactoria a kylix. "Whereas with you, I can linger for an eternity because, as you know, you have my heart." She leaned in and kissed Anactoria softly. Then she leant back and raised her drink. "To you."

Anactoria, momentarily appeased, lifted her own kylix.

3

Old Phaon sat back on his specially carved wooden klismos, mid-centre of the bow deck on his brand-new flagship, The Alabastron. This gave him the perfect vantage point to observe his fifty-strong team of oarsmen as they filed into place on either side of the lower, middle deck—not that he was particularly interested. He had people whose job it was to be interested and take care of all the details for him. What he did like about sitting there, sheltered from the elements by the splendid, newly designed canvas deck-shelter, was the air of importance his position gave him.

He, along with a select number of influential mariners both on Mytilene and in Kyme had formed a business cooperative to improve the current design of the Penteconter, originally a warship, to make it both more versatile and more fit for purpose in each of their enterprises.

His main objectives were two-fold. The first was to improve the ship's speed. More speed meant more trips and thus more money. Incorporating an extra layer of oarsmen on either side of the galley and including an extra-long sail would more than double the ship's potential power—an improvement the navy would certainly seek to adopt soon.

Phaon himself had come up with the brilliant idea of training slaves for manpower rather than using qualified freemen, in an effort to minimise the running costs. After all, brave, worthy seamen and soldiers were not needed in his business—he was not going to dirty his hands in a war. All that talk about the 'Persians are coming', in his view, was just puff. All he needed was muscle-power, and slaves were good enough for that. He did, however, concede that manning the mast and sails was beyond the average slave. So, for that, Xanthias, his trusted manservant, had hired a small band of specially trained sailors.

The second objective was to increase the ship's hold space, primarily to maximise cargo room for merchandise.

But that was not the only reason he needed the hold space to be bigger. There was another, about which he was most excited and which would revolutionise not only his business but the seafaring trade as a whole. He was sure of it. He needed the space for guest cabins.

In truth, the passenger service was the suggestion of his new 'associate', although he did not like addressing him thus. Orpheus, a legendary musician, had originally come to Phaon and requested he be employed to put on private recitals for guests on Phaon's ship. At the time, Old Phaon explained that he offered only a merchant ferry service and that unless Orpheus wanted to sing to the crew, or repay the compliment to the Sirens, Phaon's Ferries were not the platform for such frivolities.

The thought lingered though, and once Phaon started thinking about it more seriously, he had to admit that Orpheus's idea was inspirational. He immediately sent for Orpheus to come back and talk through what such an arrangement might look like and eventually decided to pursue it, in principle. He was reluctant to make a more long-term commitment to Orpheus as he was bound to demand ongoing payment, and Phaon was sure he could rustle up a few slave-dancers or some more economical entertainment once the business was up and running. After all, everyone knew that men mostly just wanted drink and sex—music was not a necessity for either of these.

Anactoria had been leaning over the bulwark of Old Phaon's new ship, watching the galley slaves file onboard and take their position in the double rows. The workings of the new double structure of the galley seats fascinated her. She was trying to figure out how the double rows of oarsmen would avoid getting their oars entangled.

As the final preparations for departure got underway, you could feel a palpable buzz of excitement grow amongst the men, not least because it was the first voyage in such a state-of-the-art vessel, but also because they were allegedly going to be ferrying some precious cargo to Anatolia for the aisymnētēs himself. Since the rumours had started, things had developed and it was now believed that "cargo" was code word for very important guest. At any moment, a very important guest, apparently the first of many, would be boarding The Alabastron to be ferried across to Anatolia.

There had been much speculation about the identity of this first guest. Some of the slaves had even wagered their next meal on the likelihood that they would be carrying Pittacus himself. So additionally, Anactoria was on the lookout for any signs of such a person.

She noticed a group of men, the new crew she assumed, gathering to one side and talking to Xanthias, Old Phaon's manservant, trusted captain of his first and all subsequent flagships.

Four characters in the gathered group caught her attention. Why exactly, she couldn't place. The only thing she could think of was that the rest were dressed in their usual chiton and cloaks. These four wore their hoods up. She assumed this was to shelter them from the midday sun and although it was not yet the full heat of the summer, this was not so unusual as to be suspicious.

After talking to these men, Xanthias led them on board where he bade them wait to one side of the deck for their official introduction to Old Phaon, as was tradition for new recruits. However, Anactoria noticed Xanthias gesture to one of the hooded figures, the smallest, to follow him down below deck.

This intrigued her. Unfortunately, her observations were interrupted by Old Phaon calling for her from where he was sitting on his throne in the shelter on the bow of the ship. He was demanding that she take up her usual position near him on the floor.

Like a dog, she thought, only a dog would have a better life.

Xanthias appeared in the shelter and, after getting the necessary nod from Old Phaon, called the ship to attention. It was time for the new crew members to be introduced.

Anactoria was used to this type of thing and she was about to return to her own private musings on the mechanics of the double row of oarsmen when her attention was once again drawn to the three hooded crewmen on the mid-deck below stepping forward to be introduced.

There was still no sign of the fourth. What had happened to him? What was Xanthias doing taking him below deck? Maybe he was their secret guest. She resolved to have a look round in the hold later. For now, she was more interested in hearing their introduction.

There was definitely something familiar about one of them, but she couldn't think where she would have seen him, and so far she hadn't been able to get a good look at him.

Then as luck would have it, he glanced in her direction and their eyes met. Instantly she knew. He was the man she'd seen climbing down from Sappho's window!

She must have gasped in surprise, which drew Old Phaon's attention.

"What's the matter?" he barked.

Anactoria's eyes darted between Old Phaon and the young man. Then she saw him discreetly lift his finger to his mouth in the same gesture she saw him make that day. It was definitely him. What would he be doing on the ship?

She quickly shook her head at her master. "Nothing, Master. Forgive me." She lowered her head slightly, in a way that she knew would help placate him. "I was just marvelling at the splendour of your ship, Master."

"Hmm," he grumbled, but satisfied that this could be true, he refocussed on the task at hand.

Finally, the first of the three men stepped forward. He was large, well built, with a distinct scar across his face, probably from battle. He also seemed to be the spokesman for the other two. Anactoria listened as he explained that he had crewed many a vessel with his two colleagues, rattling off a few apparently esteemed sea captains' names whom Old Phaon could consult for a glowing reference. He continued to explain that the smaller, lithe blond man with him was a little slow and he was his ward. He assured Old Phaon he was a very good acrobat. Due to his slowness, he had no fear and thus was a dab hand at the top ropes, the ones most sailors try to avoid, because of the risk.

When it came to introducing the third, much to Anactoria's frustration, very little was said about him. They had known each other for almost their whole lives and had apparently crewed together for many of those years. The big man made a point of vouching for his friend's skills and agility despite his slight stature.

What would a sailor be doing scaling Sappho's pillar? Anactoria thought.

The young man in question stepped forward and politely greeted Old Phaon. Anactoria could just hear his voice. Even though he didn't say much, she could hear he was softly spoken and surprisingly eloquent—perhaps too eloquent for an average sailor. This further intrigued her.

"Master, it is time to address the crew," Xanthias whispered to Old Phaon.

Anactoria prayed he was still sober enough to do that. She didn't mind seeing him make a fool of himself, but she knew for any onlooker it would be excruciating and often someone would get hurt.

Slowly Phaon pushed himself up into a standing position. "Today is an auspicious day," he announced and held up his kylix. "Remember it, as we set sail on this here ships' maiden voyage. May it be remembered well." He was about to take a sip when he realised his kylix was empty. He reached for the amphora of wine which was standing on an expensive dark crimson cloth covered table, but as he did so, he misjudged the distance and instead of picking it up he knocked it and sent it tumbling down onto the lower mid-deck where it crashed in an explosion of red wine and pottery shards.

"Herewith Master Phaon has anointed our ship The Alabastron." Xanthias announced quickly. "May this deliver good fortune upon us all."

Old Phaon had enough sense left to realise what Xanthias was doing and lifted his cup to the heavens to accept the undue credit.

"May this become a tradition on all new ships for years to come," Xanthias said.

One of the tending kitchen slaves brought over another amphora of wine and filled Old Phaon's cup.

Phaon took a slurping swig. There was an uncomfortable silence while the whole ship waited for him to resume his address. He, however, it seemed had forgotten what was happening. In a low whisper Xanthias prompted his master.

"Oh, yes. Here's to me and my new venture," he slurred and took another gulp. "I don't want any of you useless morons messing it up. If

I find anyone out of line, I will personally have each one of your eyeballs harvested for a snack and have you drawn and quartered until you beg me to suck out your brains —"

"Okay, Master," Xanthias interrupted quietly before Phaon could get further carried away with creative ways to torture his slaves. "I think they get the point and I will make sure everything goes smoothly."

Old Phaon sat down and everyone took that as their cue to get back to work.

———

Not long after Phaon's address, a tall young man in fine clothing walked up the plank and it became clear from the lavish welcome bestowed on him by Old Phaon that he was the honoured guest. He was Tyrrhaeus, the son of Pittacus.

Anactoria was surprised he had come alone, unaccompanied by the usual entourage fitting for the son of the aisymnētēs. Apparently, he was making a personal trip to Anatolia and had insisted, despite his father's reservations, on travelling alone. However, his father would only allow it on condition that they commission the best ferryman in Mytilene for the task.

This, for Anactoria however, did not solve the more intriguing riddle: Who had the fourth, small, hooded figure been?

———

Now that their guest had arrived, it was nearing the time to set sail.

Xanthias, the long-suffering servant that he was, hovered nearby, while he waited for Old Phaon to give the command. When it started to look like this might not happen soon, since Old Phaon seemed too preoccupied with drinking with his new young guest, Xanthias stepped forward and discreetly tried to get his master's attention.

Old Phaon finally noticed.

"Oh Xanthias," he slurred. "Are you still here?"

Xanthias straightened up, clearly surprised. "Yes, Master. I am. I'm waiting for you to give the go-ahead so that I can take us out to sea."

"Ah, yes. Actually Xanthias, you won't be doing that." Old Phaon said casually.

"Sorry, Master, I'm not sure I understand," Xanthias said.

"Syros. Where are you?" Old Phaon called out.

A younger, greying man with fat cheeks and over developed forearms appeared in the shelter. "Master," he said and bowed.

"This is Syros, the new captain of this ship," Old Phaon said.

"But Master, I don't understand," Xanthias said.

Old Phaon closed his eyes. For a moment it was unclear whether he had actually nodded off mid-sentence. "Of course, you do," he said. "Do you really think that you are still the hot-blooded stallion, capable of riding my new queen?"

Xanthias looked even more confused.

"Do you really think I would trust this, gorgeous, curvaceous state of the art beauty to an old nag such as yourself?" He shook his head in answer to his own question. "Now, be off with you!"

There was a stunned silence, as all those who heard the interaction tried to make sense of what they just heard. Old Phaon had just fired his longest-serving, most loyal, most trusted servant in front of the entire crew, without any forewarning.

Xanthias hesitated for a moment, but then bowed and headed towards the plank.

"Pull the plank, on your way," Old Phaon called after him. "Now, can someone fill my kylix, for Zeus's sake."

Anactoria's heart broke for Xanthias. Over the years she had always steered clear of him. Partly because she could never understand why, or how, a man like that could be so loyal to such a tyrant. She knew, like her, he did not really have a choice. But, unlike her, she never ever heard him say a word against Old Phaon. In fact, she often heard him give Old Phaon the credit for his own good ideas or kind deeds. It was as though he had made it his life's mission to defend and protect his master in whichever way he could.

And this was how Old Phaon rewarded him?

Anactoria watched Xanthias head towards the plank. She noticed him glance around one last time. At first, she assumed it was a silent goodbye. Then, she remembered the fourth hooded man.

4

———

Syros gave the command and with a loud heave-ho they set a
course for Ephesus on Anatolia. This journey was not going
to be without peril as the ship needed to leave sheltered waters and
enter the main, deep currents of the Aegean to circumvent the island
of Xios before heading back towards the mainland and docking at
Ephesus.

Almost before the ship had left harbour, Old Phaon began basking
in the joy of entertaining his captive audience. He plied Tyrrhaeus and
himself with lavish quantities of food and drink, boasting to his young
guest how the gods were shining down on him and his new venture.
Tyrrhaeus, being a timid, well-mannered young man, accepted
everything on offer most graciously and engaged in polite
conversation, while Old Phaon proceeded to get more and more
inebriated.

Once the major business of setting sail was over and the ship was
headed in the right direction, there was a lot of waiting around to be
done by the hired crew. Antimenidas ambled casually over to where
Alcaeus stood, resting on the bulwark.

"It is time," Antimenidas said and discretely passed Alcaeus a small spindle flask with a cork stopper. "I need you to put the contents of this into the wine destined for the old man and his guest."

"Why me?" Alcaeus asked.

"You said you wanted to come along. So, it is time to make yourself useful."

"But—"

"You are less conspicuous."

Alcaeus had to agree, his brother's burly shape was nothing if not noticeable and even more so if he was found fiddling around with the supplies in the hold. Cicis, though smaller, was not an option. Even if he had been up to the task, his shock of white blond hair made him too conspicuous.

Alcaeus grunted and took the flask from his brother's hand, putting it surreptitiously into the leather satchel that was slung over his shoulder.

Antimenidas nodded his approval. "Remember, make sure you are not seen and certainly do not speak to anyone. Just slip that into their next amphora and get out of there."

Alcaeus nodded and swallowed down the knot of nerves that had formed in his throat.

<hr />

Anactoria bided her time, patiently. When she thought Old Phaon was engrossed enough to not notice or mind her absence too much, she excused herself and slipped out, making her way below deck.

This area was mainly occupied by the oarsmen, cramped in double rows one above the other on either side of the galley. The space around that was divided into a further two levels. The lowest level was called the pit because its main purpose was holding sewage and refuse. Above that, a new level had been built into a space that went unused in the old penteconters. The Alabastron's stern had been modified with the creation of two large storage rooms that could be locked to keep any precious cargo safe. In a mirror image of that, in the bow, just under the floor of the new luxurious deck-shelter, not only was there extra space for storage crates and supplies, there were also small sleeping cabins, designed to give Old Phaon and his esteemed guests privacy and comfortable lodgings during their voyage.

Anactoria wandered around, pretending to be making her way down to the pit. In reality she was looking out for anyone who resembled the small mystery hooded figure she'd seen descend below deck with Xanthias.

Finally, she reached the bow area near Old Phaon's cabin. She stopped to listen when she heard sounds, like crying. It seemed to be coming from behind a stack of crates in the corner. She approached carefully. When she moved one of the crates, she found a small person curled in a ball on the ground.

"Hey, are you alright?" Anactoria asked.

The hooded figure started and looked up. She was an old woman. Tears streaked her face.

"Please. Please. Don't tell," was all the woman said, her eyes large with fear.

Anactoria bent down slowly and put a gentle hand on the woman's shoulder. "It's okay," she soothed. "I won't. What are you doing back here?"

The old woman looked at her with big eyes. "Xanthias said it would be safe. He said he'd take care of me, but he never came back."

"Why are you on the ship?"

"It's my daughter, she's in Anatolia and I need to get to her." The old woman started to cry again.

In an effort to calm her, Anactoria gently stroked her arm. "Xanthias had to leave the ship. But it's okay. I won't tell anyone. Shh. But you have to be quiet. Okay?"

The frightened woman looked up at her and nodded vigorously.

Alcaeus found it easy to locate the ship's food supplies. He was surprised to find that all was left completely unguarded, stacked in crates and on palettes not far from the bow end. Six tall amphorae stood tied into a wooden frame, separated from the squatter containers of water. All he had to do was ease out the stopper of the first amphora, tip in the liquid from the little flask and then get out of there.

That is when he heard something.

Anactoria carefully replaced the crates obscuring the old woman's hiding place.

"Hello."

Anactoria jumped. She spun round and almost knocked the man behind her over with a reflexively raised right elbow. When he regained his balance, she immediately recognised him—the man from Sappho's balcony.

"You! What are you doing here?" she hissed. "The oarsmen and crew are not allowed in this area."

He raised his finger to his lips again. "I mean you no harm. I just want to talk," he whispered.

Anactoria glanced up towards the deck-shelter. She realised she must have been gone quite a while already and even drunken Old Phaon might have noticed her prolonged absence by now.

She eyed the man in front of her, looking him up and down. Close up, even in this dim light, he didn't look much like a sailor. He was far too well-kempt—definitely more like a politician or aristocrat, but he still wore a hood, so it was hard to see his face properly.

"Why are you here? What do you want?" Anactoria asked in a harsh whisper.

"I just want to talk."

"What about?"

"You and I have a good friend in common, as you know." He looked to see if she was following.

Anactoria nodded warily, recollecting his exit down Sappho's balcony.

"I'm positive she would want you to help me. In fact, she said as much."

"She didn't to me."

"She couldn't."

Anactoria looked suspicious.

"I asked her not to. She said that when the time came, I should approach you and ask you myself."

"How do I know you're not lying?"

"She gave me this," he produced the mother-of-pearl hairpin from inside his leather satchel.

Anactoria's eyes widened. She would recognise that hairpin anywhere.

"Why do you have it? Did you steal it?"

The hooded man shook his head. "No, she gave it to me so that you would know I was not lying when the time came."

Anactoria studied the man warily. "What is it you want?"

"I need your help."

"With?"

"I need you to get Old Phaon's guest to come down here. I have to talk to him. It is very important."

"I am not helping you harm the aisymnētēs' son."

The hooded man shook his head. "It's not what you think."

"Now I know you are lying about Sappho. She would not condone this."

He nodded. "One would think so, nowadays. But boy, you should have seen her in her youth." He risked a fond little laugh. "She was great then. So much fire. So much passion. Hasn't she told you about being exiled to Sicily back then?"

Anactoria studied the man in front of her.

"We got exiled together," he added with pride.

"She never said anything about being exiled with anyone."

"Oh?"

Alcaeus could not help the little stab of disappointment. "I really thought she'd have mentioned that."

"If you *are* up to something, Old Phaon would have your head, never mind the aisymnētēs, and mine if I am seen with you."

"You won't get caught. Just ask him to come to his cabin. I'll be waiting there."

"What do you need to say to him? Tell me, and I'll tell him."

He shook his head again. "I'm sorry. I can't do that. As you said, I don't want to involve you too much." He met her gaze. "Honestly, you know Sappho. Do you think she would give her blessing," he held up the hairpin again, "if I had anything but honourable intentions? I can assure you, I, for one, am of like mind with Pittacus himself when he said, 'Achieve your victories without blood'. I'm really not here to try to kill Tyrrhaeus. You have to believe me. I just need to talk to him."

"What's going on here?" A loud voice boomed from behind Anactoria.

She swung round to see Old Phaon lumbering down the stairs towards her.

Luckily the position of the hooded man was hidden from direct view from the entrance, giving him that split second to jump through the rafters down onto the lower deck and disappear into the shadows.

Old Phaon moved surprisingly fast, but not fast enough to get a good enough look at the retreating figure.

He cursed loudly.

Then he turned and grabbed Anactoria by her long dark hair and pulled roughly.

"Who were you talking to?"

"No one, Master," she said.

Old Phaon's jealousy and suspicious nature got the better of him, even more so the drunker he was. She could smell the vile stench of stale liquor on his breath. Anactoria could see his foggy mind trying to make sense of the situation and then settle on what, to him, was the obvious conclusion.

"I see what this is. You think you could have yourself a sailor without me knowing? You're my property!" He spat at her. "I will say if, and who, can have you." Tightening his grip on her hair, he dragged her up to the upper deck.

"Friend, slaves and crew, listen to me," Old Phaon bellowed out over the galley for everyone to hear. He still had Anactoria clutched by the hair and was holding her at an awkward angle. "It seems my unruly slave here is feeling a little frisky and understandably, I think some of you would be tempted to help her out."

From where Anactoria stood, with as much composure as she could muster and trying not to wince from the pain of his cruel grip, she could feel more than see almost all the eyes from the mid and lower decks trained on her. Her shame flooded her cheeks.

"Come on, speak up. She's a great catch." He tore the thin chiton from her frame and started to roughly rip at her under garments.

Anactoria made an effort to straighten up and stand as tall and proud as she could, refusing to seem weak or intimidated.

"Don't be shy. I'm sure at least one of you has been tempted to have a taste of her," Old Phaon cooed to his men.

Anactoria caught sight of movement. To her horror she realised the blond acrobat that came on board with the big warrior was raising his hand. Luckily the big man pulled him back swiftly before Old Phaon could notice.

For a long moment the only sound that could be heard was the rhythmic splashing of the oars hitting the water.

"What about you, Tyrrhaeus?" Old Phaon whirled Anactoria round to face his guest seated behind him at the table inside the shelter. "Perhaps you'd like her—a gift to help you through the rough night."

Anactoria made sure to meet the young man's gaze squarely—an unspoken challenge.

Within a heartbeat their guest had the grace to lower his eyes and shake his head. From this close range she could see the red flush crawl over his young cheeks. He cleared his throat and pointed to the entrance to the lower deck. "Nature calls," he said.

"Well, I guess if you want something done, you have to do it yourself." Old Phaon shoved her forward, forcing her head and torso to connect hard with the table. He held her down using his substantial body weight.

She didn't need to see what was going on behind her to know what would come next.

She became aware of the old man fiddling with his garments against her rear and then she felt him penetrate her roughly. Clearly the adrenaline and excitement of the situation—new ship, new voyage, the presence of his guest as well as all that showmanship must have boosted his libido. For once, he did not need his leather olisbos. At least the sexual element of the assault would be short lived and insipid, she thought. But, rather than console her, this merely alerted her to what was to come. She was sure that afterwards, he would overcompensate for his shortcomings by inflicting more pain.

She was not wrong.

Once he had finished, he roughly pulled her back off the table. As she turned towards him, she felt a sharp thwack as the hilt of his kopis connected with her jaw. A searing pain shot up to her temple. The familiar warm, coppery taste filled her mouth. After the first blow came another and another and another followed by a number of well-aimed body blows. She lost track of how many.

It was not the violation or the pain that she found unbearable. The gods knew she had endured enough during her life as his slave. It was the humiliation. Up to now, no matter what unspeakable things he had done to her and her fellow slaves, it at least had always been in the privacy of his bedchamber. Now, this, was a step too far!

She drew on all her anger and her hatred toward him for strength to stay standing. As long as she was alive, she would not give him the satisfaction of seeing her collapse.

Once the body blows had stopped, through one swollen eye, she saw his fleshy features glistening from the exertion and looking dangerously scarlet. He was gulping like a punctured bellows. Not for the first time, she prayed to Aphrodite that his health would fail him then and there.

When he could finally speak again, he turned and barked incoherently out over the galley. "Let that be a lesson… Interfere with my property again… If I catch you, your punishment will be worse… You'll beg to die." Then, seemingly satisfied that his point was made, he grunted in the direction of the two cabin slaves who were waiting to serve the next course. "Put her where she can be seen."

The slaves swiftly sprang into action, seizing her, one on each arm, neither daring to make eye contact. They dragged her down onto the lower deck and chained her up to the central mast with thick, rusted, iron shackles.

Alcaeus used the end of the commotion after Old Phaon's spectacle to slip back to Antimenidas.

"What took you so long?" Antimenidas hissed. "Did you manage to do it?"

Alcaeus shook his head. "I was interrupted."

"What? Even with everyone's focus turned onto this freak show and you could not slip a little dram into an amphora?" Antimenidas huffed with disapproval. "Wait a bit till things calm down, and then try again."

Alcaeus shook his head again.

This shocked Antimenidas and he frowned.

"I'm afraid I can't. The flask broke."

"What?"

Alcaeus could see his brother's cheeks colour highlighting his scar.

"Sorry, I—"

"Never mind," Antimenidas interrupted. "I don't want to hear it. I'll find another way of getting that boy off this ship."

"Let me talk to him," Alcaeus said. "I'll try to persuade him to come with us."

"No! You have done enough damage!"

The air felt thick. Sappho had been extra tense all afternoon—a common feeling when she was separated from Anactoria. She couldn't help it. Her mind would fill with strange imaginings and jealousies feeding off her own insecurities. Usually, she would channel the most extreme of these emotions into a new poem or performance. However, when she found her thoughts looping and she was getting more depressed about the ills of old age and struggling with her own poetic meter, she decided it was time to give up.

She summoned Kleïs to bring their outdoor cloaks and when they were ready, the two women left her residence and turned down the road towards the sea. She tried to seem nonchalant, feigning being outside for nothing more than a recreational walk, but in reality, she had a very specific destination in mind.

Sappho and Kleïs were heading towards the harbour, directly towards me. I scanned the surroundings but found nowhere to escape. I took a deep breath and straightened up. I had not expected an overly friendly greeting as I suspected Sappho might have seen me leaving the Kallisteia with Anactoria. However, even I was surprised to notice her hands ball into tight fists the moment she saw me—so tight I wondered if she was about to draw blood.

"Good day, Sappho," I said, as friendly as possible.

"Bilitis." She nodded cordially.

"What brings you out to the harbour?" I asked, making conversation, although I was pretty sure it had something to do with the same reason I was in the area myself—the ship I had come down to see set sail.

"I came to see The Alabastron," Sappho said, "My brother, Charaxus, told me about it. Apparently, it is said to be quite spectacular."

I nodded. "Yes, it was. It's a pity you missed it."

"Oh really?"

She craned her head to see into the harbour behind me.

I nodded. "The unpredictable arrivals and departures of the ships are a nuisance. My uncle is always complaining about that."

I could see her search the jetties across my shoulder. Her eyes finally landed on the old, discarded ship, the Eleni.

She sighed. "As it is in life," she said obscurely.

"Pardon?" I asked, not sure what I was missing.

She shook her head and changed the topic. "You saw it depart, no doubt?" she asked, with a curt tone.

I nodded, "Only because I happen to have come out early on my walk," I added quickly. I didn't want her to know I was there because I had hoped to catch a last glimpse of that Adonis of a slave who was beginning to occupy most of my waking thoughts.

"Of course. You walk," she said. I was not sure if it was genuine surprise or sarcasm in her voice.

"Yes, it is so beautiful along the coast. It would be a shame not to, really. It also keeps me fit and the fresh air keeps me young." I knew I was babbling now and as I spoke, I saw her raise an eyebrow.

Then she smiled a clay smile. "Well, enjoy the fresh air. We probably should go and find some ourselves."

I did not miss the insinuation.

"Oh, of course." I said with a courteous nod.

"Come Kleïs," she said and continued past me. Her young slave girl gave me a haughty look before falling in behind her.

The large, empty gap left by Old Phaon's new flagship tugged at Sappho's heart—an empty void left by the absence of her beloved Anactoria.

Sappho glanced back at the other ship, the Eleni, again. It looked old and discarded. She doubted that the old ferry would ever make another voyage.

Internally Sappho bristled at Bilitis' words. Bilitis was about half her years, so of course she was young. Sappho could feel her blood starting to boil. The nerve! Did that little whippet think she looked old? She quickened her step in irritation, to such an extent Kleïs had to trot to keep up.

"Oh Mistress! Look!" Kleïs called next to her, dragging her attention back to the world around them.

Sappho glanced in the direction Kleïs pointed. A small fleet of merchant ships had appeared on the horizon and were heading towards them, towards the port.

Sappho stopped to watch. Oh, if only Anactoria's ship was among them now.

"Some say that the most beautiful thing upon this dark earth is a host of horsemen,"[1] Sappho said wistfully. "Some say a host of foot soldiers, while still others claim it is the swift rhythmic oars of our fleet of ships," she nodded at the horizon, "but, for me, I think it is whatever one loves most."

"Surely some things are inherently more worthy of such praise than others?" Kleïs asked "Or at least one should choose what one loves wisely."

Sappho shook her head. "Think about it. It's easy to understand. Take Helen, for instance, the most beautiful of mortals on this earth. She could choose anyone she wanted in all the world, yet she chose the man who destroyed all the honour of Troy, succumbed to his every beck and call. So doing, she even left her dear son and her family to follow him to a far-off land. Women are easily led astray by love, especially when those near and dear are not present to remind them of what they have—out of sight out of mind."

Sappho gazed sadly out at the horizon.

Anactoria, you probably don't even spare me a thought when you are away, Sappho thought. But I hope you know that you, with your handsome face and your gentle ways, you are the most beautiful to me. I would rather gaze upon you now, here with me, than all the chariots and mail-clad footmen of Lydia. I know that in this world we cannot always have everything we want; yet to crave for even a little of what was once shared must be better than to forget it.

Kleïs rolled her eyes. She knew full well what Sappho's forlorn look out to sea meant. If only her mistress could get over her infatuation with that brutish slave and notice *her*. Talk about overlooking those nearest and dearest. If anyone knew that feeling, it was her!

"Look, Mistress," Kleïs said, struggling to keep the irritation out of her voice. She pointed at the horizon again. "I think there might be a storm coming. We had better head back."

Kleïs was right. Deep grey clouds were building to the south.

Oh Aphrodite, I hope Anactoria will be alright, Sappho prayed. Then she considered what she had heard her brother, Charaxus, a worthy seaman himself, say about Phaon's new ferry and its revolutionary design. She recalled him effusing about how fast and superior it was and that it was also, apparently, unsinkable. She hoped he was right, but resolved to perform an extra special rite to Aphrodite for Anactoria's safe return, just in case.

5

Poseidon had clutched his trident, amassed the clouds and churned the ocean into a foaming frenzy. He'd roused the blasts of all four Anemoi into a stormy clash worthy of the wrath of all the Olympians.

The storm had engulfed them so swiftly that the crew barely had time to drop the sails. Not that, with a fifty-strong team of oarsmen, it had really been necessary to put the sails up in the first place, but Phaon had commanded it. Why go slowly if you can go very, very fast, he'd reasoned.

The gale force winds tugged hard at even the bare masts and far too often caught the sides of the galley-like sails. The ship's unusual, top heavy weight distribution didn't help to keep it stable in the turbulent seas, and already the lower decks were awash with oceans of seawater that had streamed in via the oar hatches and over the galley edges as it rolled uncontrollably. In the large waves the ship pitched and plunged dangerously.

Syros was in a panic. He should have heeded the old boat builder's warning when he said nothing good could come from the new design. He cursed his own ego for not paying more attention and not trying harder to persuade stubborn Old Phaon to listen. Now, the old bastard was not even there to witness the mayhem in the wake of his hubris. After his demonstration with the slave girl, and yet more kraters of wine, he'd been hardly able to stand, so he and his guest had retired to their respective cabins. Initially, Syros was glad to have him out cold, so at least he couldn't interfere too much in the actual running of the ship. But now, he was not sure how he was going to get them out of there alive.

Another enormous wave crashed over the rails of the boat, drenching the deck and flooding the rows of oarsmen in the galley.

As the boat pitched excessively once again and slapped down hard on the water, Syros heard an alarming crack. He moved quickly to see what had happened. To his horror he saw the hull was splitting at the joists. It had been made so flat and broad in order to accommodate the space needed for the guest cabins and extra cargo areas that it could not withstand the impact of slapping onto the water with such force, wave after giant wave. If this continued, the ship would be at the bottom of the ocean before the night was out.

He had no choice.

"Get everyone off the ship! We are going down." He yelled at a couple of crewmen who were wrestling with a sail-cloth a few feet away from him. They were too late; water had already started pouring into the hull at the bow. Some of the slaves, fuelled by blind terror, had managed to break free from the ship and, despite still being shackled together, had taken to the stormy sea like rats. Syros knew that almost all of them were unable to swim and, really, they didn't stand a chance.

He fought his own overwhelming instincts to follow them and save himself, but as captain of the vessel, he knew he had a duty to get the aisymnētēs' son off the ship, never mind his employer, Old Phaon himself.

What in Tartarus was keeping Cicis? Antimenidas thought.

Once he realised it was no longer an option to save the ship, he'd sent Cicis to fetch Tyrrhaeus, while he focussed on securing the life-raft. Someone had to stand guard and fend off the hordes in the event the slaves realised that such a thing existed. It was only a small raft, barely big enough for four people, as it was intended only for Old Phaon and his prized guests.

Cicis was slight and nimble so navigating his way below deck should have been relatively easy. It was not even a very complicated task. They should both have been back with him by now.

As for Alcaeus…. Where in Zeus' name could he be? He hadn't seen him since their altercation after Old Phaon's spectacle. He could only hope Alcaeus would make it back before they needed to jump ship.

Just then he heard a loud creak from the ship, as they slapped down hard after another enormous wave lifted them towards the stars. The ship was on the verge of disintegrating around them. He knew he couldn't wait any longer. He had to find Cicis and get them off the ship now!

He propelled his bulky frame as fast as he could down to the cabins to find his brother.

At first Syros could not quite understand what he saw. As Poseidon's bolts lit the night sky, he could just make out a figure hunched over something on the floor in Tyrrhaeus' cabin.

"Tyrrhaeus, come!" Syros called over the noise of the crashing waves and rushing water. "We have to go!"

As he approached, Syros realised the figure was too short and stocky to be the otherwise lanky young man. In another flash of lightning he recognised the young blond acrobat boy from the crew.

"What in—" His words caught in his throat as large hands gripped his head and snapped his neck in a clean twist.

To his horror, as Antimenidas got to Tyrrhaeus's cabin, he found the captain of the ship standing over Cicis and Tyrrhaeus who were both on the floor for reasons he could not quite fathom. His intuition told him something had gone very wrong. Years of training and instinct kicked in. In two smooth moves—a lunge and a twist—he neutralised Syros and shoved him to the side. Thanks to the next flash of lightning he realised Cicis was sitting over Tyrrhaeus who was lying on the floor and there was a large kopis sticking out of Tyrrhaeus's chest.

Cicis turned to look up at his brother. His eyes were wide. "He won't come," Cicis shouted over the storm.

"Oh Zeus!" Antimenidas said.

"I'm sorry, brother," Cicis said.

Antimenidas didn't think twice. He grabbed Cicis by the scruff of his neck and hauled him up and out of the cabin. It was all over. All they could do now was try to get out of there alive.

Alcaeus had to move quickly. He was still reeling from what had just happened.

He was trying to get himself out of there as fast as he could when he stumbled across a couple of slaves who were trapped under a fallen beam. He couldn't ignore them. After struggling for what seemed like an age, now more than ever he was determined not to give up on them, he managed to pull them free. Then he tried his best to persuade them to get out and jump ship, like the rest of the crew and oarsmen. But the one, the younger man, barely older than a boy, was too scared and wouldn't move.

Alcaeus would never forget the look of resignation and love in the older slave's eyes as he too stopped, shook his head at Alcaeus and turned back to the boy. Last thing Alcaeus saw of them was them embracing before a deluge of seawater swamped them and sucked them out to sea.

By that stage the ship had taken on so much water and sustained so much damage that the only way across to the higher edge was along the central lower deck. His progress was frustratingly slow. The ship was rolling so much and it was hard to find traction on the wet and slippery wood.

The boat plunged suddenly sending him hurtling forward towards the midship mast.

That's when he saw her—the slave girl. After Old Phaon had made an example of her, she had been forgotten and left shackled to the mast.

He heard shouts coming from further ahead and saw two figures, one large and one smaller—the unmistakable silhouettes of his brothers—fighting the wind and the water to get across to the life raft. He knew he had to hurry. Cicis couldn't swim and Antimenidas would need his help. Yet, he hesitated. He couldn't leave the slave. Not like that, tied up.

"Alcaeus, we don't have time," he heard Antimenidas bellow.

Alcaeus looked back just in time to see a third figure coming up behind them. It was Old Phaon and it looked like he was gaining on them and about to make a lunge for Cicis.

"Look out!" Alcaeus shouted.

With a large roundhouse hammer fisted swing that lifted Old Phaon clear off the ground, Antimenidas disposed of him, sending Old Phaon and his kopis flying through the air to finally land head first, unconscious, on the deck a few feet from Alcaeus and the slave.

"For the sake of Zeus hurry up and come!" Antimenidas shouted.

Alcaeus turned back to the young slave. "I'm sorry, I don't know how to get you loose." Then as Tyche would have it, as he moved to go, he felt a strap tug around his neck. He realised it was his leather satchel, still slung over his shoulder. He pulled it open and rummaged inside. Next to the miraculously still intact vial of potion he found Sappho's hairpin and pulled it out. No one needed luck more than that slave did then. He handed it to her. "If you get free, you better bring that back to me, or Sappho will kill me!"

Alcaeus turned and headed up the deck, past an unconscious, most probably dead, Old Phaon.

Just then, a very large wave crashed over the side of the ship and slammed into the raft with such force that it fractured the planks.

"Grab the biggest piece you can lift and jump," Antimenidas shouted. Cicis did as he was told but hesitated on the edge of the ship, probably taken aback by the enormous waves out there.

"I have to go get him. I can't leave him!" Alcaeus shouted over the roar of the storm. He turned and started to fight the waves and water washing over the deck to get back to the entrance to the lower deck.

"Do it now!" he heard Antimenidas shout at his brother behind him and in the corner of his eye he saw him shove Cicis forward into the sea.

Then, as if out of nowhere, he felt big strong arms grab him, pull him back and turn him round. His brother looked him square on, his lips moving inches from Alcaeus's face. "It's too late. We have to go!"

Then, his brother shoved hard against his chest and shoulders sending him hurtling backwards over the side of the boat.

———

Sappho knelt at her private shrine and tried to focus on performing her regular rite to Aphrodite, but she struggled to clear her mind. Ever since the walk to the harbour, she had been plagued with an anxious sense of foreboding. She tried to remind herself that this was not the first time Anactoria had accompanied Old Phaon on a trip in a storm. However, something felt wrong. She had initially written it off as her natural concern for Anactoria, but if she was honest there was more to it.

It wasn't only the thought of losing Anactoria to the storm, Aphrodite forbid, but her thoughts were marred by doubts about Anactoria's love. She feared she would never truly have Anactoria's heart. Despite all the reassurance she could have, the fear would not leave her. If Anactoria ever rejected her—that would be a pain she could not bear!

There was only one cure. Aphrodite *had* to hear her prayers. She lit another candle and bowed her head.

"Eternal Aphrodite, thronged in flowers, daughter of Zeus and powerful enchantress, I pray that you take this burden from me. Please hear me. Please listen and hear my pleas, as you've done before, when you left your father's house and came to my rescue and answered my prayers. I remember it well. You appeared in your magnificent chariot, drawn swiftly down from the heavens, through the pale sky by vibrant birds. You came and smiled at me with your immortal beauty and said, 'Sweet child, what troubles you? Why have you called to me? What is it you want with all your impassioned heart? Who is it you would like me to lure to loving you? Sappho, who wrongs you?'

"I told you my pained heart's desire and you very kindly answered my prayer. You said, 'If now that person flees, she soon will follow; Where once she spurned your affections, from now she will offer you loving gifts; If 'till now she had been the beloved, she will now love you. I will make it so.'"

Sappho took a deep breath and wiped at the tears that were rolling down her cheeks.

"Please, Aphrodite, come to me again, now! Please answer me again. Release me from this pain! You gave me what I'd asked for then, but now all my heart desires is fulfilment of this love, or if not then contentment—no more longing and suffering as a result of this unfulfilled desire. Oh, please, Aphrodite come to my rescue."[1]

Anactoria had learnt a number of skills in her reasonably short time on this earth. Picking locks was one of them. The problem was usually getting hold of something to do it with. Thank Aphrodite for the man with Sappho's hairpin! A hairpin was not her first choice for this task, but it would work. If only the ship wasn't rolling around so much.

She had just freed her ankles and her left arm and was now trying to do the same to her right when she became aware of movement next to her. The bastard, Old Phaon, was regaining consciousness. He was in the process of trying to sit up. Her pulse quickened as her whole being swelled with anger at what he had done—not only at what he had done to *her* but the pain and cruelty he had dished out to her fellow slaves over the years. Someone needed to teach him a lesson.

From what she could tell, it was now only the two of them left on the ship. There was no one else there whom he could turn on or hold over her. Now was her chance. He deserved to pay for his wrongs, even if that were the last thing she did in this life.

She refocussed her efforts on the lock, and just before Old Phaon could gather his wits she broke free and in a few swift moves, despite her agony and pains, she grabbed the two nearest shackles and with a couple of clunks secured them around Old Phaon's wrists.

She could not hold back her satisfaction when she saw his eyes bulge in realisation that he was now chained to his own ship.

"Thought you'd walk away from this alive?" She pushed herself up against the mast.

"But, Ana —"

"No 'but Ana.'"

"Anactoria you can't do this!"

She laughed a hollow laugh. "You know how many times I've thought that about you?"

"Ana, you can't."

"Why on earth not?"

Old Phaon shook his head and the pitiful look on his face almost made her feel sorry for him.

"Give me one good reason," she shouted. When he didn't respond immediately, she decided it was divine justice that he should suffer the fate of his ship. She pushed herself off the mast and scrabbled her way to where the three men had jumped earlier. She passed something glistening in the dark and realised it was Old Phaon's kopis. She snatched it up thinking it could be useful to fashion a raft for herself and maybe cut some rope to tie herself to it. Her strength was running low.

Carried on a gust of wind from somewhere behind her came Old Phaon's disembodied words, "You can't do this to your own flesh and blood."

At first, she was not sure if she had merely imagined it, but then the meaning of those words came into focus and once they were loud and clear in her mind, each word stung more than the salt seawater on her open wounds ever could. All the pain and humiliation she had suffered at his hand up to that moment paled in comparison to that singular blow.

She slowly turned back.

"What did you say?" She tried to keep her voice even.

She saw Old Phaon nod hopelessly.

"What did you say?" She walked up to him, her attention narrowing until there was nothing else in the world other than the pathetic lump of a man half-sitting, half-lying in front of her.

"I said, you can't do this to me…. I'm your father."

Anactoria shook her head slowly still grappling with the sense of his words.

He nodded again. "My Eleni, my only love, died giving birth to you. So, you see you are my daughter. That is why I always kept you close."

"Close?" she said quietly to no one.

He nodded. "Yes, I mean I did not sell you and you got your own chamber and I kept you with me. You were special. You were mine."

Suddenly the years of abuse she had witnessed and suffered flooded back. She remembered that when it became particularly bad and felt unendurable, she would dream little dreams of how somewhere in the world she had loving parents that were still looking for her. That she had been kidnapped and taken from them and how someday they would be reunited. She couldn't recall how often that tiny spark of hope—that someone, somewhere, out there cared for her —was her only lifeline, her only balm against the unbearable pain, and the morsel of strength she clung to, to be able to carry on.

She could feel the rage building up inside her, more violent than any storm.

With strength she did not know she had, she grabbed a spare length of chain from the shackles and wrapped it around Phaon, securing the pleading, pathetic, old man.

When he realised that his pleas were falling on deaf ears he resorted to his usual insults and verbal abuse.

"I was wrong to keep you even as a slave. I should've stuck with my original decision to have you ended like you ended your mother's life. At least I got a few more good fucks out of you as Eleni's stand-in."

Something snapped inside Anactoria. She ripped his garments from his body and with one swift swing of the kopis she sliced his shrivelled lump of a manhood clean off.

The howl that came out of him could have been heard in Tartarus. She wasn't sure if the tempest had actually dissipated at that point or whether it was just the haze of fury that cloaked her as if she stood in the eye of the storm. A calmness she had never felt before enveloped her.

She stood there with the bloody lump of flesh in her hand watching as Old Phaon went from screaming, to whimpering to eventually unconscious either from the pain or the loss of blood that was gushing from his wound.

She turned and headed to the side of the ship. There, looking out into the stormy darkness she held up the bloody member.

"Aphrodite, hear me. I offer you this, in your honour, in the hope that you may grant me this one wish… that like you… I may be reborn and rise out of the sea as you once did from your father's genitals."[2] She flung the lump of flesh as far as she could out into the sea.

All around her the ship creaked and gave a moan as if breathing its final breath. She grabbed a large plank and with the kopis cut a length of rope before she too leapt overboard.

Alcaeus's muscles screamed with fatigue and lack of oxygen. His hands and legs were so cold, his grip started to slip. Wood shards and splinters dug deep into his flesh as he tried to hang on. He didn't care. In fact, he tried to jam his hands on any protruding nail or shard that could give him even the slightest bit of traction. But they wouldn't hold. Wave after relentless wave slammed into him, filling his already searing lungs with more and more water, dunking and disorientating him until he hardly knew which way was up, towards that critical, life-giving gulp of air.

Then, Poseidon's final angry blow crashed into him, whipping the flimsy raft up into the air like it was nothing more than a dry autumn leaf and thumping it down onto the hard water where it exploded like fire sticks, trapping him in an endless tempestuous tumble of salt, sea water and desperation. A suffocated primal scream built up in his chest as darkness took over his senses.

He would certainly have drowned, had Antimenidas not been there to pull him out of the whirlpool and haul him on to the last surviving chunk of raft alongside Cicis.

6

Alcaeus jolted upright, drenched with sweat.

Where was he? Where were his brothers? Tyrrhaeus?

Panting furiously, he squinted into the dark, trying to make sense of his surroundings.

He was no longer out at sea.

He was alone.

He tried to think.

The last thing he remembered was being hauled onto Antimenidas's shoulders.

How?

When?

Then more of the memory of their watery ordeal and the events on the ship rushed back.

After what had seemed like lifetimes of drifting in and out of consciousness, they must have finally washed up onto some shore. He remembered being too tired to move. He'd have been content to die right there, but Antimenidas, as usual, was made of far tougher stuff. He used to joke with his brother that that was why he was the warrior and Alcaeus was the poet. But thank Zeus he was!

He studied his surroundings again. He was in an unfamiliar room which, from its Spartan appearance, must have been a guest house or an inn.

He made a move to get up. His body ached as though he'd been in a boxing match with the gods—well he figured that he pretty much had been, with Poseidon at least. He hobbled over to the little table standing by the window. It had a small krater and a large bowl on it. He picked up the krater and sniffed it. It was filled with water. He took a few large gulps of the cool liquid.

He felt like he had been in a desert for days. Ironic when he had practically been submerged in sea water instead. As soon as the gulps of liquid hit the pit of his stomach, they came out again with a force to match any wave Poseidon had whipped up. He just managed to puke into the bowl. He was too dehydrated to drink.

He caught sight of his hands in the moonlight. They looked dark and dirty. He poured some of the cool water over them. The large, red, angry cuts left by the wooden shards and nails stung like tongues of fire on his skin. He winced and put the krater down, wiping his hands on the cloth that had been lying folded on the table.

He needed to go and find the others.

Alcaeus found Cicis and Antimenidas sitting in an adjacent tavern, tucking into a meal. Relief flooded him and he suddenly felt so overwhelmed he had to bite back the tears to such an extent he could hardly speak. Instead, he play-tackled Cicis and engulfed him in a bear hug.

"Eww," Cicis said shrugging off the physical contact without taking his eyes off his plate of bread and cheese.

Alcaeus went to do the same to Antimenidas but the 'don't you dare' look on his big brother's face caught him short.

Alcaeus lifted his hands in surrender and backed off.

"All right?" Antimenidas said, more in the manner of a casual salute than a question, before returning his attention to the chunk of bread in his hand.

Alcaeus nodded and swiftly dried a tear off his cheek. "What have I missed?" He took a seat next to Cicis.

"Ant said, 'princess has finally woken.'" Cicis smiled with a full mouth.

"He did, did he?" Alcaeus eyed his two brothers.

Antimenidas huffed and stuffed his final hunk of bread into his mouth.

Alcaeus's stomach grumbled. He couldn't remember when he had last eaten. "How did you get food?"

"The waitress said it's on the house," Antimenidas said with a mouth full of bread.

"I asked for mine on a plate." Cicis added, rearranging a chunk of cheese on his slab of bread.

"Great, I need some too."

He looked up and gestured to the small, buxom woman, with ears that protruded through her long, wiry dark hair, not dissimilar to the handles of the skyphos she had just delivered to the only other table with occupants.

"Can I have whatever they had," Alcaeus said when the woman got near, nodding at Antimenidas's plate.

She huffed in a manner suggesting a world-weariness that could only be acquired after a lifetime of serving transient strangers in a coastal tavern.

Alcaeus watched her waddle over to the large hearth where round, fresh loaves had been stacked like a mini Lesbian wall[1] in order to stay warm.

"So, are either of you going to tell me what happened and where we are? Where are the others?" Alcaeus looked around the small tavern, making sure that he had not overlooked anyone else. The two weather-beaten old men at the nearby table smiled toothless smiles at him and then slurped loudly from their skyphoi.

Antimenidas nodded slowly. "I have missed your enquiring mind, brother." Then, in a deliberately low voice, he proceeded to bring Alcaeus up to speed.

Once they had run ashore, Antimenidas managed to drag them to a nearby coastal inn. The story he had spun was that they were fishermen and their little boat had been no match for the storm. Fortunately, the innkeeper was the doting father of two budding fishermen himself, so he was naturally sympathetic, offering them a room and food on the house until they were well enough to make their way home.

As for their location, Antimenidas confirmed that the storm currents had pushed them back, northwards, and strong Eurus had blown them west until they washed up on the southwest coast of Lesvos, on the beach of the coastal town of Skala Eressos.

Alcaeus chuckled.

"And what could possibly be funny?" Antimenidas asked.

"Nothing." Alcaeus shook his head. "I was just thinking that Sappho would not be pleased if she knew I was here. She'd find it somewhat ironic that it took a storm and Poseidon's wrath to finally get me to see her birth place."

Antimenidas brought his hand down hard on the table, so hard both of the other guests turned to look. "Do you not understand how serious this is?" he hissed through gritted teeth.

Just then the waitress approached with a skyphos of wine for Alcaeus. He suspected her timely arrival was intentional—a tactful way to avert what must have looked like an imminent brawl. He accepted the skyphos and gave her a grateful smile but, not wanting more projectile vomit at that point, he ignored the cup once it was on the table.

Antimenidas picked up his own drink, one of his large warrior hands just about wrapping around the big cup. He took a gulp while he waited for the woman to depart out of earshot.

"Where is everyone—the other survivors?"

Antimenidas shook his head and then he muttered into his drink. "There are none."

"What do you mean? None?" Alcaeus frowned, pin pricks of shock working their way up his neck. "Phaon? Syros?"

Antimenidas said nothing, just stared at his drink.

"Not even a few of the slaves?"

Antimenidas shook his head slightly.

Alcaeus felt his rage and sorrow bubble up with tears, stinging the corners of his eyes.

"Besides, it is better that way," Antimenidas said stretching out his hand and gently placing it on the back of Cicis's neck, soothing him. "If anyone can do as much as place us on that ship, Pittacus would not think twice before he executes us. No questions asked."

Alcaeus sat stunned. Then he slowly shook his head willing for the truth to be different. His brother was right. If Pittacus so much as got a whiff that they had been present on the ship on which his son had died, they would immediately be blamed, regardless of the truth to the contrary.

Antimenidas let go of his little brother's neck and refocussed on his drink. "We can only pray to any of the gods that might be paying a sand-grain's worth of attention to our pitiful lives that there are no survivors and no witnesses that can tie us to Tyrrhaeus or the ship."

The waitress arrived back with a large plate of bread and some very smelly cheese.

Alcaeus was suddenly not hungry anymore. He wanted to stand up and shout the building down or if not, pummel the walls until his hands hurt more than his heart. But, instead, he started to pick at his bread. "So, what happens now?" he asked.

"Nothing. We wait. We see if any of the gods answer our prayers."

"And if they don't?"

Antimenidas banged down his skyphos, sloshing wine over the edge. "Then we deal with it." Antimenidas held Alcaeus's gaze. His meaning was crystal clear: there could be no witnesses.

Antimenidas took another gulp of his drink, before he continued more calmly. "In a few days we can head back to Mytilene. We will pretend to have arrived back from Anatolia. There we can spread the word of happy sightings of Tyrrhaeus in Ephesus."

"As if nothing went wrong?" Alcaeus's voice cracked.

Antimenidas nodded. "If there's no body found, or at least if people think he's still alive and well, there could've been no crime to investigate."

"What about the ship? That was big news. Will people not ask what happened to it?"

"Well, unless there are survivors, there will be no-one to ask. It can become one of the greatest mysteries of our time. Maybe you can write a poem about how The Alabastron found its way to Atlantis."

Alcaeus wasn't sure whether he detected sarcasm in his brother's tone or not. But he decided to let it go. His heart felt crushed as he thought of young, trouble Tyrrhaeus, the two devoted slaves in the Pit and the slave girl on the deck. He wondered if by some miracle of the gods *she* could have survived. The chances were about as high as finding a painted glass shard in a desert. Either way, he was not going to share any of his thoughts with Antimenidas right then.

I hadn't slept very well. So, I got up earlier than normal and took my regular walk along the beach road from my uncle's villa, north towards the port. I stopped off at the kittens and was relieved to see that they had survived the unforgiving night.

I didn't know why I did it to myself. The whole point of accepting Old Phaon's gift of the young slave was to get over the heartache of Mnasidika leaving me. The idea was not to fall for yet another beauty —be it a completely different sort. I compared Mnasidika and Anactoria in my mind's eye. They were nothing alike. Mnasidika was small, petite and very sweetly feminine. Anactoria, on the other hand, was really so much more a female Adonis—handsome, strong, androgynous.

I found myself smiling at the memory of our night together—the feeling of those strong hands enveloping me, caressing me, and taking me to heights of pleasure I had only previously dreamed about.

Oh, I longed for her to get back soon so she could do that to me again. Old Phaon would no doubt want top drachma for her now, but she was worth it. I didn't have much else to spend my allowance on anyway.

I looked around and took in the beautiful morning view of the calm, mirror-like sea, now barely lapping at the shore. The morning sky was crisp and clear. One would never have guessed that only the previous night this coastline had been pummelled by such a spectacular storm. The only sign was the inevitable flotsam that had washed up on the beach, driven here by the ardour of the Anemoi. Most of the debris consisted of seaweed and organic matter. I always used to dream that someday a big treasure would wash up on these shores and I would be the one to discover it. "Maybe something from Atlantis," I once told my uncle.

He just laughed at me.

He was a practical man, not particularly religious—a fact he kept to himself. Anyone who was not devoted to at least one deity was frowned upon in these parts. When I was little he explained to me how, as a result of his travels, he had been exposed to so many different people and cultures, each with their own deities and beliefs. I remembered him saying, "How could any man decide his deities were any more real than another man's?" As a result, he concluded they were probably all either equal, all existed or none did. Who was he to decide?

I was happily caught up in my own reverie and idly scanning the beach when I noticed some larger fragments of wood had washed up with the seaweed. Oh dear, I thought, I hope Poseidon hasn't claimed some poor, unsuspecting fisherman and his boat last night.

That is when I saw it.

It looked like a... a hand.

My heart raced in my chest.

I ran over to where it protruded from a clump of bladderwrack and splintered wood. Soon I had excavated the thin, naked figure. It was a youth... no, a woman! That was unusual. A woman's place was generally on land, in the home.

I carefully rolled her over and turned her head up out of the sand, wiping away the tangles of dark hair. Her face had been badly damaged. But as I studied her face, I realised there was something familiar about her. Then, I almost fainted as panic gripped my heart.

It couldn't be!

Frantically, I began to call Anactoria's name, repeatedly beseeching her to wake up. In desperation I grabbed her shoulders and shook her violently.

My new found love could not be dead!

I got no response from her body, no sign of life. How could this be happening? How could she too leave me?

"No, Poseidon, you cannot have her!" I howled out my distress.

Suddenly, my sorrow was displaced by rage—an incredible wave of rage. I let her drop to the sand and began to pummel her? She was not going to leave me too!

"No!" I cried out and with a fist balled in anger I banged down hard on her chest. I wanted her to feel it all the way in Tartarus. How I thought that would work, I don't know. I guess, on some level, I believed that for a while after our death we still retain an ethereal connection with our bodies and this life, at least until we have been ferried across the Styx. I prayed she had not reached there yet.

I slammed down hard once more.

And then, one of the gods must have heard my pleas, for Anactoria's lifeless body began to move. She started to convulse, gasping for breath and coughing wildly in an attempt to expel the water from her lungs.

Astounded, I helped her sit up. Relief coursed through me. She was alive!

As soon as her coughing had calmed, I clutched her to me, hard, as if I could infuse my life force into her being.

I'm not sure how long I sat like that, with her in my arms, saying prayers of thanks to every god I knew. But eventually, to my horror, I realised she was not moving anymore. The terror that she had actually slipped away in the end, while I was prematurely celebrating her return, almost paralysed me. But luckily, sitting with her like that, I could feel her soft breath on my shoulder. She was alive but unconscious.

I needed to get help.

I tried to lift her. She was too heavy. I needed something to transport her in.

Thank Tyche, a slave was passing on the road just off the beach with an empty cart—probably on his way to the harbour market. I used some of the hundred drachma I had on me as leverage to get him to help me pick up Anactoria and put her in his cart.

But, where to take her? Who would treat a slave? Unless she was accompanied by her master who could foot the bill no one would even look at her.

I could take her home, to my uncle's place. But I had no experience in nursing people back to health and there was no telling the extent of her injuries.

Then it occurred to me. The young slave might know.

At first, he looked blank, then a guarded expression crossed his face.

"What?" I was getting impatient. "If you know somewhere, you *have* to tell me now."

He shook his head.

"I promise, nobody will get in trouble. But this is urgent."

"I'm not supposed to say." He looked around nervously.

I approached him square on, and took his bony shoulders in my hands so that I could look at him directly. I searched his deep, dark eyes. "Listen to me. This is a matter of life and death. If you know somewhere where this young woman can be treated you have to tell me."

He blinked a couple of times. Finally, he licked his lips and glanced around again before he said really softly. "My aunty once got help from Lady Sappho."

"Lady Sappho?" I asked, astounded. "Sappho, wife of Kerkylas?"

He nodded. "But please, I don't want to cause any problem. She is very kind, especially to young girl slaves, and has helped a number of them when they are in trouble. But we're not supposed to say."

I nodded. "It's okay." I squeezed his thin shoulders again. "Thank you. Now, do you think you can help me get the cart to Sappho's villa without arousing suspicion?"

Again, he looked unsure, but finally he nodded. He picked up a large, empty sack from the bottom corner of the cart and gently threw it over the alarmingly frail-looking, unconscious, Anactoria.

I followed the slave with his cart as fast as I could through the rough, uneven street to Sappho's villa.

If Sappho really was helping young slave girls, I understood why this would need to be kept quiet. Anyone found meddling in the business of another citizen, including interfering with their slaves unbidden, would be in deep trouble and likely sued for property damage. So, I was careful to remain discreet, refusing even to tell Sappho's personal slave what business brought me there.

The young girl showed me to the gynaeceum.

I couldn't help but pace impatiently, while I waited for Sappho to arrive.

I'm not sure what kept her, whether it was genuine other pressing business or merely a tactic to assert dominance—I suppose I will never know. But after a not insignificant wait, Sappho finally showed herself.

She, being such a talented actress, hid her feelings very well about seeing me in her home, but when I insisted on speaking to her in private, she looked suspicious.

What all her acting skills and professionalism could not hide from me was her reaction to the contents of the cart. Without a word she sprang into action. She dismissed the house slave and bid me and the slave pushing the cart to follow her. She led us a short way along the hall from the gynaeceum to a guest bedroom. Here, she showed us in and closed the door behind us.

Up until then, I hadn't really thought through how Sappho, personally, would react to seeing Anactoria in such a state; so far my entire focus had been on getting Anactoria to desperately needed help. Only when I saw the colour drain from Sappho's face and her stagger slightly in shock that I knew Anactoria was no ordinary slave to her.

"I was told you sometimes help slaves in need, so I decided to bring her straight here. For that reason, and the fact that I believe you are familiar with this one, and her situation, I thought it best to see you privately," I explained.

"Quick, help me get her into the bed," she said.

We did.

"Wait here," she said to me. Then she led out the young slave with his cart and returned a short while later with a basin of water and cloths.

I helped her move Anactoria so that we could wash her, and with obvious, practised efficiency, Sappho set to work, tending to her most urgent injuries. Honestly, until that point, I hadn't realised the full extent of Anactoria's wounds.

I'm not sure how long I was there, observing, rinsing cloths, passing on ointments and generally doing what I could to help.

On one level, I knew I'd made the right decision to bring her to Sappho. There was no doubt that she was safe, in competent hands. But, on another, I wished that I could've taken her home and cared for her myself. As I watched Sappho tend to poor Anactoria I tried not to let pangs of jealousy cloud my judgement. The important thing was that Anactoria should get better.

After she had finished, Sappho stood back with a worried expression gazing at the still unconscious Anactoria.

"We have done as much as we can for her. Now we wait." Then, she looked around suspiciously even though we were the only two people in the room. She jerked her head, indicating that I should follow her to the far corner, out of earshot of Anactoria and any passers-by beyond the door in the rest of the house.

"It doesn't take much to assume that finding her like this raises a number of uncomfortable questions about the ship and what could have happened on it. So, you were right about acting with discretion. We should keep this just between ourselves."

I nodded. "Of course."

She held my gaze for a moment longer, as if to assess the level of my commitment.

She was right. We had no idea what really had happened to Anactoria. For all we knew, she could have jumped ship, or more likely been cast off as punishment by her cruel tyrant of a master, and not been intended to survive at all. Not only was Anactoria's future at stake, but the penalty for anyone assisting someone else's condemned slave was extremely high. We needed her to regain consciousness soon, in the hope that she could tell us what had happened.

After seeing how Sappho tended to Anactoria, I knew that in many ways I had made the right decision to bring Anactoria here. It was clear that Sappho would do anything to help her. So, with a lighter heart than when I had arrived, I allowed Sappho to show me out. I left with a promise to visit the following day to see if I could help.

Once the door closed behind Bilitis, Sappho headed back to Anactoria's chamber.

Kleïs heard Sappho see her guest out, so she went to meet her, to resume her duties of attendance.

"No, thank you, Kleïs." Sappho said without pause, "I don't need you tonight. You can get on with your other duties. And no one is to go into the guest room, is that understood. And by that, I mean *no one.*"

Sappho was so preoccupied that she didn't notice Kleïs's dejected reaction. Instead, she headed straight back to Anactoria's bedroom, securing the door firmly behind her.

Anactoria hadn't moved since Sappho had finished cleaning and dressing her wounds. Sappho's heart creased to see her beloved so broken. But, right now, she was not there for that.

When she and Bilitis were removing the flimsy shreds of garment that had survived on Anactoria's body, Sappho had glimpsed something hard and sharp stuck in the material. She thought she recognised it, but there had been no time to inspect it then. If it was what she thought it was, she didn't want prying eyes on it. So, she'd quickly stowed it to one side for inspection when she had a private moment.

The cloth was wet and cold to the touch and covered in stains of Anactoria's blood. Sappho gently unfolded it. She let out a small involuntary gasp. She was right. There in the bloodied cloth lay her own mother-of-pearl hairpin.

How did that end up here, with Anactoria?

She must have crossed paths with Alcaeus.

Sappho thought back to Alcaeus's last visit. What did he say? Something about a mission for which he needed luck. Could that mission have involved going on Old Phaon's boat?

What had happened on that ship?

She sat down on the bed next to her love and took hold of her hand. She wished, now more than ever, that Anactoria would recover swiftly. She needed to know what had gone on. This was a delicate and troublesome situation, not least because it was illegal to save a slave. If Old Phaon had intended to dispose of Anactoria, Sappho had no right to stop it. Then a terrible thought struck her. What if Alcaeus had been on the new boat too and something had happened to the whole vessel?

Something else niggled at the back of her mind: Bilitis. What was her interest here?

She was very grateful that Bilitis had rescued Anactoria and brought her to her. It was the why that bothered her. Why would Bilitis care enough to rescue someone else's slave? What was Anactoria to her? The most worrying thing was the way she'd seen Bilitis look at Anactoria. She couldn't misinterpret that look. She knew it well. She had seen it so many times in her life, when one human being looked at another with devotion.

The thought was too much to bear.

Sappho got up abruptly.

Could Bilitis have designs on Anactoria? She remembered seeing Anactoria leaving with Bilitis on the day of the festival. What happened? How long had they been spending time together?

She turned to her sleeping love.

Could the feelings be mutual?

Sappho felt nauseous at the thought. Surely not? She had to believe *not*. She couldn't cope with the pain. By the gods, Aphrodite could not be that cruel.

The following day, after another very restless night of worry, I rose early and as I had promised, went straight to Sappho's house. I was desperate to find out if there had been any change in Anactoria's condition.

Unfortunately, I was met by Sappho's gatekeeper, Kleïs. She wouldn't show me into the house and kept saying that her mistress did not want to be disturbed. She said she would tell Sappho that I had called and she was sure Sappho would send word when she could see me.

It really irked me to be brushed aside like that, but there was nothing I could do without risking exposing Anactoria, so I went for a long walk to clear my head.

I tried again the next day and the next.

Eventually, I reassured myself that Sappho's behaviour was good news. She would only keep me in the dark if Anactoria had survived. I also knew that Sappho would not be able to keep Anactoria hostage like this forever. So, all I could do was stay calm and bide my time.

For the next few days, Sappho didn't leave Anactoria's side. She spent every moment with her, behind the closed doors of the guest room, personally tending to her every need. While Anactoria was unconscious, Sappho curled herself around her sleeping form, cocooning her to give her comfort, and when she finally regained consciousness, Sappho fed her, bathed her and changed her dressings devotedly.

When Sappho felt Anactoria was strong enough, she sat her up and gently broached the topic of what had happened the night of the storm.

Anactoria initially struggled, or perhaps was reluctant to remember, but eventually, through tears of terror and shock that streamed down her chiselled face, she told Sappho everything.

At the sight of her lover's distress, Sappho drew her into her arms and held her tightly.

"You're safe now," Sappho said softly. Both women knew that was very far from the truth, but neither were ready to tackle that reality. Instead, they collapsed back onto the bed clasping each other as if it were their last embrace. Soon their chaste hug morphed into gentle, then more passionate and urgent caresses, which ignited insatiable fires.

They spent a number of days and nights making love, drowning all their worries in each other's bliss.

Then one morning, Sappho woke up distracted—so distracted that she hardly noticed Anactoria's kisses migrating down to the soft, dark curls of her delta. Nor did she notice when Anactoria started licking and sucking at her most intimately, in a way which normally brought Sappho cascading to the height of her ecstasy within heartbeats.

The reality of their situation, the knowledge of what the future could entail and what could happen to Anactoria if anyone found out she was alive, had finally settled like a dark cloud over Sappho.

"There must be a way we could make this work!" Sappho suddenly said and sat up.

A bewildered Anactoria pushed herself upright. "Clearly I've lost my touch," she said, only half joking.

Sappho realised what she meant. "Oh, your touch is more magical than you can imagine, my love." She sat forward and cupped Anactoria's chin. "But we have to work out how to make things right," she said.

"What are you talking about?"

"I have just realised that, if what you say is correct, and Old Phaon is definitely dead, you don't have a master to claim you."

Anactoria looked glum. "Yes, what will happen to me?" She rolled away onto her back. "I can't be sold on before we make it clear that he is dead. The moment I tell people he is dead, they'll condemn me to death for his murder, or at best I'll be placed on auction and who knows where I'll end up, or who my new master will be." Anactoria sat up and took a drink from the cup of water next to the bed.

Suddenly a thought struck her. "Actually…" she said turning back. "Maybe you can just say that Phaon had agreed to sell me to you and that I now belong to you?"

Sappho got up and started pacing at the foot of the bed. "No, I've thought about that, but he has been too public, telling anyone who wanted to listen that he would only sell you to me 'over his dead body.'"

Anactoria scoffed at the irony. "Yes, well—"

Suddenly Sappho's face lit up. She rushed over to Anactoria "Oh thank you, thank you, Aphrodite!" she addressed the heavens as she went. She sat down in front of Anactoria and took a deep breath.

"I know this sounds crazy, but hear me out. The night you were on the boat in the storm, I prayed to Aphrodite to take away my pain, my longing for you." Sappho looked guilty. "I had meant for her to make me care less for you since it was obvious that Old Phaon would never allow me to buy you."

"You wanted to care less for me?" Anactoria looked hurt.

"Yes, and I regret that now. I don't know how I could ever have even contemplated that thought. You bring me such joy and although sometimes equal sorrow, I would never want to lose you." She stroked Anactoria's cheek gently. "I think Aphrodite knew my heart better than I, so rather than answering my prayer as I wanted it, she came up with a different solution." Sappho smiled. "And I think she has, as usual, exceeded my expectations!"

Anactoria was still confused.

"You see, it is a shameful fact that no one, no free person, pays much attention to individual slaves." She grabbed Anactoria's hand and helped her up from the bed to come to stand in front of the mirror. She stood behind Anactoria. "With only a little bit of effort we could turn you into someone else... A free woman." She gathered Anactoria's hair up into a bun away from her face.

Then something occurred to her. "Or even a man." They both stared at the young, androgynous form and boyish face that reflected back at them. "No-one would look twice at a beautiful new young man in town. As a free man, you can come and go as you please. No one would need to own you. This way you can be free, have money, a business and a life of your own." Sappho considered what a beautiful young man Anactoria would make. "Or maybe they would look more than twice." Twinges of jealousy twisted in her gut. Then she brushed off the thought.

Anactoria still looked blank, "What does this have to do with Aphrodite?"

"Don't you see." Sappho turned Anactoria to her, clasping both her hands. "She has given us a means to take away my pain and longing, just not in the way I had expected, which was by making me care less for you. Instead, she has given us a far, far better solution."

Anactoria thought back to the ship and her own prayer to Aphrodite to be reborn. Could it actually be possible?

Suddenly fear gripped Sappho's heart. Would Anactoria still be with her if she had a free choice? She pushed the thought aside.

Anactoria was still not convinced. "Even if we go with this, what would I do? I have no money to start a business and no real skills." She moved off, back to the bed.

Sappho started to pace again, thinking hard.

"I know!" Sappho burst out. "Why not take over Old Phaon's business?"

"What?" Anactoria shook her head vigorously.

"This is perfect." Sappho clapped her hands. "I mean, you have lived with that man your entire life. You know his household, his people, and you also know his trade, from being his shadow almost everywhere he went. At the time you thought it was your curse, now you can turn it into your fortune. No one could know how to be him better than you."

"Be him? Either there is seriously something wrong with your eyes or Aphrodite has enchanted you. I do not look like an ugly old man! I would never be able to pass as him."

Sappho nodded, still processing ideas. "What do we have? Tell me again. The fourth hooded man. That was actually a stowaway Xanthias had let on the ship?"

Anactoria nodded.

"What happened to her?"

Anactoria shrugged, ashamed that she had not spared the old woman more thought after being caught out by Old Phaon and dragged up to the deck-shelter.

"Okay. What if we invent a story? Thanks to Old Phaon's fat, loose lips we all know he had started ferrying special guests. What if he didn't only take illustrious, wealthy citizens? What if on this occasion he let an elderly, frail lady on board? But rather than being just any old woman, this time it was Aphrodite in disguise."

Anactoria shook her head.

Sappho held up a hand stopping her from interrupting. "And, even though she could not afford to pay, he agreed to take her. In exchange for his kindness, in a miracle befitting her greatness, she granted him his youth and your good looks." Sappho beamed at Anactoria, very pleased with her idea.

"There is only one problem," Anactoria scoffed. "Everyone knows that it will be a cold day in Tartarus when greedy Old Phaon would agree to ferry anyone for nothing, let alone a kindly old woman."

"Exactly, a deed so uncharacteristic deserves a miracle reward." Sappho smiled. "Don't knock the power of a good story. People are far better at accepting miracles when the recipient either really deserves it… or the odds of it happening are most unlikely. If we want them to believe someone like Old Phaon was granted your youthful good looks, then we need to make it seem very unlikely and his behaviour very uncharacteristic, to warrant such reward."

Anactoria just stared, unable to respond.

Sappho smiled and came over to Anactoria and kissed her chastely on the lips. "He would've had to have done something truly superhuman for him, in order to deserve being rewarded so handsomely… as you."

Anactoria pulled away. "So, you think I should pretend to be this new, younger Phaon?" Anactoria asked, her naturally deep voice rising a little.

Sappho nodded and sat down next to her on the bed.

"And you don't think that people, his household, would recognise me? I've been living with them too, for my entire life. Even if I fool them for a bit, what happens when I get caught? Then I not only get put to death for killing my master, I also get put to death for impersonating a citizen. I'm not sure which one they would try me for first. Either way, I will end up dead!"

"As I said, take it from me, most people outside of your household would definitely not recognise you. No disrespect but most free men don't pay much attention to slaves, not even if they are up close and personal, being pleasured by them." Sappho nodded again, acknowledging Anactoria's concern. "As for Phaon's household, I'm sure there is not one slave in it that would be sad to see him gone. They would all have a vested interest in going along with the ruse."

Anactoria thought for a moment. "Well, at the villa there is Kalliope, Kora, Eunice, and Ephoney. On the boats he is only close to Xanthias." She thought about how Old Phaon had treated Xanthias the day they departed. Hopefully that was enough for Xanthias to be pleased to see him dead too. If not, Xanthias could be a problem.

Then something occurred to her and her expression clouded. "What about Aphrodite? Would she not punish us for tarnishing her reputation?"

"I think as long as we make up a story worthy of her cunning and glory, we would have her blessing. Besides, she would probably enjoy the drama, not to mention getting the credit for working such an artful miracle."

Sappho leant in closer to Anactoria. She gently took hold of her chin and looked deep into her eyes. "We can do this…. *You* can do this." She closed the gap between them and kissed Anactoria.

This time, within moments, their kiss had ignited their passion. Anactoria raised herself up and pushed Sappho back onto the bed. Then she started to trail hot kisses all the way down Sappho's body, directly to her delta. She picked up her ministrations where she had been interrupted earlier. Within a few short heartbeats Sappho was moaning and writhing in pleasure, begging Anactoria for more.

7

*S*appho and Anactoria knew that if they were going to make their plan work, they needed to move fast. They couldn't risk anyone finding Anactoria at Sappho's residence, not even Kleïs.

Sappho, on account of her theatre and performance work, was a skilled make-up artist and master of disguise. As a result, she also had all the necessary tools and materials to hand and later that very day, she went about cutting Anactoria's hair into a short cut as was fashionable for a young man. Then she swept up all the offcuts and collected them in a little wooden box.

"Have you developed a new fetish, or is there a reason you're keeping that?" Anactoria asked, clearly puzzled by Sappho's actions.

Sappho laughed quietly. "There is a very good reason. You'll see. Now get some rest. I'll be back later and I'll wake you when it is time to get ready." Sappho took the box and left.

A while later Sappho returned with a bag of supplies, to find Anactoria still awake. She had been too nervous to sleep.

"First, I need to bind you. We need to tie the strophion tighter than normal to flatten your breasts." Sappho took out a long linen cloth from the bag and began to wrap it tightly around Anactoria's chest. Then she picked up a chiton she had selected and secreted away from Kerkylas's wardrobe. "I chose these based on what I can remember of Old Phaon's dress," Sappho helped Anactoria into the tunic and then fastened a woollen himation over the top. She had opted for the bulkier look of a woollen cloak over the linen to bulk out Anactoria's slighter frame.

"Do you really think this will work?" Anactoria asked.

Sappho didn't answer immediately. Instead she finished fastening the last few fibulae that held the cloak in place over the shoulder and arm. Then she took Anactoria by the hand, kissed her knuckles and gently pulled her around to look at herself in the mirror.

"Oh, my Artemis!" Anactoria covered her mouth with her hand in shock. She couldn't believe her eyes. Before her stood a person she hardly recognised. Her usual full chest was almost completely flat—the curve that remained under the tight cloth looked like nothing more than well-defined men's muscles. The combination of that, the male garments, her short hair and her naturally tall, athletic build, had turned her into a very convincing, all be it adolescent, young boy.

Sappho took hold of Anactoria's hand, bringing the younger woman's attention back to her. "Now, I can dress up the facade, but you need to bring the substance. You have to act the part and act like a man, or the illusion will crack instantly."

"How do I do that?" "There are a few basic rules. One, never touch your face unless you are in ostentatious, deliberate contemplation. Two, men generally are economical in their movements. Think big efficient movements, not little flutters as women do. Three, when in doubt don't speak. More wisdom and power, signs of truly respected men, are perceived in silence than in all the scholarly orations and writings."

Anactoria nodded repeatedly.

Sappho caught her chin. "Just once."

Anactoria obeyed with a more deliberate, single nod.

"Good." Sappho smiled. "Men also disagree more often than woman. It's showmanship. If you agree, sometimes it might be best not to respond."

Anactoria made an effort to suppress the nod.

"The final rule is that men take up space—to give them presence. To pass as a man, you are going to have to commit completely, take a leap of absolute faith. Call their bluff. Make it big, make it strong, even if it feels unnatural. In reality, it is even unnatural to men, but they practice hard for years. Unfortunately, we do not have years. But I know you can do this. You naturally have an inner presence—a match for any man. Let it prosper."

Anactoria gave another slow, deliberate nod.

"Now for the final touch," Sappho turned and opened the little box in which she had stowed the off-cuts of hair earlier. She pulled out something that looked like a small pelt. "I had my best artist make it. Of course, he does not know who it is for," Sappho explained as she went about fixing it to Anactoria's chin and jaw with a warm, waxy substance that felt soothing on her skin.

Once done, Sappho moved out of the way and Anactoria stared at her reflection. "Wow!" With the addition of the beard fashioned from her own hair, on top of the already convincing attire and short haircut, she was sure no-one would ever guess she was a woman, unless they actually saw her naked. Sappho had worked her magic.

"As I said, I can create the facade, but the rest is now up to you." Sappho squeezed Anactoria's shoulders gently.

Anactoria turned and grabbed Sappho strongly around the waist, pulling her toward her and kissed her firmly, almost forcefully.

"Will that do?" she said, with a wicked twinkle in her eye. When she finally released a breathless Sappho, Sappho could do nothing more than nod.

Under the cover of darkness, a striking young Phaon slipped out of Sappho's villa and made his way to Old Phaon's house.

They had decided that it would be best to break the news of Phaon's return to his household first to allow the initial rumours to circulate and get people used to the idea before Phaon made a public appearance in the harbour.

Anactoria managed to deal with the return to the villa fairly easily because it was such familiar territory. However, she was shaken by the looks of initial fear from the slaves and servants that greeted her. Although, given Old Phaon's behaviour, this did not surprise her. It chilled her soul to be on the receiving end of such trepidation. Pretty soon though, she was met more by surprise and quizzical looks when she was found to be mild tempered and kind.

A few days later, it became time to put into action the next part of the plan: young Phaon's unveiling.

Sappho had agreed to meet the disguised Anactoria in the market and to walk down to the harbour with her, pretending to be discussing business.

"Ah, good Sappho," Anactoria said more loudly than was necessary as she neared Sappho in the market. "You wanted to talk?"

"Yes, Phaon," Sappho said, playing along.

"Please, come." Anactoria bowed her head slightly as a sign of respect, "Walk with me, I unfortunately don't have time, I am needed in the harbour."

Sappho was amazed at the transformation. There was no sign of Anactoria the subservient slave woman under that facade. This person, this man before her, was confident, assertive and charming.

"What is it I can do for you?" Anactoria asked. "Is this about my lovely Ana, with whom you are obviously quite taken?"

Sappho did not miss the hint of a smile curling Anactoria's lips under her dusting of facial hair.

"No, Phaon," Sappho said. "I have far more important things to discuss, today."

"Oh... more important than that slave you hanker to buy from me?"

"Yes. Let's just say I'm more focussed on the master today." Sappho knew she was playing a dangerous game. She couldn't be seen to be flirting with Phaon in public, but the increased stakes of the situation were intoxicating and making her bold.

"Oh, really." Anactoria stopped walking and pinned Sappho with her dark eyes—the one thing no disguise could ever change. Luckily not many people ever looked into the eyes of their slaves—not as she had looked into Anactoria's.

Startled for a minute by a flutter in her delta, Sappho cleared her throat. "Ah, yes. I'd like to discuss bigger business with you, back at my villa, with my husband present."

"That does sound intriguing," Anactoria smiled again. Then she nodded. "I shall come to you as soon as I have concluded my business in the harbour. In the meantime, why don't you join me for the walk."

As they passed through the market, Sappho noticed the looks they received. It was obvious that the new young man in town was turning the heads of almost every girl, woman, boy and man they passed. She swallowed hard and tried to bury the serpent of jealousy that was twisting in her belly. She couldn't blame them. He certainly was striking and, even more arousing, was the secret knowledge that this handsome man, under it all, was her woman.

"Remember, don't act, be the great Phaon," Sappho coaxed in a whisper as they got near to the harbour.

Anactoria nodded. "'think and behave as if I am him'" she whispered back and took a deep steadying breath. "I have just come off a shipwreck and I'm pleased to be alive and back." Anactoria frowned. "Just one problem. I don't know if I can be as mean as the old man."

Sappho shook her head. "You don't have to be." On seeing the turmoil in Anactoria's eyes she had to work hard to resist squeezing her arm or taking her sweet, handsome face into her hands. "You have just had a near death experience and that can transform a man, even one as evil as Old Phaon."

"I hope you're right" Anactoria said.

Just then Anactoria caught sight of Xanthias standing on the quay, next to Phaon's dilapidated old Eleni. "Well, here goes," Anactoria muttered. She pulled her shoulders back, straightened up and headed over towards Xanthias with purpose.

"Xanthias, my friend," Anactoria said stretching out her arms and giving Xanthias the biggest manly hug she could, slapping him on the back. "You old daimon. It's me, Phaon. Don't you recognise me?"

"No," Xanthias said blandly.

"True, I'm a much-changed man. You will not believe what has happened to me, and it is you I have to thank."

"For what?"

"Do you remember the stowaway you smuggled onto The Alabastron?"

Xanthias shifted uncomfortably. "Yes, yes. I found out about her. It is not as if I didn't know you were stowing the poor away on my ships for years. But the point is, *she* turned out not to be who she seemed. In fact, she was the Divine Aphrodite herself in good disguise. During the journey to Anatolia she, in the form of the old woman whom you smuggled onto the ship, was discovered where she was hiding behind the crates on the lower deck. To this day I'm not quite sure why, but perhaps I was feeling generous, so I decided to show her mercy and allowed her to continue on the journey with us. My generosity must have impressed her and she chose to reward me well." Anactoria slapped Xanthias on the shoulder. "Thanks to you, she gave me back my youth."

Xanthias's gaze remained unflinching. "Where is The Alabastron now?"

Anactoria nodded, acknowledging Xanthias's obvious question. "Well, it seems Adrestia, Aphrodite's daughter, did not agree with her mother's reward and imposed her own retribution. Shortly after that my ship was caught in an epic storm and I fear, sadly, if it had not been for my newly acquired god-given strength and youth, I might not have survived. I actually suspect from what I have heard that I might be The Alabastron's sole survivor." She couldn't help feeling a genuine guilt and sorrow at the truth of that. She was pleased Old Phaon had got what he deserved, but she couldn't forget all the slaves, the crew and the poor old woman who had just wanted to get to her daughter.

When Anactoria looked up, having finished her story, a large group of eager listeners had gathered around her and Xanthias. Murmurs of scepticism bubbled through the crowd.

"Why would Aphrodite suddenly be interested in rewarding you for that? She is the goddess of love and matters related to marriage and romance, not virtue and propriety or in a habit of rewarding people for them," one man in the crowd shouted.

Suddenly afraid and feeling quite helpless, Anactoria glanced at Sappho, who was standing to one side, observing the crowd.

Sappho stepped forward. "Surely you do not question the power of Aphrodite?" She said sternly. She was widely known to be a devout follower of the goddess. Some even called her the Chosen of Aphrodite, and if anyone could be trusted to speak for the goddess, it was Sappho. "We cannot begin to imagine that we, as mere mortals, can understand the capricious nature of the gods. They are inscrutable to us. Ineffable. Who knows what lesson there is in the bestowal of this particular gift on this man?" Sappho went on to cite a number of examples where Aphrodite and other Olympians' actions were open to misunderstanding.

Much to Anactoria's relief, a few people in the crowd began to nod slowly, but she doubted Sappho's argument would be enough to sway the whole crowd.

Alcaeus headed to the port of Mytilene again. So far, there hadn't been news of any survivors from the ship to worry about. After a couple of weeks, when there was no return of The Alabastron, the town's folk had naturally become bemused at its long absence. Yet, the commonly-held belief that the ship had been built to be unsinkable prevented anyone from giving a sinister explanation much consideration. At most, a few jaded old mariners had been heard scaring little children with invented tales of dragons and daimons that could swallow the biggest ships on the ocean in one gulp.

Also, fortunately, word had not yet got out that Tyrrhaeus, son of Pittacus, was amongst the missing occupants of The Alabastron. Alcaeus thought Pittacus wouldn't want that known until it was absolutely necessary. There was no doubt that Pittacus would have immediately suspected villainy and had probably already started enquiring behind the scenes as to his son's whereabouts. But it was never good for a ruler to seem weak or affected before his foes, so he certainly would not make his enquiries publicly known until he was absolutely sure there had been foul play.

In order to combat that, Antimenidas had asked Alcaeus to start a rumour that Tyrrhaeus had been seen in Anatolia. The story he had spun was that Tyrrhaeus, unable to stand the pressure from his father, as aisymnētēs, had eloped with his new lover to Anatolia, where he was now happily enjoying his new freedom. If only that were true, Alcaeus thought, a lump forming in his throat. It was likely that the embarrassment of having his son choose to live a life deliberately away from him would be enough to stay any further attempts by Pittacus to track down his son. Alcaeus was pretty confident that things would stay this way, provided that the stories of sightings of Tyrrhaeus thriving on Anatolia continued to circulate. In devising these invented tales, Alcaeus tried to give sweet Tyrrhaeus the best life he had always wanted.

Despite there being no sign of further developments for some time, Antimenidas's overly cautious nature had caused him to insist Alcaeus keep patrolling the harbour, just in case there was news. Alcaeus had tried to persuade Antimenidas that his time and efforts could be used in myriad other ways to better help their cause and keep them out of trouble.

Alcaeus had even started to believe that their meddling could have negative consequences if they continued. During a few of his forays out to the harbour, Alcaeus had narrowly avoided bumping into Xanthias, who it seemed had taken up residence on the Eleni, probably because he now had nowhere else to go since his dismissal from duty as captain of Old Phaon's new flagship. Alcaeus couldn't tell Antimenidas why he thought this because he knew that if he told him, Antimenidas would have him finish Xanthias off. So far, Alcaeus had calculated that Xanthias was not a real threat. After all, Xanthias was fired before the ship ever set sail, and although he would probably recognise Alcaeus and his brothers if pressed, as long as there was no cause for suspicion, all that meant was that they crewed on The Alabastron until it got safely to the next port. There, as the story that he and Antimenidas had agreed on went, they disembarked and took on gainful employment until they eventually returned to Mytilene on a different ship travelling back, towards the northern Aegean.

Alcaeus also reasoned to himself that it might be useful to have a witness to their presence on The Alabastron, whom they could call upon at some point later, if they ever needed to lend credibility to their version of the events.

Alcaeus was just about to head back home to face down Antimenidas and insist that it really was a waste of his time, and counterproductive, to keep patrolling the harbour when he noticed a crowd gathering near the Eleni.

His heart started beating faster as he feared the worst.

That drunken old bastard must have the entire pantheon on his payroll. Could he really have survived after all?

Alcaeus rushed over to the crowd, making sure to stay in the background, just far enough back to be able to hear what was happening but not attract any unwanted attention.

He was surprised to see a young man in the centre of the commotion and was about to guffaw at the youth's unlikely tale when he saw Sappho step forward. What would she be doing in the harbour with a man claiming to be a young Phaon raised from the dead? Could this really be Phaon? Even if it was Phaon, why would Sappho have anything to do with this? He took another long look at the young man claiming to be a renewed, youthful Phaon. He had a slight resemblance to Phaon, that was for sure, but there was something else, something familiar, about him.

Alcaeus glanced back at Sappho. Then he noticed it. Her hair was tied up with the familiar mother-of-pearl hairpin.

"How the —" he said under his breath.

He looked at the young man again.

It suddenly made sense. Could this really be her? For a long moment he studied the short hair, the beard, the boyish figure. If anything, Alcaeus prided himself on having made a detailed study of the male form, but he had to give it to her.... She was good! Very convincing, but not convincing enough for a trained eye like his. Although, she must have been helped by a professional… Of course —Sappho!

He was so engrossed in studying Sappho's handiwork that, for a moment, he forgot about the true danger. The young slave knew of his interest in Tyrrhaeus! She could tell the authorities and report him and his brothers. She might not know who they were, but he was sure she would recognise him, if she saw him again. Or, considering Sappho now had the hairpin, the chances were the slave girl had already told Sappho who gave her the pin, so it was very likely that Sappho also knew too much by now.

Tension coursed through his body as he tried to decide what to do.

Sappho was passionately addressing the crowd. He listened more closely.

It was clear that Sappho was working with this slave girl, working hard to sell her illusion. Why?

Alcaeus thought back to the first time he had laid eyes on the slave. It was outside Sappho's house. Then he remembered Sappho had confided that she was quite taken with one of Phaon's slaves. Was this the one?

Regardless, if anyone caught wind of their deception, the young slave would surely be put to death for impersonating a free man. He was not sure what would happen to Sappho for assisting her.

On the positive side, for them to be so bold, it must mean that they were pretty sure Phaon himself, or anyone else from the ship, was not going to turn up and spill the beans.[1] And, as long as Sappho and the slave had a vested interest in this subterfuge, neither would do anything stupid that would jeopardise the girl's identity.

He realised that the best course of action for them and for him and his brothers was for this crowd to believe their story.

The crowd was restless.

He needed to act fast.

"Good gentlemen," Alcaeus spoke up, causing the crowd to turn towards him, "such a spectacular story surely cannot be dreamt up by mortals alone. It must have had divine inspiration." He scanned the crowd and then met Sappho's eye briefly. "Nevertheless, no one can blame us for being a little amazed. This is an unusual event. However, I for one must confess I can certainly see the likeness to Old Phaon. Surely you can too. That would be too much of a coincidence, would it not?"

Taking centre stage now, a place he always felt most comfortable, he walked up to young Phaon and slapped him on the back. "No offence good man, but old age did not treat you well… new youth however…" He made a show of glancing at the young Phaon's backside and then turned and winked at the gathered crowd. "I…" He smiled, pausing for further effect, "…am delightfully surprised."

All, except for Xanthias, laughed heartily, nodding their agreement and slowly the majority began to disperse, murmuring amongst themselves about the miracle they had just witnessed.

When Anactoria saw the man from the ship appear out of the crowd, she was convinced her fate was sealed. She was sure he was about to blow her cover and it would all be over within seconds. How could she have been so stupid as to let Sappho talk her into this mad little pipe-dream? She was about to step forward and confess, to save herself the humiliation of being unmasked by someone else. As she went to move, something stopped her.

Afterwards, she could not be sure what it was. It might have been the cocky smile he had on his face, or the way he glanced at Sappho. Whatever it was, it stopped her and, thank Aphrodite, it did.

However, when she turned to assess the crowd, she noticed the continued look of scepticism on Xanthias's face. He was going to be a hard nut to crack, and she also saw that a number of Phaon's remaining crew from the Eleni were watching and taking their cue from him. She realised that without his acceptance, she would still be doomed.

Xanthias was a very simple man, with simple beliefs. He, like most sailors, had a healthy respect for the four Anemoi and the sea currents and he was a follower of Poseidon, more out of necessity than any particular choice.

Anactoria remembered hearing a story from one of the old kitchen slaves when she was a small girl, about how Xanthias had grown up with Old Phaon and was destined to be his manservant, but Phaon soon realised his talents would be wasted on putting out his garments and making his bed. On one of their first trips out at sea together, it became apparent that Xanthias, with his calm nerves and astute sense of direction, was an uncannily good sailor. And once Xanthias had proved that Phaon could trust him with his life, the latter decided that very day to make him first captain of his ship. Despite how Old Phaon's treatment of him that last day, Anactoria had no doubt Xanthias was probably the closest thing Phaon had to a friend... and confidant.

"I owe you an apology." Anactoria said to Xanthias seriously. "I should never have dismissed you like that, the last time we were here. You did not deserve to be so treated by me."

"Look, I don't know who you are, but you are not my Master Phaon," Xanthias said and turned to walk away.

"My friend, you doubt me." She said as calmly as she could. She had no choice. This was the biggest gamble of her life. "I'm pleased. I wouldn't have expected anything less from a loyal friend who has known me and guarded my deepest secrets all these years, something for which I've never thanked you either. But I'd like you to know that it has always been appreciated."

Xanthias turned and looked at Anactoria with a quizzical look on his craggy face.

"I am likely to be the sole survivor of The Alabastron." Anactoria held Xanthias's gaze. "So, I also know that you, out of everyone, as the person who has kept my secret, will know how much I've lost since I last saw you." She allowed her words to settle, hoping he would pick up on her meaning. She guessed that if anyone had known Old Phaon's biggest secret then it would be Xanthias.

Xanthias's stern expression wavered for a moment.

"So, my loyal friend, forgive me if I'm not the man I used to be, but from now on, I hope to be better." She held out her hand towards him.

Finally, Xanthias's face contorted into a smile and he grabbed Anactoria's hand roughly, pulling her closer into a half-hug. "Thank Zeus, you are alive!"

Anactoria nodded and smiled at Xanthias. Then she slapped him on the back. "So, now my dear Xanthias, let's not waste more time. First order of business…"

Anactoria turned towards the loitering crowd. "Gentleman, I wish you to bear witness that I hereby publicly declare that my Xanthias, my trusty slave to this day, is hereby manumitted and shall from now on be deemed a free man."

Anactoria turned back to Xanthias and saw a complete look of horror on his face.

"Xanthias, what's the matter?"

"Master, you do me a great honour, but you also punish me too severely."

Anactoria frowned.

"I have been your faithful slave all my life. I have nothing else. I know nothing else. I have lived in your house or on your ships and worked for you every moment of my waking days. If I'm not your slave, I am nothing. If you banish me, I cannot live."

Anactoria, rested her hand on Xanthias's shoulder. "My good man, I do not banish you. I need your help, now more than ever, to ready the Eleni. We have a business to run and I need you at the helm as soon as possible, not as my slave, but as my business partner."

I wasn't sure what caught my eye first. On my usual walk along the coast to the harbour, my mind was preoccupied with Anactoria and how I was going to oblige Sappho to allow me to see her. She was surely better by now and there was only so long Sappho could keep her hidden, all to herself, in that house of hers. Then, as I reached the harbour, I noticed a crowd gathering on the dock.

The moment I saw the young man addressing the crowd I knew it was her.

Stroke of genius!

I had no doubt Sappho probably orchestrated it, with the help of her theatrical expertise. But, even so, it was a very Spartan thing to do, completely fearless. I had to admire Anactoria for her guts. I immediately loved and respected her even more. If she managed to pull this off, she would be set for life.

This also meant that Anactoria would now, more than likely, have returned to Old Phaon's residence—away from Sappho as gatekeeper.

I decided it would be best if Sappho did not know that I was aware of their little ruse just yet. I needed to bide my time, to see Anactoria on her own, probably at her home. So, I ducked out of sight and left the harbour as quickly as I could.

Once the crowd had dissipated completely, Alcaeus sidled up to Sappho.

"Hello, my sweet Sapph—"

His words were cut short by a loud slap across his cheek.

"Don't you 'sweet Sappho' me!" she hissed between gritted teeth. "First, you make me think you are dead. Then, I find out that you and your brothers are somehow involved in this mess in the first place, and then you swan in here as if you have just arrived fresh from the Elysian fields."

"Look, I can explain," he tried to say, rubbing his smarting cheek.

"You are damn right, you are going to explain, but not now. Right now, I have more important things to take care of. But don't for a moment think you are off the hook."

As Alcaeus entered the small villa that he shared with his two brothers, he was instantly accosted by a furious looking Antimenidas.

"What is this I hear about Phaon's miraculous return?"

Alcaeus had to bite his tongue not to laugh at his brother's scarlet features.

"Relax big brother, I have it all under control."

"What do you mean relax? What do you have under control?"

Alcaeus shook his head. "Sorry, I can't tell you. For once, you are just going to have to trust me."

"Trust you?" Antimenidas repeated incredulously. "Let me remind you it is not just ours but also your other brother's freedom and life at stake here!"

Alcaeus nodded. "I know that as well as you do, big brother, but I would rather not risk the lives of both my brothers by giving one information that could put him in danger, in the process of trying to save the other."

Although Alcaeus was being light-hearted and was enjoying winding up his brother, whom he knew hated not being in complete control, he was also very aware that he was only half-joking. If word came out about Anactoria's deception, those that knew would also be implicated.

8

Sappho had decided it was best for Anactoria to keep a low profile and stay out of the public eye for a few days, to allow the dust to settle on her revelation and for people to get used to the idea of Phaon's miraculous transformation. All her life as a slave, she had never been on her own for more than a small part of a day, so after a week of rattling around at home alone, Anactoria couldn't stand it any longer. She needed to see Sappho. Sappho had forbidden her from just turning up at her house unannounced, especially if Kerkylas was not around. She had said it was for Anactoria's safety.

Anactoria began to rack her brain for an alternative plan of how she was going to be able to see Sappho. Finally, she had an idea. If she planned it carefully, based on what she remembered of Sappho's routine, she might be able to catch her while she was out and about on her errands to the market, where she went regularly to procure silks and supplies. It was a long shot, and she might end up walking around the open area of the market for ages—not what Sappho would call keeping a low profile—but it was worth the risk. What was the point of having a new life as a free person if she could not live it?

Sappho felt the unexpected, soft caress on her neck.

She swung round and her heart soared as she recognised Anactoria, in her dapper disguise. Sappho was about to fling her arms around her lover's shoulders when she suddenly remembered they were out in the market, and panic stopped her. Instead, she gently pushed Anactoria away, biting back the ache she felt. She had missed her with every fibre of her being, every minute of every day, since they parted at the harbour.

"What?" Anactoria said, her brow creasing in distress.

"We can't do that. Not here!" Sappho chided in a fierce whisper.

"Why not? I've missed you."

"We're in public!"

"You've never had a problem with public places before." Anactoria winked suggestively.

"That was before." Sappho glanced around nervously, pleased to see Kleïs was well out of earshot where she had asked her to wait to receive the new silk roll she had just purchased. "Then you were a girl. No one pays much mind to affection between women, especially when one of them is a slave girl. Now, you are a respected member of society and I'm a married woman. Attention like this from you could cause a scandal." Her tone softened a little. "Besides, Kerkylas would not react well to being cuckolded by the new, handsome man in town."

Anactoria nodded and reluctantly stepped back allowing for a more acceptable space between them. "Sappho, may I walk with you?" she said a little louder so passers-by could hear. "Perhaps I can help you carry your purchases home. I am actually heading that way, since I've business to conduct with..." Anactoria searched for and settled on the only reason that came to mind, "with your husband."

Sappho nodded cordially, "That would be most kind," she said in a stage voice. Then she whispered, "That's more like it." She winked.

As they set off back to her house, Sappho was acutely aware of all the eyes on them. This was dangerous not only for Anactoria, but for her too. She was not jesting when she pointed out Kerkylas would not take kindly to being cuckolded by anyone, least of all a young man half his age and so much more handsome. He was a powerful man, and the consequences for her and Anactoria could be dire if Kerkylas thought there was anything going on. Nevertheless, Sappho had to admit, the raised stakes made even this simple walk home incredibly exhilarating.

Kleïs, like most of Mytilene, had heard of Old Phaon's miraculous transformation. Even so, the reality of seeing him in person shocked her. It certainly was a transformation for the better. The younger version of Phaon was very handsome and very charming. It really was remarkable. Whenever she had the opportunity, she'd glance surreptitiously at the young Phaon, trying to see if she could catch a glimpse of the Old Phaon in there somewhere. There was a definite likeness, but it was hard to believe this is what he was like in his youth. Not only were his looks different, it was as if his whole attitude and manner had also changed. He seemed kinder, more friendly, generally a much nicer person. Kleïs guessed that if anyone underwent such a dramatic transformation as he had, it was bound to change their life perspective and behaviour.

Having said that, the thing she found even more surprising was Sappho's new attitude and behaviour towards the young Phaon. Sappho had previously made no bones about her intense dislike for the old man. However, since his transformation, their mutual disdain had evaporated. In fact, if you did not know otherwise, judging by the way they were with each other now, you could be forgiven for mistaking them for secret lovers.

If it were true, Kleïs would hardly blame Sappho for being unable to resist such a handsome man. But Kleïs knew otherwise. As Sappho's personal slave, it was only natural that she was familiar with almost everyone Sappho interacted with, both in and out of the bedroom. In all the years that she had been with her mistress, she had never known her to take another male lover. Sappho loved her women and had many of them as lovers, but she was always faithful to her husband. Whether that was out of loyalty or because she knew Kerkylas would have the other man's head if he found out, Kleïs could only speculate.

And yet, there was something else that bothered her about young Phaon. Whenever she was in his company, which was only briefly, Kleïs had a strange feeling, which she just couldn't shake. There was something very... familiar... about him, his mannerisms, the turn of his head—like she knew him. But that was not possible. During all her mistress's dealings with Old Phaon, she had only ever seen him from a distance and then only quite briefly. There was no reason why she should feel like that.

After taking another veiled look, she concluded that seeing a younger version of someone was bound to feel strange and slightly contradictory. It was pointless breaking her head trying to decipher a miracle.

Imagine her surprise when Sappho showed her guest into her private gynaeceum next to her sleeping chamber. The only man whom she'd ever invited there was her childhood best friend, Alcaeus. Not even Master Kerkylas was ever really entertained in there.

"That'll be all, Kleïs," Sappho said as Kleïs set down the tray of fruit and wine, which she had requested from the kitchen for her guest.

At first Kleïs was not sure she had heard correctly. But when Sappho stood waiting expectantly for Kleïs to leave, Kleïs nodded and made for the door.

"And close the door behind you," Sappho said. "I don't want to be disturbed under any circumstances, Master Phaon and I have important business to discuss."

What was going on? Again, she'd been dismissed—this time it left Sappho in the solitary company of a young man! Master Kerkylas would not be pleased! Not that she would betray her mistress by informing on her, but why would Sappho do that? Did she not trust her anymore? Kleïs racked her brain to think if there were any reason that could have caused her to lose favour with her mistress.

The door had hardly closed behind Kleïs before Sappho leapt into Anactoria's arms.

"It has felt like forever, since I've tasted your sweet lips," Anactoria said, sounding more husky than normal.

"Really?" Sappho asked.

"Yes, really." Anactoria frowned a little and stared down at the woman she had longed to hold almost every moment of every day since they parted. "Why do you sound surprised?"

"Well, I'm old." Sappho pushed herself out of Anactoria's arms. "And you are young and beautiful. I see how the young women and young boys look at you now."

"Now? Why now? I'm no different from before."

Sappho nodded slightly. "You were always very beautiful and striking. But then you were a slave, someone's possession, and people saw you that way. Or rather they did not see you. Now, they see you as an eligible, successful young man in society. They want to be with you. I see it in their eyes. Men want to conquer you, and women dream that you would marry them."

Anactoria shook her head. "No, they do not." She moved closer and pulled Sappho to her. She kissed her. "I can assure you. Nothing has changed. You have my heart."

Sappho shook her head. "You say that, but soon you will realise your power and begin to contemplate the new doors that are open to you now. When that happens a young man like you would not want to be with an old woman like me."

Anactoria moved quickly. In one smooth move she picked Sappho up off the floor and started to carry her out of the gynaeceum.

"Wait. Stop. What are you doing?" Sappho squealed. "Where are you taking me?"

Anactoria kicked open the door to Sappho's bedchamber. "You told me that as a man I needed to make my actions speak louder than words." Anactoria threw Sappho onto her bed, causing Sappho to giggle nervously. "So, I'm going to show you just how wrong you are and how much I adore this gorgeous, ageless body you have."

Anactoria bent down and started kissing Sappho's neck, her collarbone and her chest. She undid her robe to expose more skin and continued to adore the rest of her body one kiss at a time.

Soon all discussions of age and beauty were forgotten, as both surrendered to their need to love and to ravish the other.

A commotion outside the bedchamber woke Sappho. Then she heard a knock at the door and Kleïs calling from the other side. "Mistress, Sappho." She knew it must be important for Kleïs to disobey an order not to disturb her.

Sappho got up quickly and threw a robe around her before she headed to the door, hoping not to disturb her sleeping lover.

"What is it?"

"Mistress, I'm really sorry to interrupt you, but I thought you might like to know that Master Kerkylas has arrived home."

Sappho nodded and tried to remain calm. "Thank you, Kleïs. If he calls for me, tell him I've been having a nap and I'll be out shortly."

Sappho closed the door and then hurried over to the bed where Anactoria was still fast asleep.

"Anactoria, wake up!" Sappho hissed. She picked up Anactoria's tunic and threw it at the adorably tousled woman in her bed. "You need to get up and get dressed. Quick! Kerkylas is home early."

"Why?" Anactoria asked puzzled. "He doesn't usually mind me in your bed."

"He might be fine about me entertaining young women like this, but it would be a completely different story if he found a gorgeous young man in my bed."

"What about Alcaeus?" Anactoria asked starting to get up.

"Quick! You've got to hurry." Sappho waved off her question. "Kerkylas tolerates Alcaeus because he knows I'd never in a million years sleep with him and Alcaeus is clearly more interested in boys than women."

"But I'm not dressed as a man —" She waved at her naked body. "Maybe we should just tell him I'm a woman. That way I can stay with you."

"You arrived here as Phaon. People saw you. In the eyes of the world you are Phaon. We cannot afford to let anyone put two and two together. If he finds out you are not Phaon but a slave impersonating a free man, or even worse, a woman impersonating a man," Sappho rubbed her face, struggling to stomach the thought, "you will be a dead woman and that is without even looking into what really happened on that ship. As you know Kerkylas has Pittacus's ear."

Anactoria moved quickly and got dressed. Once she had her disguise in place, Sappho led her to the window and let her out. Memories of that day rushed back to her. It now seemed aeons ago, before all this began, when she'd first seen a hooded Alcaeus descend the balcony pillar.

PART II

9

I left it for a few days before I decided to make my move. Under the cover of night, I made my way to Old Phaon's house. At first it looked rather dark and quiet and I feared she was not going to be there.

Old Phaon's slave, Eunice, answered the door and asked me to wait while she announced me to her master.

I later learned that Anactoria's first order of business, on her return to the house, was to manumit all Old Phaon's slaves. Most, barring a few who chose to stay and help her look after the house out of gratitude, had left to build new lives for themselves either in Mytilene or in neighbouring villages.

A few minutes later Eunice returned and escorted me to the andron. Probably wisely, Anactoria had kept up appearances as Phaon, even in the privacy of her own home.

If Anactoria was surprised to see me, she didn't show it. Instead, she welcomed me almost cordially and invited me in to take a seat.

"I tried to visit you while you were convalescing at Sappho's." I began, feeling a little uncertain.

"Yes, sorry. Sappho felt it was best if we keep things as quiet as possible until we had decided what to do."

"Well, I am impressed. I think it is a genius idea. To hide in plain sight. I saw you in the harbour. You were spectacular."

"It was Sappho's idea," she said looking a little embarrassed.

"You are pulling it off nicely." I felt I needed to do something to break the ice between us. I got up and moved closer to her, to where she was still standing rather stiffly clasping an empty kylix like it was a battle shield. "However, I would much rather pull off this disguise altogether." I tugged at her chiton slightly.

Anactoria laughed a little nervous laugh. She shook her head and refocussed on pouring me a drink. "Bilitis, you are possibly the most direct woman I know."

"Well, I've learnt nothing comes from waiting around." I smiled.

She shook her head, looking more serious as she handed me a filled kylix. "I can't, Bilitis." She turned and topped up her own drink. "Things are different now that I'm no longer a slave. I need to act responsibly."

"Oh, I'll let you be responsible for me all night," I teased and held up my kylix to toast her.

She wouldn't look me in the eye, keeping her focus on her drink. I reached over and took hold of her free hand.

Her hands weren't big, exactly, but they were strong, and I could see the blue veins on the back, slightly proud just below her quite pale skin. I gently ran my thumb along the length of one of her veins. For some reason I found this insanely appealing. I turned it over and examined the calluses on her palms—evidence of hard labour in Phaon's house or perhaps even on his ships. I remembered what it was like to have her rough hands stroking and caressing my body.

I felt, before I saw, her fingers press gently on my chin lifting my face to look at her. I was instantly captivated by those dark eyes. I marvelled at everything they must have seen in her short life. For some strange reason I also wondered what she saw right now.

I realised that I had truly stopped thinking of her as a slave. To me she was my Phaon—strong, powerful protector in a woman's body.

Before I could stop myself, I had leaned in and pressed my lips against hers. The sensation, the taste of the wine on her lips, was so utterly intoxicating. I had to have her. I slipped my shoulders out of my chiton and allowed it to drop to the floor, right in the middle of the andron.

When she pulled back and saw what I had done, she shook her head and laughed. "I'm serious, Bilitis. I can't."

I stepped forward and pressed my body into her. "Of course you can." I kissed her again, feeling her resolve melt. "I know you want to," I whispered in her ear, "to know what it's like to have me as an equal."

She pulled away again. I saw the confusion and indecision dance behind her eyes. For a moment I was sure she was going to turn me down. I don't exactly know what swayed her, but after a long pause she held out her hand. I took it and then she picked me up and carried me from the andron to her bedchamber.

She gently lay me down on the bed. As if she'd heard my thoughts, she began to stroke and caress my now almost burning skin with her cool, callused hands, covering every inch, as if committing me to memory. Maybe she had intended that to be our swan song—her way of saying goodbye to me.

My pulse and my body reacted without my permission, and I found myself wishing she would both hurry and slow down her explorations. I willed the fierce beast in her breast, the Hecatoncheires, that I'd had the pleasure to get to know that first time we were intimate, to return. My heart began to race as I imagined her hard calluses raking over my nipples. I must have moaned. I felt her strong arm slide in underneath my back and lift me off the bed slightly while her other hand made light work of untying my strophion.

My breath caught as her fingers slipped into my loin cloth, one hand on either side of my hips. Before I had a chance to lift off the bed, she ripped the flimsy material from my body. The cool night air hit my hot, moist flesh and struck me breathless as does the icy Aegean, during that first crisp spring swim.

I froze in anticipation, squeezing my eyes closed, and I waited.

The first thing I felt was her short hair tickle my inner thigh. Without any preamble, her lips firmly closed around me and I felt her strong tongue flick and lash across my most sensitive skin before settling into that maddening, incessant rhythm that drove my desire higher and higher. It felt like Poseidon's lightning bolts were coursing through my body, ripping me apart from inside out.

"Oh, Aphrodite!"

After nearly being found out by Kerkylas, Sappho and Anactoria resolved to be more careful. They decided to limit their time together to when they knew they would definitely not be interrupted.

After one such stolen afternoon of lovemaking, Sappho sat at the dressing table combing her hair, getting ready to return to her house before Kerkylas came home.

Anactoria got up out of the bed and came over. She bent down and kissed Sappho's shoulder gently. When their eyes met, Sappho noticed an uncharacteristic seriousness about her.

"What is the matter?" Sappho asked.

Anactoria hesitated for a moment. "Sappho, my love," she began gently, "I am struggling. I don't know if I can keep going on like this."

"Like what?" Sappho put her comb down and turned and took Anactoria's hands in hers.

"Like this," Anactoria glanced around the room, "sneaking around. This can't be my—our—life from now on. I'm finding it hard to keep up this charade, even though most people seem to have accepted our story, I'm still gawped at where ever I go, like the freak show I am. It's like I've come back from the dead."

"Well, according to our story, you have," Sappho tried to lighten the mood.

"Seriously, Sappho, I can't live like this. The only way I will have a life is if I leave Mytilene and begin again somewhere, where I can just be a normal young man."

"You're wanting to leave?" Sappho frowned. "Where will you go?"

Anactoria shrugged and gripped her hand a little tighter. "I don't *want* to. I have to. I'm working on getting Old Phaon's old ship seaworthy. It is taking time, but as soon as it is done… I want you to come with me."

Sappho felt stunned. She shook her head unable to comprehend where Anactoria was going with this.

"Please, Sappho. Come with me. We can go anywhere you want. As long as it isn't here, the whole world is ours."

"I can't leave." Sappho scoffed.

"Don't you see?" Anactoria pleaded. "We could be together now, as we always wanted."

"Things are different." Sappho sighed.

"What do you mean?"

"For us to be together, for us to go away, you want me to leave my husband, my life, my school, everything?"

Anactoria nodded. "Yes, so we can build a new life together. You are very talented and well known. You can start a new school somewhere else."

Sappho shook her head. "Other places are not like here, Anactoria. Here, I have a life. As a woman, I have more freedom than anywhere else. Other places don't afford women this kind of life and the ability to come and go as we please, to speak freely, to learn, to make decisions. In other places you are governed by your husband— regarded as no different from a house dog."

Now it was Anactoria's turn to shake her head. "But you'll be with me. I will look after you. Of course, I will give you all the freedom you want."

"My dear, Anactoria." Sappho stroked Anactoria's cheek. "I have no doubt you will look after me… for as long as you are in love with me."

"I will always love you."

"Can you not see? I can't take that chance. You are young and beautiful. You can have anyone and any life you choose. When you tire of me, and you will, I'll have nothing. I've always been very independent. Life here allows me to be that."

"I keep telling you, Sappho. How can I make you believe? There is not, and will never be, anyone else for me."

Sappho laughed softly. "I have eyes, my darling."

"And what is it that you see?"

"I see how people look at you." Sappho took a deep breath. "Even the day Bilitis rescued you, I could see the lust in her eyes, and that was when she knew you as a mere slave girl."

Anactoria felt a pang of guilt over her recent encounter with Bilitis. She hadn't really wanted anything to happen between them, but it was as if she just didn't know how to stop it. Perhaps she still wasn't used to being in a position to be able to say no in the first place. But that was a lame excuse. She knew it. It had felt as if, on some level, she owed something to Bilitis. After all, she was the reason Anactoria was alive. No, that wasn't it either. There was more to it. Even though she loved Sappho, she did like Bilitis, and had honestly enjoyed the intimacy with her. It felt good to have the opportunity and choice. She wished she could somehow make Sappho understand the difference, but she knew Sappho wouldn't, or perhaps even for all her worldly wisdom, couldn't understand, since she herself had never been a slave to anyone.

"Now that you are an eligible young man in society, things are so completely different," Sappho continued. "Like Bilitis, there are hundreds of beautiful young women looking for a good husband. She will soon, if she has not already, figure out our ruse and will make you an offer you can't refuse. After all, you are her perfect suitor—a gorgeous and successful young man. Your coupling would make for a prosperous alliance, with her uncle being such a successful trade merchant already."

"Come on Sappho. Stop that! That is just paranoid jealousy talking now." Anactoria backed away, running her hand through her hair in exasperation. "I have free will too, you know. Do you pay me no respect?"

Sappho didn't answer.

Anactoria knelt down in front of her lover. "Sappho, do me this favour: Please just think about my request."

***

Once again under the cover of night, I went to Anactoria's house. As before I found her in the andron. I was quite giddy with anticipation. The combination of the danger in the subterfuge and the memory of our last, passionate night together brought a flush to my cheeks.

"Bilitis," was all she said, when she saw me enter. Her voice sounded flat and matter of fact.

"I had hoped for a little more enthusiasm," I said. "After all, it's not often you are visited by someone who holds your secrets dear."

"Leave us, Eunice" Anactoria commanded her slave who had been hovering to take any requests for refreshments. Then she turned towards me. "What brings you here so late?"

"I came to see how my lovely young friend and most handsome young man on the island was doing." I went right up to her and cupped her slightly prickly cheek. I couldn't help it. She really did look so handsome in her Phaon disguise.

"Bilitis, you shouldn't have come." She turned away from me.

I put my arms around her. "Oh, but I had to. I've been unable to think about anything other than us since I was here last."

"There is no us. I told you then. My heart is taken." She turned to face me, dislodging me from her back.

"Yes, yes I know. It's not your heart I'm after. I'm after these powerful hands," I reached for her hands and stroked them again gently with my thumbs. Then I pulled her into me, "...and that dextrous, talented tongue... and the way you play me like an enchanted lyre." Just the thought of what she had done to me the last time I was there was enough to cause a tremble in my depths.

"Bilitis," she said seriously as she turned and freed herself from my grasp, "I can't." She sounded almost desperate, which surprised me.

"Why on earth not?" I laughed at the lunacy. "Tell me, have you, by some cruel twist designed by Aphrodite, lost your touch or your voracious appetite?"

Anactoria shook her head and answered seriously. "I just can't."

"Can't. Why?"

She didn't respond.

"Come on. You didn't seem to have a problem last time, or even right at the beginning when Old Phaon loaned you to me."

"That was different."

"How?"

"I didn't feel as if I had much of a choice, especially when I was still Phaon's slave."

Not immediately sure how to respond I bit my lip. "Are you saying that all that extra time you spent in my bed, not going home until the last minute was under duress?" I guffawed. "Or the last time I was here. You didn't feel you had a choice? I don't believe that. Are you saying that you don't like what we do? Am I not a good lover?"

Anactoria had the decency to look embarrassed. Then she shook her head. "No, it is not that. You are a very good lover and I enjoyed what we did very much."

"So..." I moved in to kiss her, anticipating the incongruous feel of her stubble on my cheek.

Instead, she pulled away.

"What then?" I asked, surprised at her genuine resistance. I was not accustomed to being rejected like that.

"I've just been thinking, and it might seem stupid, but I have realised that now that I'm no longer a slave, I have free choice, but also responsibilities that I have never had to deal with before."

I waited, still not quite understanding.

"I need to guard against imprudent choices that might have a negative impact on... people I love."

I scoffed. "Wow, that was quick." Then a realisation struck me. "Was the other night just a way to keep me quiet about your little secret? Did you think that if you were intimate with me you could stop me telling people who you really are? Do you really think that little of me?" The hurt bubbled inside me, engulfing my heart.

"Bilitis," she said earnestly. "I'm sorry. The other night shouldn't have happened. I was confused and scared and I'm not used to being able to say no."

I took a long look at Anactoria. I could feel the hurt tightening its grip until I felt my heart begin to crack. "Whoever it is, she really does have you under her spell."

Anactoria looked me straight in the eye. "Yes, she does."

I nodded slowly, uncertain what to do next. I wanted to run out of there, screaming. It was not until that moment that I realised how far I had fallen in love with her. Yes, I'd told myself that I was just after the great sex and the excitement of the deception, but I hadn't been entirely truthful.

"So, where does that leave us?" I asked.

The darkness in her expression suddenly lifted. "Can we be friends?"

Oh, how I wished that that look of glee on her face was associated with seeing me in the first place.

I felt myself nod slowly. Almost unable to speak, I turned and was about to head for the door when I felt her hand on my shoulder. I was too stunned to pull away. Within a few seconds her arms folded around me. "Thank you! I'm so relieved," she said.

I just nodded, my cheek rubbing against her fake beard.

Just then Eunice re-entered the room. "Master Phaon, apologies. You have another visitor."

Anactoria let go of me immediately and straightened up. "Who is it?"

"It's Sappho, Master."

I caught the quick glance Anactoria threw in my direction, as if she was considering where to hide me. My heart broke a little more.

"Show her in," Anactoria said.

The moment Sappho saw me, you could have cut the air with a falcata. Instantly, my worst fear was confirmed. It was *she* who held my dear Anactoria's heart.

The irony struck me: Even if she had not been in love with Sappho before her ordeal, I was the one who delivered Anactoria directly into Sappho's claws from the beach. It is hard to find fault with the person who nursed you back to life. Anactoria probably didn't even know or remember that I was the one who found her.

"Well, thank you for the clarification." I said to Anactoria in a business-like tone, in response to which she looked overly relieved. The air felt thick and I needed to get out of there. "I'll leave you two to get on."

Anactoria nodded. "Thank you for coming. I'll show you out." She started escorting me towards the door.

"No need," I said. "I can find my own way." I strode out quickly, before the tears I felt building could break their banks.

———

Anactoria rushed over to Sappho and took her into her arms. "What's wrong? What are you doing out so late?"

"You're right. It *is* late. What is *she* doing here?" Sappho asked not even attempting to hide the suspicion and disdain in her voice.

"She came to see if I was okay, after what happened," Anactoria said.

"How did she know it was you?"

"She saw us together at the harbour. It didn't take a great leap for her to make the deduction. She came here because, apparently, she had come to see me at yours but you refused her entry."

Sappho diverted her gaze. "I didn't want anyone upsetting you or risk news of your recovery getting out. I was just protecting you."

Anactoria pulled Sappho into her. "Thank you. I wasn't blaming you. I was just answering your question. I can't thank you enough for everything you have done for me. Without you I would probably not be here." Anactoria smiled and gestured towards the room around them. "And, I *certainly* would not be *here*."

Then she refocused on the more urgent matter. "What brings you here so late into the night? Is Kerkylas not home yet?"

Sappho nodded. "I had to come. I told him I was going to see Alcaeus about a symposium. There is a problem. You are in danger." It was clear Sappho was very distressed. "It's Tyrrhaeus. His body has been found, washed up on the shore of Smyrna on the coast of Ionia. They think he was murdered. Pittacus is beside himself and on a war path. You have to leave—to get as far away from here as possible."

"Shh." Anactoria held Sappho. "It's okay."

Sappho shook her head. "Word is Pittacus is going to send for you and question you."

"But why me? There is no reason Pittacus would suspect me. I, nor Old Phaon, could have had anything to do with his death. I'm not even sure he died on the ship with the rest. Rumour has it he was spotted in Anatolia after that. If he had been murdered, any of more than a hundred people who despise Pittacus, or even just bandits in a foreign land, could have done it."

Sappho swallowed. "But you, Old Phaon, were one of the last people to see him alive."

Anactoria took a few seconds to absorb what Sappho meant. Even if she was not a direct suspect in Tyrrhaeus's death, answering awkward questions about their voyage, ship, and her miraculous survival would be very dangerous. She finally nodded, thinking quickly. "The Eleni, Phaon's old ship is almost ready. I could probably sail in a week."

Sappho shook her head. "That'll be too late. He'll be sending for you tomorrow. The order has already been given. You have to get out of here *now*! Maybe hide somewhere safe until the next ship out. But it can't be Old Phaon's ship. You cannot leave a trail. Pittacus will leave no stone unturned. He might seem like a fair and wise leader up to now, but I doubt he will be as reasonable when it comes to the death of his only son."

Suddenly Anactoria looked serious. She clasped Sappho to her. "Come with me."

"What?" Sappho resisted. "You know that's not possible. We've spoken about this. We need to focus on getting *you* off the island."

"You said it was only not possible because you were not sure of me." Anactoria took a deep breath. "What if I asked you to marry me? Would you be sure of me then?"

Sappho shook her head, dismissing the idea. "Don't be silly."

"I've never been more serious in my life. I mean, putting practicalities aside, which we would need to work out together. Come with me, be my wife. You said it yourself. I can now live as an eligible young man. This is our chance, our gift from Aphrodite."

"What? Go with you and be your concubine?" Sappho half-laughed.

"I know you have a good life here; you have your students, your fame, your husband and wealth and a position in society, but you yourself said, 'the thing that you love the most you value the most'." Anactoria let the challenge hang between them.

Deep inside her chest, Sappho's heart pounded furiously. Could Anactoria really mean that, that she would want her and continue to want her? Even now, with everything Anactoria had gained and all the new potential she'd acquired? It would be everything Sappho could ever have wished for. Deep in her heart she knew she could do it. She could leave Kerkylas and her life on the island and follow Anactoria wherever she went, in an instant, just as Helen left with Paris for Troy —if only she could be sure Anactoria's heart was true.

"Do you really mean that?" Sappho asked hesitantly.

Anactoria extended her hand. "Please, come with me."

Sappho couldn't resist such a plea, nor her chance for her dream to come true, any longer. She threw herself into Anactoria's arms. They kissed deeply.

When they finally pulled apart, Sappho began, cautious once again. "If I go with you and I allow myself to truly fall in love with you... I fall hard. You had better mean it."

Anactoria nodded, her cheeks starting to hurt from her smile. "I've never meant anything more in my life."

Sappho's heart swelled. She would have loved for that moment to last forever, but they needed to be practical. "So, how are we going to get off the island?"

"Can't we just leave Mytilene and find refuge in a town on the other side of the island, until the dust has settled?" Anactoria asked. "Or maybe I can take on another identity until my boat is finished."

"Fooling commoners once, with the whole new identity charade, is one thing. Pulling that stunt on a rampaging Pittacus is quite another. You're going to need more than a couple of mountains between you and Pittacus if you want to survive and escape unscathed. No, we have to get as far away as possible."

"But where? I've only ever lived here with Phaon. I have travelled with him on his ship, but I was never allowed off at the various ports."

Sappho thought for a moment. "Why don't we go to Sicily? I have contacts there from when I lived there in exile with Alcaeus during the reign of Myrsilus."

"How do we get there though? How did you get there before?"

"On a trade-ship to Sicily. Charaxus stowed us."

"Can you ask your brother to do that again? Or, even better, maybe he could give us a ship. I do know my way around one. If he did, we could go anywhere we wanted."

Sappho gave a dry laugh. "There is little love lost between Charaxus and me."

"Oh, I thought you said Charaxus owes you?"

"Yes, I suppose he does, but this is personal. Unfortunately, after our return from Naucratis in Egypt, I got into an altercation with him for being so foolish as to pursue matters of the heart that blindly, and ransoming family wealth for that Egyptian courtesan, Rhodopis. No, I can't go to him with this. There must be another way."

Anactoria ran her hands through her short hair as she racked her brain. Suddenly she stopped. "Of course. The only other person to ask... would be Bilitis."

"No, absolutely not!" Sappho crossed her arms.

"Why?" Anactoria asked. "After all, she already knows my secret and she is the niece of one of the wealthiest merchant traders on the island. Maybe she could arrange for us to have safe passage on one of her uncle's ships."

"You just told me you want to marry me and in the next breath you want to involve Bilitis in our plans.... What was she really doing here earlier?"

"Sappho you must stop being so suspicious and jealous. Bilitis rescued me in the first place and what is more, she brought me to *you*.... Surely, that demonstrates her honour?"

Sappho remained quiet for a long time, her mind reeling. She really did not know what to think anymore.

"I really cannot think of any other way. Can you?" Anactoria asked.

Sappho finally sighed.

"Okay, well then," Anactoria said. "I'll go and see her first thing in the morning."

"No, you can't. Pittacus's men will be out looking for you by then. We have to go now. Have you got rid of all your slave clothing?"

Anactoria shook her head.

"Good. I think it best if we change you back into a slave girl, just until we've safely left these shores. Hopefully, if we are really careful no one will think to look for one of Old Phaon's slaves."

Sappho led Anactoria into Old Phaon's bedchamber, where she helped her transform herself into a woman again. Anactoria's androgynous features were previously softened by her long dark hair. Now that was gone, she was in danger of merely looking like a boy in a dress. Sappho looked around for something to help. If only she had one of her wigs with her. She caught sight of Phaon's expensive silk curtains. She rushed over, lifted the corner and inspected the seam. Then, with one hard yank, she ripped off the bottom panel.

"Here, take this." She draped the silk cloth over Anactoria's head and around her neck. "That's better."

Anactoria grabbed Sappho's hand and they slipped out of the villa and headed for Bilitis's uncle's home.

10

I had just managed to drop off to sleep when a commotion in the atrium woke me. I was surprised to find Anactoria and Sappho mid-altercation with my personal slave, Abra. I schooled my expression, dismissed Abra and led the two women through to my gynaeceum.

I was horrified to find out that Pittacus was looking for Anactoria and, my personal disappointment about my earlier confrontation with Anactoria aside, of course I was willing to do whatever I could to help. The problem was that my uncle's ships didn't sail directly to Sicily. The only ship leaving Mytilene in the coming few days was one headed west to Lefkas, but at least it would take them part of the way.

"You'd have to disembark there and wait for another ship southwest-bound, towards Sicily," I said. "But at least you will be off this island."

I could see Sappho was not comfortable about the idea. She kept glancing between Anactoria and me.

"You can't really afford to wait around here," I added.

It was clearly not only the detour to Lefkas that was making Sappho uncomfortable. I sensed she was trying to make sense of something. I wondered if Anactoria had said something to her. I doubted it, because it would be stupid to evoke the jealousy of someone like Sappho and I hoped Anactoria would have more sense than that.

Eventually, realising they did not have many other options, Sappho agreed.

"I'll find out from my uncle exactly when the next ship is due to leave, but in the meantime, where are you going to hide?" I asked Anactoria, "I mean, you can't return to Old Phaon's house."

Sappho frowned. "I know. I was going to take her back to my house. No one would question a young slave girl in my quarters."

I had to stop myself from smirking. "That might be all too true and would probably have been a good plan, if you had not been seen together in public and you had not defended young Phaon's miraculous return so vocally in the harbour."

Anactoria and Sappho shared a look. They knew I was right.

"You might be Pittacus's right-hand man's wife, but I doubt even that would shield you from scrutiny under the circumstances," I continued. "Instead, I think he will use every stone he can lay his hands on to execute anyone whom he believes has had even the smallest involvement in any of this mess."

Sappho knew I was right. They had been noticed together, and it would not take much for Pittacus's men to come knocking at her door. She would struggle to convince them that she didn't know his whereabouts, let alone be able to hide Anactoria if they insisted on searching her home.

"Do you have any suggestions?" Anactoria asked me.

I swallowed. I had to play it cool. "Well," I said trying to sound nonchalant, "you could stay here with me. There is no logical reason that Pittacus's men would associate you with me. I have not been seen with Old Phaon since the Kallisteia, and certainly not since your return. If you did want to hide here, when the time comes, I could easily smuggle you onto my uncle's ship and send word to Sappho to meet you there in time to set sail."

I observed the meaningful glances they exchanged. I could tell Sappho was not in favour of the idea, but once again she was also unable to offer a better alternative.

Eventually Sappho shrugged, almost imperceptibly.

Anactoria turned her beautiful brown eyes onto me. She nodded. "Thank you, Bilitis."

"Okay, that's settled. I'll go and get Abra to arrange a bed for you."

I knew there was a perfectly prepared bedchamber ready for any unexpected guests, but I thought they needed a little privacy to say their goodbyes. The last thing I wanted was to have to stand there and observe them. Perhaps, in hindsight, I should've used the excuse of not having a bed prepared as a reason to lure the lovely Anactoria to my own chamber.

I have to say, if nothing else, I had to admire Sappho's nerve. After she and Anactoria had said their goodbyes, Sappho came to find me in the kitchen where I was fetching Anactoria some wine.

"Ah, Sappho let me show you out."

"That won't be necessary, thank you. I can find my way. I just came to say, privately, one worldly woman to another, you had better look after her as though your life depended on it. If something were to happen to so much as a hair on her head, you will wish you had not been born."

I managed to hide my surprise. "Sappho, I can assure you. I am determined. I will let nothing happen to her." I tried to smile in a disarming manner. The last thing I wanted was for things to escalate. It seemed to work.

She turned and made for the door. As she got to it, she stopped and glanced back. "Oh, and remember, she's not a slave anymore and she no longer belongs to Old Phaon… So, keep your philandering hands off her."

I nodded.

I often wonder whether things would have turned out differently had she not come into the kitchen that day and threatened me. I don't react well to threats.

On her return home, Sappho immediately instructed Kleïs to pack her travel chest.

No amount of questioning would get Sappho to share her reasons. From what Kleïs could tell, Sappho's plans did not include Kerkylas. In fact, she was sure that whatever this was, it was that trouble-maker, Alcaeus's doing. She had asked those she knew and no one had heard of an upcoming symposium, never mind one at which Alcaeus and Sappho were likely to perform. Something else was afoot between her mistress and Alcaeus.

What was more, judging by the things Sappho had asked her to prepare, this did not feel like an ordinary, short business trip. If Kleïs had been feeling unsettled by Sappho's strange, secretive behaviour of late, this thought sent her into a spiral of confusion. What if Sappho were planning to leave for good? This wouldn't be so bad if Kleïs could be sure that Sappho was planning to take her along. In earlier times, Kleïs would not have doubted that for a heartbeat, but in light of Sappho's recent behaviour, Kleïs was more than uncertain.

Without Sappho around as her mistress, Kleïs genuinely feared for her future. It was not only that Sappho treated her well and allowed her more freedom and privilege than she would have had from any other mistress, she had also always protected her from Kerkylas and from having to participate in his entertainment evenings with his political friends. Kleïs did not dislike men: she had secretly hoped to get married to a nice young man, perhaps one like that young Phaon, herself one day. And it was not that she particularly minded Kerkylas, but some of his so-called friends were nasty, cruel, old men whose power, as they got older, had gone to their heads as much as it had left their phalluses, and in order to compensate their shortcomings, they became more and more sadistic.

No! She couldn't have Sappho desert her. She had to do something. She was just not sure what, yet.

At first light, I went out to the harbour to meet my uncle whose ship had just docked from a trip to Egypt. He was so delighted to see me there to greet him, it creased my heart that I had not thought to do this more often—only now that I wanted something from him. He however, did not seem to take it to heart that the reason I was really there was to find out about the next ship leaving the harbour and to ask for passage on it, but that I could not tell him why I needed it.

He confirmed that the next ship out of Mytilene that could have room was due to depart in two days. Then he looked pensive. "Bilitis, you are my favourite niece. I have always thought of you as more my own daughter than your mother's and I have always supported you and your wilful independence. But now, I have to ask you whether I can trust your judgement."

"Uncle, this is important. Although I cannot tell you the details, I can tell you this involves someone I really care about."

He looked at me with a long, cool stare. Then he nodded. "Well, at least that's something. You have been my ward for a few years and it has worried me how detached from life and people you have been, since you left Pamphylia. It's good to know you have finally found something or someone you care enough about to take action."

"Thank you, Uncle."

"I just hope this will not cause difficulties for me or the business. If it does, you are on your own. Is that understood?"

I nodded. "Yes, Uncle." This was no idle threat. I knew that a woman like myself was nothing, if I were neither married nor the ward of my uncle.

After that conversation, he headed on to the market to attend to his business before making an immediate departure for Crete later that afternoon, while I headed straight home to tell Anactoria the good news.

As soon as I got home, I sent Abra to Sappho with a message to meet us on the harbour by noon, in two days' time. Then I set to work, personally packing up a crate and supplies for Anactoria from my own clothes and a selection of my uncle's wardrobe. Once that was done, it was time to relax, to enjoy this precious time with my love, before she left and I would probably never see her again.

Those two days together did not disappoint. Even though we weren't intimate, it was so very wonderful to have her undivided attention all to myself. I was amazed at how much she knew and had learnt in her time as Old Phaon's slave. Being ever present and invisible certainly gave her an insight I could never have imagined. I'm sure there were also huge and possibly unspeakable disadvantages, but she never mentioned those.

On the morning of departure, Anactoria and I left my uncle's house very early. I wanted to make sure we could get to the safety of the ship well before sunrise, particularly because Pittacus's men would be out and about looking for young Phaon, and we had decided that it would be safest, and afford her most freedom, if she travelled in her young Phaon disguise. All going well, she would adopt the Phaon persona from this day forward, for the rest of her blessed life.

As we approached the harbour, I noticed a lot more activity on the ship than I had expected so early. When I spoke to the captain, he told me that a big storm was approaching and so they had a change of plan and were to set sail as soon as possible.

Anactoria flew into a panic. I had to physically restrain her to stop her from running to Sappho's residence herself. I said I would send Abra to take the urgent message to Sappho.

I often ask myself what brought me to act as I did in that moment —a decision that would set a series of events in motion which would change the course of my life, and the lives of Anactoria and those around us, forever.

Once out of Anactoria's earshot, something happened. It was as if without her presence by my side—a presence that made me a far better person than really I was—I was suddenly overcome by my own selfish thoughts.

It occurred to me that I had reached a crisis point. I was standing on a precipice. Right there and then, I had the power to make all my dreams come true in an instant. Everything I ever wanted—to have someone all to myself, someone who would care for me, and whom I could love and cherish for the rest of our lives together—was within my reach. All I had to do was… do nothing.

The alternative, to condemn myself to a lonely, isolated existence, seemed unbearable. Why did I have to deny myself happiness?

So, rather than send Abra on to Sappho, I bid her goodbye and instructed her to return to my uncle's house and to say nothing of our departure to anyone until well after midday.

Now, I often wonder what others would have done in that situation?

I also wonder what life would have been like had I had sent Abra with that message, if I had been the one left standing on the pier, waving off the happy couple as they set sail on their new life together. Who would be telling this story, then?

When I returned to Anactoria's side I found her fraught with worry. Her nerves were as frayed as old rope and she was frantic, desperate for solace—solace I could and would gladly offer. I wallowed in her need to be comforted by *me*. I was the hero coming to her rescue. It felt so right, and in that moment, I had no doubt that I had made the right decision. She needed *me*. *I* could look after her and in time she would grow to love me more. In time our lives would be good together.

As the time for departure drew nearer, and of course there was still no sign of Sappho, Anactoria became more and more distressed.

"Where could she be?" she pleaded.

I couldn't bring myself to lie. So, I said nothing. Instead, I squeezed her shoulders gently and pulled her into my arms. She didn't resist.

One of the shipmates whistled down to us. That was the signal. It was time to board.

"Anactoria, we cannot wait any longer. It is time to go. You need to get onto that ship to get you to safety. Sappho would never forgive me if I didn't make sure you got away from Pittacus to somewhere where he won't find you."

"No, we can't leave without her!" She was almost in tears. "Where is she?"

"Look, I know this is hard." I hugged her again, trying to communicate all my love and reassurance. "Perhaps Pittacus's men did come around and she realised she couldn't lead them straight to you." I shook my head trying to think of a few more feasible explanations, but I couldn't. "Or, there could have been half a dozen other reasons why she couldn't get here. All we can do is stick to the plan and hope, if she can, that she catches you up."

"You don't understand, I don't want to go on my own."

The gods were smiling on me.

I turned her to face me, "what about if I go with you as far as Lefkas? We can wait there for her. If for some reason she has been detained, she would surely follow on the next ship out."

I could see her grappling with the inevitable. She knew she didn't have a choice but to get on that ship.

"You know Sappho is a remarkable and resourceful woman. If she has the will, she will find the way."

"She does have the will."

I saw the flicker of uncertainty in her eyes. However, my reassurance was apparently enough to coax her onto the ship and within a few heartbeats the ship was headed out of the harbour.

It saddened me to see her eyes fixed on Mytilene, even long after the harbour was no longer in sight.

As for Sappho, would she really follow? I had no idea. I couldn't see how.

Even if she did, at the very least I had bought Anactoria and I a little time—a little window in which I could help her learn to appreciate me and everything I could offer her, and so, if it came down to it... choose *me* instead.

Sappho had organised her deception with military precision. She had divided up her plan into separate actions and bade different slaves to carry out each part. She had asked Kleïs to pack her personal belongings because there wasn't anybody else who could do that. Beyond that, she had arranged for two different sets of porters to take her travel chest, along with a consignment of wine and wares, first to the market and then to the harbour as if it was an ordinary chest destined for export. She had sent another one of her messenger slaves to the harbour to intercept the chest and make sure it was taken to the correct quay, from which Bilitis's uncle's ship was due to set sail. All that was left was for her to get herself to the quayside before midday. She decided it would look the least suspicious, and buy her the most time, if she waited until Kerkylas had left for his work before she sent Kleïs on a suitably lengthy errand somewhere, potentially out of town, while she made her way to the harbour on her own.

Since the very moment she had said yes to Anactoria, she had deliberately not allowed herself the luxury of contemplating the greater consequences of her imminent departure at any length. Instead, while her gut churned with excitement, she kept her mind focused on the plan and on making sure she would not get caught before she was safely on board that ship heading to her new life with her young Phaon.

It was only afterwards, when she was back home, lying curled on her bed and crying her heart out, that the full magnitude of what she had been planning to do dawned on her all at once. She had been about to give up *everything* for Anactoria. Yet that was nothing compared to how it felt to experience Anactoria's betrayal. Before that moment, she'd had no idea what it would feel like to *really* lose everything that mattered to her, and that at the hand of someone she trusted with her life.

She could not blame Kleïs for being disturbed to find her in such a state. She allowed Kleïs to help her sit up and drink some water while

Kleïs combed her long dark hair—an activity that usually soothed her tempestuous spirits.

Why would Anactoria do that to her?

Was it Anactoria's doing? Or was it that harpy, Bilitis, who had orchestrated this from the start? She should have checked the departure schedule with the harbour master herself. She had thought about it, but decided it would draw too much attention to that ship if she were found to have been asking questions. It was bad enough she had to get her messenger to take her chest to that quay.

Her mind circled. Why? How could Anactoria let that happen? Her heart broke at the thought that her dearest love was now gone forever.

Why had she let Bilitis near them and their plans? Why had Bilitis been their only chance of getting off the island? If only she'd had a choice. If only she had a ship!

Oh, the pain was too great, the suffering too severe. Anactoria had left her. She couldn't bear it. Oh, but for a physical wound that could overshadow the pain of her broken heart. She glanced around for something sharp. Anything. The only thing to hand was her hairpin. She grabbed it and started stabbing at the palm of her hand in an effort to draw blood.

Almost instantly, Kleïs' cool hands caught her wrists and held them tight.

"You don't understand, I can't bear it," Sappho sobbed.

"Even though I am uncertain what exactly troubles you so, I do understand pain, Mistress. Believe me I do. But inflicting more is not going to make the other go away."

Sappho collapsed into Kleïs' small frame and sobbed.

Later, once Sappho's tears were all spent and she had calmed herself a little, Kleïs went to fetch her some more water.

Sappho studied her reflection in the mirror. She imagined she felt like an island would feel, after being pummelled by a storm. She took a deep breath. That is where it had all started, the storm. She remembered her prayer to Aphrodite that night. Her goddess had forsaken her. This pain and suffering were exactly what she'd sought to avoid. She felt a hopeless exhaustion about to overcome her.

She sat down again to rest, lowering her head in her hands and accidently hurt her brow with the hard mother-of-pearl object she was still holding.

Memories of finding the hairpin on Anactoria's rags flooded her mind. She remembered how overwrought she had been at the time with fear that it might be too late—that she might have lost her love forever. She recalled how she had given Alcaeus the hairpin only a day or two earlier and wondered what his part in all this could have been.... Alcaeus and his stupid brother's schemes, whatever they were, were always bad news. As Sappho brooded over Alcaeus's involvement, literally like a ship appearing out of the fog, a clear, simple idea came to her.

Kleïs hurried to the kitchen to fill the krater with water from one of the amphorae.

She made sure to hurry and returned directly to Sappho's chamber. She didn't want to leave her mistress unattended in her current condition. She had no idea what had happened that morning while she was on her own. Whatever it was, she had not seen Sappho that unsettled since she lost her first born all those years ago.

She was astounded when she returned and found Sappho had, almost miraculously, transformed from helpless wretch on the verge of suicide to a fiery daimon.

"Kleïs, get me Alcaeus," Sappho barked.

Kleïs nodded and rushed out to find a messenger to send to Alcaeus. Of one thing she was now absolutely certain: whatever had upset Sappho, it clearly had something to do with Alcaeus. Kerkylas was right. He was bad news and could not be trusted.

Alcaeus was usually thrilled when Sappho sent for him. This time his gut told him to act with caution. What happened on that ship and the matter of young Phaon hung between them like a preternatural cloud, weighing heavily on their life-long friendship. He was sure she had summoned him now to hear the explanation that she had demanded that day in the harbour. If he could avoid that right now, he would, at all cost.

But all personal resolutions he might have made on his way over to Sappho dissolved instantly when he saw her dark rings and red, puffy eyes.

"What is it, Sappho? What happened?" He rushed to her side. "You look like Morpheus has avoided you for days!"

Sappho's well-aimed palm connected with Alcaeus's cheek with a resounding slap.

"Ouch!" Alcaeus cried out before he could stop himself.

"Very perceptive, as usual, Alcaeus." Sappho's tone was vulnerable but icy. "Kleïs, that'll be all. I'll call you when I need you."

Kleïs made a swift retreat.

"What was that for?" Alcaeus asked, still holding his smarting cheek.

Sappho slowly opened her palm to reveal the hairpin. "This," she said evenly.

"What is that?" He shrugged feigning ignorance. He had so hoped that that hairpin would not come back to haunt him.

So far Sappho hadn't asked him anything about the ship but, judging by Sappho's outburst in the harbour that day, the slave girl had told her some of what happened. How much the girl knew or what of that she'd told Sappho, he was uncertain. He wondered if Sappho knew *he* was the one who left her beloved slave on the ship to drown, and it was only by the grace of the gods that she survived. In addition, he really didn't want to have a conversation about what he and his brothers were doing on the ship in the first place. He wanted nothing more than to try to put the whole devastating experience behind him, if he could. There was not much chance of that, he knew. What happened on that ship would haunt him for the rest of his life.

More than that, until Sappho had dragged the facts out of him, he wouldn't have to account to his brother about how much she knew and whether she would, or could, give them up. In the old days, back when they were clearly on the same side, exiled in Sicily together, Antimenidas would have had no doubt that Sappho could keep their secrets. But since then she had married Kerkylas who was Pittacus's right-hand man, and this pulled Sappho squarely into the ruling faction and placed them directly on opposing sides of the ongoing feud. This made questions of loyalties a lot less certain.

Sappho held up the hairpin so he could see it more clearly.

His heart sank. "It's a hairpin," he said stating the obvious as matter-of-factly as possible.

"That it is." Sappho took a deep, exhausted breath. "If you recall, it is a very specific hairpin. It is the one I gave you the day before your big secret mission for which you claimed you needed luck."

Alcaeus shook his head. "I'm so sorry I lost it. I will buy you a new one. I was meaning to come tell you about it and apologise."

Sappho shook her head. "No, it's not lost. This is *that* hairpin. You see I know it is, because it is unique. It was made for me and given to me as a gift by a young woman, whom I tutored years ago, before she married and moved to Egypt." She took another deep breath and let it out in a slow, long sigh. "So, Alcaeus, please, don't treat me like a fool."

Alcaeus frowned and was about to deny it when she continued.

"You see, our young Phaon returned it to me. How do you think he got it?"

Before he could answer she continued again.

"Actually, you don't need to explain. I know all about how you lost it. I know all about you and your brothers being on Phaon's ship. And this is proof. You were there and, as usual, up to no good. What were you wanting with Tyrrhaeus, of all people? And now he is dead!"

Alcaeus gave a fake laugh, and shook his head. "It is not what you think, Sappho! I can assure you. That," he pointed at the shiny object in her hand, "doesn't prove anything. You only have a hairpin and an unreliable account."

Sappho nodded slowly. "Yes, but it was a fairly detailed account and it makes pretty good sense—enough to convince me of its truth. And, I think Pittacus will want to hear my story. Don't you? And, once he has heard it, what do you think he'll believe?"

Alcaeus shook his head in disbelief. "You wouldn't do that to me."

Sappho held up her finger to stop him talking.

"And, just to reassure you, I'm one step ahead of you. In case you or your brothers come up with any alternative ideas, I will hide the hairpin or give it to my slave for safekeeping, with instructions about what to do in the event that she never sees me again...." Sappho nodded and swallowed hard. "But, you're right. I certainly would prefer not to have to do any of that."

Alcaeus let out the breath he'd been holding. He studied Sappho. "So, what is it you really want, my sweet Sappho?"

Kleïs's ear was hot and red from how hard she had been pressing it to the door. Suddenly she became aware of approaching footsteps echoing off the surrounding walls. Someone was coming. Quickly she pushed herself off the door and rushed away down the corridor, her heart pounding in her chest.

She hadn't heard everything her mistress and Alcaeus had said, but she'd certainly heard enough to know this was serious. To calm down, she forced herself to walk a full circuit around the inner atrium.

By Artemis! What had she just heard? She had not missed the mention of the aisymnētēs's son. She had heard the other house slaves talking of his disappearance and the recent discovery of his body on the shore of Anatolia somewhere. Apparently, the last time he was seen was getting onto Old Phaon's ship which was headed that way. This didn't make any sense. What would any of this have to do with her mistress? She couldn't believe her mistress would be involved in anything of the sort.

And, what was all that about a hairpin?

When Sappho spoke again her voice was filled with resolve. "I want you to help me commandeer my brother's ship."

"You what?" Alcaeus could not help the wave of laughter that burst from within—probably a combination of tension and incredulity at such a preposterous idea.

When he realised Sappho wasn't laughing too, he stopped. "Sorry, for a moment there I thought I heard you say that you want me to help you steal your brother's ship."

Sappho looked him straight in the eye.

Alcaeus's smile faded. "You can't be serious about this!"

"I've never been more serious about anything in my life."

"I can't do that." His voice rose a little higher than normal. "Seriously, Sappho, no matter how much I want to help you with whatever plan or troubles you have, what does a poet like me know about ships, let alone stealing them." He scoffed. "I won't even mention the fact that you are asking me to steal it from your own brother! What has got into you?"

Sappho turned towards him before she spoke. "Alcaeus, I don't have the energy for games. I really need your help. I'm prepared to be nice and ask you from the bottom of my heart, if you value my friendship...." She let the personal entreat register. "But also, don't forget, I know a lot about what you and your brothers have got up to over the years, in your fight with Pittacus—stealing a ship is a small feat by comparison."

Alcaeus swallowed. "After all these years, our friendship boils down to blackmail?"

Sappho shook her head. "Believe me, Alcaeus, you are my best friend, closer to me than either of my brothers, and I would not be asking you in the first place, unless I absolutely had to."

Alcaeus studied Sappho. She looked so tired, so vulnerable, so *desperate*—not a word he thought he would ever associate with his usually feisty and formidable best friend. He knew he had no choice but to try and help her or, if it came to it, probably die trying.

―――――――――

From Sappho, Alcaeus went straight to his brother, to persuade Antimenidas to help with the plan to take over Charaxus's ship.

As expected, Antimenidas was very resistant. More accurately, he reacted so badly to the whole proposal that Alcaeus feared he would burst a blood vessel.

"Okay, you can keep shouting at me, or telling me how you told me this would happen, but that is not going to help us right now, is it, brother?" Alcaeus asked patiently.

Antimenidas seemed to capitulate. A lifelong battle warred within him—the urge to wipe the smug expression off his brother's face, versus the knowledge that he was right.

"As you know, Sappho is not only a very influential woman in

Mytilene, she is married to Kerkylas who also happens to be the right-hand man and chief criminal prosecutor of our aisymnētēs, Pittacus—the man whose son was found dead and who will want to have all three of us, no questions asked, hanged for his son's murder. So, unless we want to end up deeper in the pits than we already are, we need to come up with a plan."

"A plan? You want me to help you come up with a plan?" Antimenidas asked, still on the verge of exploding.

Alcaeus nodded.

"Well, in that case, I suggest you go and steal that bloody hairpin from Sappho and we call her bluff. It will be her word against ours."

Alcaeus shook his head and smiled fondly at the thought of his remarkable Sappho. "She said you'd say that. She is far too clever to let that happen. We don't really have another choice but to help her, big brother."

From the day Anactoria and I, on my uncle's ship, sailed out from Mytilene, it took us almost a whole moon to reach the shores of Lefkas. Our route took us through the Aegean, through the Cyclades into the Mediterranean Sea around the headlands of Laconia and Messenia, north through the Ionian Sea, bypassing the attractive coastlines of the islands of Zakynthos and Kefalonia, past the little island of Ithaki, until we finally reached the unique half-island, half-mainland outcrop that forms Lefkas, with its notorious white cliffs which can be seen for miles, rising out of the ocean like giant crocodile teeth. It was the island's unique connection to the mainland as well as its reach, far out to sea, that made it a very popular trading post, despite how extremely treacherous the final leg around the island's promontory and into the safety of the bay could be. Many ships had run aground in that location, within a stone's throw of their destination.

Luckily, we made it.

Exhausted and cold, we stepped off the ship. I found us lodgings in a small inn, not far from the port, to the west of Vasiliki Bay. I had hoped that we could use our short stay there to rest and recover, before moving on to our next destination on another of my uncle's ships, which was due to head north from Lefkas in just a few weeks. There was no way I was going to stay with the original plan to head on to Sicily. It had far too great a burden associated with it, as the destination Anactoria was aiming for with Sappho.

Anactoria, however, had other priorities. Her feet had hardly touched solid ground, before she insisted on heading along the thin, rocky path that ran along the promontory, up to the highest vantage point on the top of the famous white cliffs. This was a good long walk from the inn—a journey she would, from then on, undertake religiously every morning just as dawn lit up the sky, only returning as darkness fell in the evening. She spent every daylight moment searching the horizon for a ship that might be bringing Sappho to her.

It hurt to see her so focussed on the absent Sappho. I longed for a fraction of Anactoria's attention, never mind affection or gratitude.

I consoled myself that it would just take a bit more time for Anactoria to grow tired of her vigil or, perhaps, to become ready to admit to the reality that Sappho was not coming to her. I needed to be patient and kind and let her come to me when she was ready. Then, I could gently escort her on the next leg of our journey, where we would be safe from Sappho's hold over her.

I had no doubt that once Anactoria was ready she would realise that I could give her a far better life than any she would have had with Sappho. I was single, had means of my own and was able to devote my life to her, if it came down to that. Sappho had a husband, children, pupils, a school and a full life which tied her to Mytilene. Even if she did manage to wrench herself away, she would never stay with Anactoria. She might have said so in the heat of passion. She might even have meant it at the time. But I knew. I had seen these things before. Promises like that, fuelled by passion, never last. I had to make Anactoria see sense.

A few days later Alcaeus headed back to Sappho's house with a spring in his step. He was looking forward to reporting on their progress. He and Antimenidas had finally come up with a plan to take control of one on Charaxus's ships in the dead of the night, with the help of a thirteen strong army of mutineering crewmen who were hoping to change their fortunes.

"So, we're all set, if you are still determined to go through with this," Alcaeus said. "As you know the stakes are very high. The consequences could be dire for you and for all of us if we should get caught or you later decide you wish to return to Mytilene."

Sappho nodded. "I assure you Alcaeus, if I decide to return, this will all be on my head. I will see to it."

Alcaeus believed Sappho; although his brother did not have the same faith in her, he also knew there was nothing they could do about it. They had to go through with this plan to help her and that was a risk they would have to take.

But now was also the time to call in a favour. "In that case," he said cautiously, "can I now have your word you will hold your tongue and leave the whole Tyrrhaeus issue alone."

"You fulfil your promise and it is all as good as forgotten," Sappho said.

In shock, Kleïs pushed herself off the door. "...not return to Mytilene?" Kleïs's mind was spinning. So, they *are* planning to leave. Leave from where? To go where? When? With the possibility of never returning to Mytilene....

She was annoyed that she'd missed such a large part of their conversation while she was on her circuit of the atrium, but there was no time now to find out all the answers. She had to do something. She could not have Sappho leave her. She needed to stop whatever they were planning!

With the plan and their agreement on Tyrrhaeus settled, there was still something that really troubled Alcaeus. He took a seat on the couch. "Forgive me my friend, but I have a question that has been plaguing me." He frowned slightly. "Why, Sappho? Why are you doing this?"

"What do you mean?" Sappho asked.

"I mean, why are you doing this? I've asked you a number of times to go away with me and you've always said a definite no. You said you would never give up your life and privilege in Mytilene with Kerkylas. You've also said you would never do what Helen did, and leave your children or your pupils. So why now risk it all?"

"Alcaeus, don't take this the wrong way." Sappho's tone was calm but resolved, as she stood in front of him. "No wealth and good standing can ever compare to the pain inflicted by Cupid's careless arrow. True love does not adhere to logic." She paused and looked affectionately down at Alcaeus, cupping his cheek like she would a small boy's. "My friend, I hope someday you find your true muse…. Or maybe, if you have already found him, that you notice him and he can make your heart sing, so that you too may be content to fulfil your true potential as a great poet and leave all those delinquent dabblings to your brothers. That is not you! Your soul is pure…. Then you will understand."

For a moment Alcaeus bit his bottom lip, steeling himself.

After another moment Sappho turned to walk away.

"Have you considered that she only asked you to marry her to get you to help her?" Alcaeus blurted.

Sappho's rage erupted and in an abrupt turn she slapped Alcaeus hard.

Stunned, Alcaeus clasped his smarting cheek. He was relieved to see she looked shocked herself at her own outburst.

"If I ever hear you say that about her again," Sappho's voice was laced with a chilling menace, "I will take that hairpin and my story to Pittacus and see to it that you are stoned, myself."

Later that night in the darkness of reflection, Sappho lay awake considering Alcaeus's words. Even though she reacted with impulse to his impertinence, they were now playing on her mind.

Could Alcaeus have been right?

Until now, she had convinced herself that the recent deception was all Bilitis's doing. That she, with her cunning ways, had devised a trick to finally win Anactoria all to herself.

But what if Anactoria had her own part to play? What if she had intended to elope with Bilitis all along? After all, Sappho did see her leave with Bilitis at the Kallisteia. Who knew what had happened between them since then? But if so, why then make a play–and such an earnest one—for Sappho's affection?

What to do? What to think? There are two warring states of mind in me[1], Sappho thought.

It was true, Sappho was the only other person, who knew Phaon's true identity. Could this have been a complicated ruse to stop Sappho exposing the young Phaon for who she was? Could it be that Anactoria had just been using her? Could this have been part of their plan all along, to get Sappho to help her and then at the last minute to mislead her, so that Anactoria and Bilitis could escape together?

No! She hit the pillow hard next to her head. She could not allow herself to imagine Anactoria doing that to her. She had to believe this was a mistake, or mix-up, or that Bilitis had duped her beloved Anactoria. If she didn't, she would surely die of a broken heart.

Days had passed since we first arrived on Lefkas. Still there was no sign of Sappho and still Anactoria persisted in her vigil, climbing to stand watch, every day, on the cold, windswept, hostile cliffs. The day of my planned departure on my uncle's next ship was drawing near and I knew it was time to talk to Anactoria, to start to prepare her for the change in our plan. So, that afternoon, I wrapped up warmly and made my way along the promontory, past the temple of Apollo, to the clifftops.

I found her sitting slumped, sheltering from the icy winds in the lea of a boulder that looked as if it had landed there as the result of a wild throw in a discus game of the gods. She looked so vulnerable, so exhausted.

Seeing her sitting there, so sorrowful, almost broke my heart. I found myself on the very edge of giving in and suggesting that we return to Mytilene—anything to end her suffering. But then, I realised that Anactoria needed me now more than ever to be strong and do the right thing—for both of us.

"Anactoria, my darling, you need to give yourself a rest. Sappho would surely not want to see you like this."

Anactoria shook her head, her jaw clenched, as she refocussed her eyes on the horizon.

I stood watching her for a while, not quite knowing the right thing to say.

"Anactoria, I know this is going to be hard to hear," I began cautiously. "At some point you will have to face the fact —"

Anactoria shook her head violently. "I won't give up on her. She said she will come."

I took a deep, steadying breath and continued tenderly. "Anactoria, it has been well over almost a full lunar cycle since we arrived here. At some point you have to consider the possibility that she's not going to come."

"I won't believe it! I won't believe she has deceived me. She said she loved me. She said she'd marry me."

I sat down on the ground next to her and put my arm around her trying to imbue her with my own heat, love and affection. "It is a big decision to make… to leave your husband, your children and your secure lifestyle. It is a lot to expect her to do for you—for an uncertain dream." These were harsh truths, but I believed they were true. I would have given anything to take away all her sorrow and hurt.

"She said she loved me…." Her voice cracked.

"I know." I said and gently stroked her hair. "I have no doubt she did love you very much and she had every intention to leave with you, but surely you can see how huge the sacrifice is that you were asking of her. Is that fair of you?"

As the reality of the situation began to sink in, tears started rolling down Anactoria's cheeks.

I pulled her closer into my arms and stroked her gently like I was soothing a little child, while she cried softly on my shoulder. Finally, she sat up and nodded.

"Come," I said, "let's get you some food and you need to sleep."

Then, she allowed me to lead her down the hill, all the way to the small room we shared in the inn.

*W*ith resolve, Kleïs headed directly to Kerkylas's andron. She couldn't remember ever having been inside it. That was the domain of men, and those few women who were invited in, were *invited* for the sole purpose of delighting men with carnal pleasures. So far, because Sappho would not allow it, she had thankfully been spared that ordeal.

She stopped briefly in front of the door and slipped her chiton slightly off her shoulder. She ruffled her hair, pinched her cheeks and rubbed her lips as she has seen some of the other slaves do before they went in to entertain Kerkylas. When she felt she was ready, she knocked quietly.

"Come," Kerkylas called from inside.

Kleïs entered, sporting her most alluring pout and batting her eyelids—also something she had seen the other slaves do.

He glanced up from the papyrus he was reading. If he was surprised to see her, he didn't show it.

"Have you forgotten your way around the house? Sappho's gynaeceum is down the hall." He dropped his gaze and continued reading.

"No, Master, I haven't."

"Well, I don't remember calling for you," he said, not taking his eyes off the document before him.

"No, but, Master, I have some information that I thought would interest you."

Kerkylas looked up. "Oh? And what information could you possibly have?"

Kleïs could feel him taking in her dropped sleeve, her coy smile and slightly tousled look.

"I'm pretty certain I already know everything about my household and my wife that there is worth knowing."

"Master, what I have to tell you would only take as long as reading a few lines of your papyrus." She hoped she sounded more confident than she felt. "If you already know what I have to tell you, that is all you would have lost. However, if you don't, then I believe it could affect you for the rest of your life."

"That is a very bold statement." He put down the scroll. "Well, if you think you can enlighten me, I'll give you a hearing, but if you're wasting my time there'll be a warm sixteen lashes coming your way."

Kleïs nodded and stepped forward around the decorative wooden desk that stood between them. Careful not to interfere with his documents, she leaned back against the table and tried to smile a coy, hooded smile as she smoothly lifted one leg off the floor. With a suggestive flurry, she wriggled her foot free of her sandal before nestling her toes into the space between Kerkylas's knees on the chair.

She was hoping to make a good seduction out of this. Instead, he seemed to look more bemused. She had never had to do this; women did not seem to need to be seduced like this, in the same way that men did. She was losing confidence but decided she had gone too far now to back out.

"I thought you might like to know that my mistress is planning on leaving Mytilene."

Kerkylas frowned. "Leave Mytilene? What for?"

"Not sure." Kleïs shrugged coyly. "I do know that she is planning to leave with…" she wriggled her toes against his inner thigh hoping to distract him, "Alcaeus."

She observed with satisfaction the expected jealousy flare behind his eyes.

"Don't be ridiculous!" He banged his fist down hard on the arm of his chair, startling Kleïs. "You're lying!" He roughly took hold of her foot and started to twist it unnaturally, causing her to whimper with pain and shock. "She would never do that without telling me."

"Please, Master. I promise, I'm not." She pleaded, wishing she had just stayed at the door, as any messenger would have done. "I heard them talking in her gynaeceum."

Through her discomfort she could see he was at least considering her words. This was the critical part. He *had* to believe her.

"Tell me exactly what you know," he said sternly, not releasing the pressure on her foot.

"I don't know very much, but… my mistress has asked me to prepare a travel chest for her and has been talking to Alcaeus privately," she gasped at the pain as he gave her foot another twist, "s-sending me away each time. It seemed suspicious and I feared Sappho might be in danger, so I tried to listen in on the conversations. I did not hear much, but I thought I should come and tell you."

He eyed her intently. "Go on. When did you hear this?"

"Earlier, when Alcaeus called, Master."

Kerkylas bristled. "What exactly did they say?"

Kleïs tried to remember and repeated as much of the conversation as she had overheard. Not everything made sense, but as long as Kerkylas stopped them, she didn't care.

Kerkylas was quiet for a long moment as he clearly considered her and the truth of her account. Finally, he seemed to adopt a more ponderous air that contrasted starkly with the vice like grip he still had on her foot.

"I'm sure there is a perfectly good reason for what you've heard. Sappho is not like other women. In many ways, she is a man in a woman's body, with the accompanying intellect and sophistication, although she draws on her creative wiles for her theatre," he said almost conversationally. "I've always given her her freedom. And, on this occasion, I am already aware of her travel plans.

Kleïs could not suppress her surprise.

"I believe there is a symposium near Petra they are to perform at and if she intends to travel elsewhere with Alcaeus, I'm sure she would have told me herself."

"I bow to your judgement, Master. If that is indeed all, then I humbly ask your and my mistress's forgiveness, but that would not explain my mistress's distress."

Kerkylas thought for a while. Then he suddenly let go of her foot and got up, almost sending her toppling over sideways. "I will deal with it." He announced and headed over to his krater where he poured himself a large kylix of the rich, diluted wine his servants brought to his office every day. "That will be all."

Kleïs bowed slightly and limped for the door, sandal in hand, her heart pounding in her chest and her foot aching.

"Oh, and speak of this to no one or I will have your tongue," he said not looking back.

She bowed again and hobbled out as fast as she could.

Kerkylas resolved to confront Sappho during the evening meal.

When she didn't arrive for dinner, he headed straight to her gynaeceum.

The gynaeceum's door was closed. This usually meant she was busy with a client or a pupil.

Back when she started teaching—amongst other things, giving private lessons to well-to-do women in society in the art of love-making—she made him promise to respect her privacy. She had pointed out that the esteemed husbands of her clients, who had sent their women to her in the first place, would not take kindly to his intrusion and that he did not want to open himself up to accusations of cuckolding them or interfering with their wives.

He had seen her point and thus far had never interrupted her sessions, despite at first being very curious to know what female secrets and dark arts were being imparted behind that closed door. However, in time he got accustomed to having a procession of women, some the wives of the most powerful men he knew, stream in and out of his house for private tuition. He even secretly felt a little proud and enjoyed the kudos and respect it gave him amongst his peers to have landed such a skilled wife.

At the time, he had conceded not to interrupt her unless it was absolutely necessary.

On this occasion he reasoned that it was necessary.

He knocked.

"Kerkylas?" Sappho said when she opened the door. She seemed rather pleased to see him, despite him breaking their rule.

"Ah, Sappho, I apologise for the interruption." He suddenly felt tongue-tied. He didn't want to cut straight to the chase, because he had no idea who was in the gynaeceum with her and he didn't think it was prudent to share their dirty linens with the world, particularly if there was even a breadcrumb's truth in what the slave girl had said.

"That's okay, Kerkylas," she said patiently. "What is the matter?"

He shook his head. "I need to talk to you, in private. Are you working all evening?"

He saw her glance back, clearly assessing the situation behind the door. "Yes, I think so. Probably well into the night."

He nodded. "In that case, please could you see me first thing in the morning, before I go to work."

He could see she was a little annoyed at his request. He knew she liked to sleep in after a late night's work.

"It is important."

She seemed to relent. "I'll see you at breakfast." She smiled apologetically and closed the door.

Seeing Sappho in her usual work mode like that went a little way to allay his fears. After all, if she were planning something more sinister with that slimy little effete weasel, she would surely not be carrying on with business as usual.

Most probably, for whatever that impertinent little slave overheard, he was sure Sappho would have a perfectly good explanation. Although he felt uneasy about leaving it until the morning to find out, he knew it could not be helped, unless he wanted to create a potentially unnecessary scene in front of a respected audience. He suddenly felt an enormous amount of anger towards that insolent little cock-tease. She had put him in this situation. In fact, he had a good mind to go and work off some of his tension by giving her those sixteen lashes himself.

Nevertheless, he took a deep breath and resolved not to take action until he had a chance to hear Sappho out. Sappho would never forgive him for punishing her personal slave unnecessarily.

The next morning Kerkylas sat at the table pushing around pieces of the fried pancake that formed his usual breakfast. He wasn't hungry. The previous evening, after his visit to Sappho's chamber, he had sent a messenger to invite a local friend to join him in his andron to drink wine and relax in order to take his mind off his troubles. His friend had stayed quite late and thanks to the quantities of wine they had consumed, Kerkylas managed to pass out, leaving his troubles to be dealt with in the morning.

Sadly, now morning had come and he had been sitting there for some time, trying to decide how he was going to broach the subject with Sappho. He knew she would be livid if she found out that her slave had betrayed her to him. She would be furious with him for listening to such slander in the first place. He also feared that she would laugh at him again, as she had done on the only other occasion he had tried to confide in her that her relationship with Alcaeus made him feel uncomfortable.

When the kitchen slave finally reappeared for the fourth time to clear away his plate and there was still no sign of Sappho, he decided she had probably overslept. Now he couldn't wait any longer.

He got up and headed for Sappho's chamber.

When he got to the corridor, he was surprised to find Kleïs curled, asleep on the floor in front of Sappho's bedroom door.

"What are you doing there?" he barked.

Kleïs startled and immediately jumped up. "Sorry, Master, I —"

"Aren't you meant to warm Sappho's bed once her clients have gone."

"I am." Kleïs looked at the floor, shame colouring her cheeks. "My mistress never called for me last night."

What did that mean? Kerkylas worried. Could she still have a client there? It was not unheard of that sometimes they stayed overnight, since it was often difficult to get home if they finished late. Should he leave it? He eyed the young slave in front of him. No, he needed to get to the bottom of this.

He stepped forward and knocked on the door gently. When there was no answer he knocked louder until eventually he lost patience and barged in!

In front of him stood Sappho's bed. Empty. Unslept in. There was no sign of Sappho anywhere.

Behind him, he heard Kleïs's sharp intake of breath as she realised the bedroom was vacant. He turned swiftly and landed a powerful backhand on her cheek, so hard it made her stumble. "You had better pray to every god you can that what you said yesterday is not true." Then he stomped out.

Sappho had set off a good a while before dawn, this time armed only with the clothes on her back and the coins she could carry. She reasoned that this was enough to tide her over for a while and when she needed more, she could sing or perform in Lefkas or Sicily. She had intended, the previous evening, to go and find Kerkylas and make a big show of feeling unwell, so that she could easily dismiss Kleïs and be left in peace with good reason, all with the aim of buying her time to pack and to get ready to head to the ship.

However, when Kerkylas arrived and knocked at her door even though it was closed, she knew something was up. She was not sure what, or how, but her gut said he knew. She had to move quickly.

She'd dismissed Kleïs, saying she would call for her when it was time for bed. Then she got dressed and let herself out of her own window. It was a little trickier getting down the pillar than she had imagined it would be and far harder than either Alcaeus or Anactoria had made it look.

She took the road down to the harbour, walking swiftly, and was relieved to find that, unlike at her previous attempt, Charaxus's ship was still at the quayside and Alcaeus was waiting for her on board. They had not conferred about the actual voyage arrangements, but she had to admit that when Alcaeus announced he was going to be travelling with her, although it initially irritated her, her heart felt lighter. As a single woman, to have the protection of a trustworthy male companion amidst a crew of likely amorous delinquents was a relief. Secretly, despite her recent quarrels with him, she also valued the reassurance of having her life-long friend by her side.

The ship set sail quickly, without incident and managed to make good progress. It reached Crete within less than half a moon, and took on supplies of fresh food and water. The rest of the journey took longer and was far more perilous, with numerous storms testing the skill of their ragbag crew and the sturdiness of the boat.

Throughout the journey, Sappho's mind was focussed on other troubles. With each league they progressed, Sappho battled with her own turbulent feelings. The daimon of doubt raged inside her. On one hand she despaired, and felt it pointless to be following Anactoria. How could she be sure Anactoria had any intention of being with her? At those moments, she wished that Poseidon would make quick business of claiming her and their ship in a spectacular storm.

On the other hand, with every day they got closer to Lefkas, she felt more positive, a little more hopeful that, despite this initial setback, which would be easily explained, they would resume their plans to start a new life together. She owed it to Anactoria to cling, with all ten of her fingernails, to every morsel of faith she had. After all, optimism, like smoke of a sacrificial fire, is what carries our prayers up to the gods, and entreats them to rain down good fortune upon us.

This also reminded her that she had not yet quite shared with Alcaeus the next part of the plan, which involved setting sail on Charaxus's ship to Sicily.

Her turbulent thoughts must somehow have vexed the gods, because before the following daybreak, the ship was caught on the edge of the most nauseating swell from a circling storm that she had ever experienced.

"We are reaching the coast of Lefkas," the captain announced with a foreboding grunt. "These waters are notorious for the number of souls it has claimed, and it gets worse the closer we get to the cliffs." He pointed into the distance.

Sure enough, there on the horizon, rising out of the depths of nowhere, loomed the white cliffs of Lefkas.

"My darling Anactoria, hold tight. I'm almost there," she whispered into the wind.

Suddenly she realised what the captain had said. "Why is it worse the closer we get?" As it was, the ship was already rolling and pitching to an alarming extent.

"This is a place of great power, bestowed by Zeus himself. It is said that anyone tormented by love can throw themselves off these cliffs and so, find relief from their woes—one way or another."

"Through death we find solace?" Sappho said knowingly.

The captain shook his head. "Not like that. It is said that some don't die." He shrugged. "But none that I've seen. Even if the fall does not finish you off... and I am a believer in miracles... there are also the dangers of the sea. Once Poseidon has you in his clutches, he rarely lets you go."

Sappho nodded.

"You had better take cover, and start praying to whichever deity you can that we get through this," the captain said.

Sensing Sappho's growing anxiety, Alcaeus, who had not left her side at any point during their journey took her arm and said, to comfort her, "It will be all right, Sappho. We will get there." Then he pulled her close to him and guided her to take shelter below deck.

here was not a single person on that ship who doubted for a moment that they would all meet Poseidon that day. Why the gods didn't end Alcaeus's and Sappho's lives during that voyage, only they know. Perhaps they too wanted to see what would happen next in this momentous tryst.

Afterwards, with true mariner showmanship, the ship's captain sucked his blackening teeth and boasted that he and his boys had been through far worse.

Once she had solid ground under her feet, all thoughts of the ship and the voyage were gone from Sappho's mind. All she could think about was where on the island Anactoria might be. She had to find her!

It wasn't hard. A beautiful man like young Phaon, accompanying a striking, tall, blonde woman like Bilitis, was doomed to be conspicuous and turn heads everywhere they went. So, it didn't take long for Sappho to find the little inn where they were staying.

The rotund innkeeper, answering to the name of Xenia, with hands like small octopi that rested on her hips when they were not doing something specific, eyed Sappho and Alcaeus with caution. She seemed suspicious about what they would want with her prize guests. Vasiliki Bay, on account of its location and renown as a trade port, did not have very many long-term guests and she was clearly suspicious of anyone who might shorten their stay.

To simplify things, Sappho explained that they were family and had planned to meet on the island before continuing on their journey together to Sicily.

"Sicily?" the innkeeper said. "You sure? Not Illyria?"

"Look, we've come a long way. We just want to see our family," Alcaeus interjected.

"Okay," she said, looking them up and down, "but you will need to take two rooms for the pair of you."

Alcaeus found it odd that she could so easily assume they were not together. Was that so hard to believe? But before he could object, she continued.

"Breakfast, a simple meal of bread and wine, will be available at dawn, and dinner, the main meal of the day, is just before sunset. For them I charge extra. No tip-toeing around after dark and also, I do not allow locked doors in this establishment. Is that understood?"

Sappho nodded rapidly, clearly keen to get through the formalities so that she could see Anactoria.

Xenia paused for a few moments, assessing her two new guests. Finally, her two little octopi came to life, and the whole of her swayed into motion, resembling a much larger sea creature. "Right, I'll go and see if they are in." She started off towards the back of the inn.

Sappho immediately followed, with Alcaeus in tow.

When the innkeeper realised this, she commented, conversationally, "They tend to be out most of the day." It sounded more like she was describing a species of wildlife she had been observing, than a pair of her guests. As she glanced back again and realised that Alcaeus was also following, she stopped, folded her octopi hands over her arms and tutted. "Unless you have a room, men are not allowed back here."

"Alcaeus, why don't you go and sort out our rooms. I'll be fine. You heard the innkeeper, Anactoria is here." Sappho patted his arm.

Alcaeus hesitated for a moment, but on seeing the innkeeper's stern expression, decided that it was best he did as suggested.

Xenia frowned. "Who is Anactoria?"

When it became clear Sappho had no intention of delaying them by satisfying her curiosity, she continued down the corridor and along a thin, oblong atrium, barely large enough to provide sufficient daylight to see where they were going.

Eventually, the innkeeper slowed to a stop in front of the second to last door.

"It's this one," she announced, "but, if they are in, I don't think they would want to be disturbed, if you know what I mean." She winked at Sappho. "I did give them the bridal suit." She chuckled and her whole body seemed to wobble.

Sappho's world slowed down and closed in around her. Her peripheral vision shrunk to a small tunnel of focus, barely encompassing the sight of her own hand reaching for the handle, twisting it and pushing open the door.

"Hey, you can't just go in. Don't you knock where you come from?"

The innkeeper's protests floated towards Sappho's ears like sound through water. With tunnel vision her eyes searched the room for one thing and one thing only—her Anactoria.

The problem with tunnel vision is that it is very hard to make sense of a bigger context or situation. But the truth is, no matter how broad her vision, she would never have been able to make sense of what she saw.

On the large, gaudy, crimson covered bed in front of her lay Anactoria, head thrown back, breasts bouncing rhythmically, mouth agape in a manner Sappho had seen so many times before—a sight she adored and one she wallowed in whenever she had the opportunity to pleasure her young lover. Her first instinct was to be pleased her darling Anactoria was safe, happy and clearly enjoying such bliss.

Then, slowly her critical factors kicked in and she started to scan the room for the source of her lover's ecstasy. It was the motion that caught her eye. There between her loved one's legs, directly over her exquisite delta, a white-blond head bobbed furiously.

The rush of blood and ringing in Sappho's ears blocked out all sound.

She saw Anactoria's head slowly turn, her expression change, the look of shock, followed by the slow motion of Anactoria reaching for the sheet to hide her shame. Her lips mouthed Sappho's name.

Sappho couldn't breathe. She turned and fled.

In the main atrium, Sappho ran into Alcaeus. By then she looked as white as bleached papyrus. She collapsed into his arms.

"Sappho, are you all right? What happened?" he asked, frantically.

Sappho wailed in his arms, too distressed to speak.

Moments later an equally distressed Anactoria, wrapped in nothing but a large crimson sheet, followed Sappho.

I didn't know what to do, so I hung back and watched the scene in horror. As for the other onlookers, it didn't take a genius to work out what was going on.

"Guess you were pinning your colours on someone else's mast," the innkeeper, who had joined the fray too by then, remarked reproachfully. "What will that cute husband of yours say when he hears?"

Anactoria started clutching and hanging onto Sappho and beseeching her for forgiveness. This clearly distressed Sappho even more, causing her to cry harder and clasp on to Alcaeus tighter.

"Take her away," he shouted at me, "Take her away!"

This snapped me out of whatever shocked haze I had entered and I managed to drag Anactoria off Sappho and back to our room.

Alcaeus eventually managed to escort a distraught Sappho to her own room. Here he eased her onto the bed and continued to hold her in his arms until she eventually stopped sobbing. Unfortunately, when the crying stopped, she remained more or less unresponsive. He just about managed to get her to drink a few sips of water. She lay on her bed and stared into the middle distance as if her mind had escaped to a different world and it was just her body left, barely breathing, on the bed.

A few times that evening the innkeeper, obviously concerned about the reputation of her inn and what people would think of the recent drama, popped in to fuss ostentatiously and offer unhelpful advice.

Alcaeus finally, quite brusquely, told her to leave them alone.

After that Alcaeus stayed with Sappho, watching over his friend, until well into the night. When it became clear that Sappho's seemingly catatonic state was not going to change soon, he decided that perhaps if he stopped hanging over her like an overeager nurse, she might relax more and get some sleep.

He doubted if he, himself, could sleep under the circumstances, but decided to go to his room until the early morning, when he would check in on her again.

Once in his room, Alcaeus lay down, but he tossed and turned more than Charaxus's ship in that last storm.

He couldn't stop worrying about Sappho. She had already been very tired and vulnerable, even before they left Mytilene, and in all the years he had known her, he had never seen her in such a state. Whatever happened had shaken her world more than he would ever know. All he could do was hope that she would come through this.

As he often did when Morpheus eluded him, he got up and went to sit at the tiny table in the corner of his room, took out a parchment and started to write.

In the room down the hall, Sappho sat up. Her eyes stared blindly out at the world through her window. Her mind reeled on a loop, churning a single, ineffable concept—loss.

As the crisp glimmer of dawn started to colour the hills, Sappho got up. Barefoot and dressed only in her thin shift, she moved to her bedroom door. She opened it and slipped out into the corridor. If there had been anyone around to bear witness, they might have mistaken her for a ghostly apparition—her thin, bare limbs and feet seemingly impervious to the piercing morning cold.

Outside she turned right, past the corner of the inn and strode out taking the path along the promontory, past the temple of Apollo and up the hill. The same path that Anactoria had walked every day for all those weeks, waiting and watching for her.

Later, Alcaeus would recall hearing something outside his door, but at the time, he dismissed it as the sounds of the pre-dawn comings and goings of an inn.

Not even writing poetry was helping to calm his mind. Finally, he gave up, got up, stretched and stared out of his window.

The morning light had almost pushed away all of the darkness. A cloying sea fret hung in the bay, shielded from the strong ocean winds by the protective arm of the promontory. Despite it being still early, he could see a person walking way up on the hills, along the path towards the cliffs. It must have been freezing out there, and he was grateful to be in his room in the inn and not on that blustery hillside.

He watched the walker for a moment. There was something familiar about her. The way her long dark hair blew in the breeze. The lilt in her step that made her hips sway ever so slightly.

He would know that walk anywhere.

In an instant his blood ran cold in his veins and before he could finish his last thought, his legs were moving—he was running out of the inn, along the road to the path leading up towards the clifftops.

Sappho had a good half league lead on him. He pushed himself to run as fast as he could, and then faster until his legs threatened to give way and his lungs burnt with a fire stronger than Hades.

How had he not heard her? He should have listened to his instinct and stayed with her, watched over her. He shouldn't have assumed that Sappho, would just lie down and go to sleep. He knew her better than that. When had she ever been that compliant? What was she doing heading up to the cliffs? He prayed to every god he could that she was not about to do something stupid.

Perhaps she just needed to get some fresh air, he tried to calm himself.

Yet still, a nasty, nagging foreboding clawed at his gut and he pushed his legs harder up the hill.

As he reached the top plateau, he could just make out her small, pale figure standing on the edge of the cliffs, her thin shift billowing to the side from the stronger winds up there.

"Sappho!" he called as he tucked his shoulders low and lurched forward against the wind. His face and eyes burnt from the cold air but he refused to take his eyes off her. "Sappho!"

As he got closer, his heart sang with relief to see her turn. He imagined he could see her smile at him, as if pleased to see him. She looked at him for a long moment, watching him getting nearer and nearer.

It's going to be okay, he thought.

Then, as he got to within twenty paces from her, in slow motion, he saw her move. She seemed to lean away from him. For a moment it confused him. Then he realised she wasn't leaning... she was falling!

She was falling!

"No!" he shouted as he dived forward, reaching for her.

1 4

When Alcaeus brought us the devastating news that morning, Anactoria went crazy with grief and despair. I had to grab her and again hang onto her with all my might to stop her running off and following Sappho over those same cliffs into the afterlife.

Eventually, I managed to lead Anactoria back to our room in the inn. I offered her a drink of wine from the krater in our room to help with the shock. She refused. I took a long drink to steady my own nerves. I was shaken to my core. I would never in a god's lifetime have guessed we could have ended up in this situation. In an instant everything about my life, our lives, had changed. It was not about anger or guilt or jealousy anymore. The whole lie of the land had changed. There suddenly seemed no space for me anymore. Sappho might have been the one who jumped, but I was the one left without a foothold. It felt as if a giant crater had opened up beneath me.

I'm not exactly sure now how long we stayed in that room. All I remember is that when my guilt and my need to flee finally began to overpower me and I started towards the door, I was stopped by

Anactoria's barely audible plea. "Please, don't leave me." She had been lying on the bed, quite unresponsive up until that moment.

Those four little words felt like a life line. The smallest, frailest bridge had been extended towards me across the void. She needed me.

I made my way over to the large crimson bed and lay down next to her. She looked so frail and forlorn. I would have given anything, everything, to make it better, to take away her pain. I lifted my arm so she could lie in the crook of it. She did.

She shifted right in, almost lying on top of me. The glorious weight of her body pressed into me, her warmth soaking through the cool, wet fabric of her chiton where her tears had drenched it. Her strong arms, now so uncharacteristically frail, wrapped around me, clinging onto me.

I imagined Anactoria's need, the need not only of the flesh but of Psyche, being the voracious beast that it was, so ravenous, starting to feast on my own life force, my own desire. I liked it. I liked that I could feed and nurture it. Perhaps I liked it a little too much.

Memories of sweet, needy little Mnasidika came back to me—the endless time I spent worshipping her, showering my love on every inch of her skin, driving her to the heights of ecstasy, in the hope that a mere drop of my love might seep in and nourish her.

I became aware of Anactoria's body gently moving against mine from the dry sobs of her grief. Her strong hand innocently cupped my breast. Like the swell of a large wave before the crash, I felt my desire build and my delta began to throb. In that moment I knew I was everything to her, all that she had left in this world. A hunger began to rise up in me—a hunger to be more. I wanted to save her, possess her, ravish her, show her the heights and depths of my love and affection for her—I wanted us to fuse as one—to truly feel alive in our passion.

I turned my head and slowly started to kiss away the remnants of the salty tears on her eyes, her cheeks, her chin. I then kissed her lips. My kisses grew deeper, leaving us both breathless. I tried to see her eyes but they were closed, her face veiled.

She posed no resistance when I gently nudged her over onto her back. I loosened her chiton to expose her breasts. I began to lavish each one with soft, warm kisses and caresses as I knew she liked. When her beautiful large nipples stood tall, I started to kiss my way down her body heading for the ambrosia that I knew would await me at her delta.

"Please," I heard her whisper. I felt her hands gently pushing at my head. My own desire was by now burning like the fires of Hades. I knew, she had the strength. If she wanted to, she could overpower me. I took hold of both her hands and firmly pressed them down on the bed on either side of her narrow, boy-like hips. I lowered my lips to her centre. Using my tongue and nose I pushed my way into her sweet-scented delta. I lapped at her rich, fragrant nectar, drinking from her like I was Tantalus himself quenching his eternal thirst. I sucked at her most precious little gem, coaxing it tall and hard and finally I forced my tongue inside her most intimate recess in a rhythm I knew could not be denied. I tried to look up and see her face. I needed to see that look of utter surrender as she succumbed to me, knowing that in that moment she was completely powerless to prevent the inevitable. I longed to see her desire burn in those beautiful dark eyes.

It was not long before I felt her body tense. Her climax began with a slight tremble, building swiftly to a shudder that wracked her body.

Finally, as I felt her relax and my pulse calmed, I withdrew my, by now deliciously aching, tongue and mouth, lathered in her ambrosia.

I needed more than life itself to see that familiar hooded look of surrender and adoration that had previously followed our intimate moments.

Instead, I found she still had her head turned away from me.

I pushed myself further up off the bed. That is when I saw she had her eyes still closed and fresh tears lined her cheeks and her chest was trembling slightly.

At first confusion struck me. How could she still be experiencing aftershocks?

Then, horror paralysed me, and shame disembowelled me. I had mistaken the tremors of her sobs for ecstasy.

Oh gods! What had I done?

Panic mixed with shame in my veins, creating a river more toxic than Phlegethon, which pulsed through my body and blazed stronger than any passion I had ever had, propelling me into a madman's rampage.

I don't quite know how I got there. I remember one minute standing up off the bed and observing the carnage I had created in my poor Anactoria's moment of need. Then next I found myself on a bench in the little port of Vasiliki where we had arrived from Mytilene, at a time in the past that seemed like a lifetime ago.

I think, had there been a ship ready to set sail, I would've left those shores then and there. I would have done what I had done before in Pamphylia—run far away and fast, from everything that caused me pain.

I sat staring out over the harbour, watching the sailors prepare the ships for their next journey. There weren't many. The port was smaller than Mytilene. One I recognised from my days watching the ships come and go in Mytilene when I first arrived on the island. It must be the ship that brought Sappho to the island. I watched as muscular seamen offloaded and reloaded large crates of cargo, probably supplies or trade goods they were taking on to their next destination.

It struck me how similar we are to ships. Our lives take us places, or we decide to go, but always, we take our cargo with us. Even when we choose to leave a place or the past behind, we pack up our memories and take them too. Our memories, our shame and our guilt, we cannot escape.

What Anactoria had needed was for me to nurture and protect her as you would a crippled roe deer or an injured lark. I see that now. I wish I could have given that to her. I have never known how. Perhaps, if I had stayed and nursed my own baby, I might have learnt the skill of a mother caring for her child. But, I didn't. My father had died before I was born and mother, perhaps struck by her own grief, never warmed to me, unlike to my sisters. Then when I had my own child, I fled before I barely knew her.

You would be right to think that my overpowering guilt and remorse over my part in the pain caused to Sappho, and in Anactoria's resulting grief, should have quelled any passion.

But, with my current, clear hindsight, I can almost make sense of it, though not so far as to condone my behaviour.

The only way I had learnt to show and receive love in my life, was through passion.

The first person to show me more than affection was my young teenage Adonis, Lycas, in Melas. He was the first boy who took any interest in me and this was long after most of my friends and sisters had all been married off.

He and I did not really talk much. I met him on my long walks in the countryside which surrounded my mother's home, and we would lie together in the sunlight meadows, touching, exploring each other. I thought I loved him, but I knew my mother would not allow us to marry, as he was not as wealthy as we were. Each time we met our caresses became more heated, more intimate. Then one afternoon in the woods, he pinned me down and it became obvious he wanted me. At first, I let him touch me, but then I felt ashamed and embarrassed so I said no, and hoped that he would stop. But by then his passions had been fuelled too far and he couldn't stop. He tried to kiss me to make it better but I turned my head and his kisses did not meet my lips, nor did desire spread between my legs. I remember the throbbing, stabbing pain deep inside my delta, momentarily obscuring the pain in my chest where my heart beat like a frightened bird against my ribs.

Afterwards he asked my pardon and kissed my hair.

I remember feeling his hot, panting breath on me. Then he left, leaving me in the clearing in the suddenly lonely wood. Around me the earth lay trampled from our afternoon of passion and I gnawed at my fists till they bled, in order to stifle my sobs.

I knew I had stayed out too long to return home. My mother would never believe it took me so long to look for a lost girdle. Besides, my chiton was stained with blood. I had no choice but to go to find Lycas again in his little cottage on the edge of the wood.

When I got there, he was asleep. At first, I did not know what to do. I desperately wanted his love, his affection to surround me, envelope me and push away the fear and loneliness. I stripped off and carefully lowered myself onto his body. He woke and I could see his brilliant smile in the moonlight. It filled my heart and I knew then I would gladly give myself to him again and again to feel the radiance of that smile on me once more.

His chest pressed against my breast and he crushed me so hard that I thought I would break, frail little creature that I was back then. It didn't hurt this time and once he was in me, nothing else existed. I could have had my four limbs cut away without awakening from my ecstasy.

A number of long passion-filled days followed.

Eventually, I borrowed a chiton from him and took mine to the local washerwomen to clean and remove the blood stains. Lucky I did, because it was those same washerwomen who came to my aid in my time of need a few moons later.

As the weeks passed, while I lived with him, I began to believe that I had finally found my earthbound Elysian Fields.

But, unknown to me, things slowly started to change. I began to feel different. At first my passions soared, which he relished, like a baby terrapin rescued after a long drought. But soon, my body started to morph, and it became clear that I was with child.

Whether that was the cause or whether it was inevitable, I do not know, but he started to change too.

He would go out for long days and eventually evenings, leaving me to wait at his cabin for his return. One evening he came home with another girl—Selenis. That same Selenis who I had called my friend, who came to lie with me and pretended to be my Lycas long before anything ever happened between Lycas and I. The same girl who also liked Lycas, who I played and beat with a cast of Aphrodite in a game of dice for him.

"Seems he has finally chosen me," was all she said, with a smug giggle and a shrug.

When it became obvious that I was upset, in some kind of consolation, he entreated me to join them in their passion. I couldn't bring myself to share what he and I had had.

Instead, I stepped out into the night and took a long walk in the woods, looking for solace, for somewhere that was dark enough to shade the images of them together from my mind, where the rivers would be loud enough to drown out the murmurs of their ecstasy and numb the feeling of his caresses that should have been meant for me.

I didn't return that night, but took refuge with the washerwomen who, on seeing my condition, took me in and tended to me like they would to unclean laundry, without compassion or regard, doing only that which was absolutely necessary.

At night, I couldn't help myself, I would creep out and go to his cottage, to see if he was alone. Most nights she was there. But one night I found him alone. I slipped inside and again, like that first night, I sat watching him sleep. My lips longed for the feel of his and my body ached for his touch, and before I could stop myself, I had kissed him and stretched myself on top of him again. He awoke and tried to sit up but I held him down. At first, he scolded me, then laughed and was soon caught up in the heat of the moment. He took me, even though he knew it was me and not her, a number of times that night. How I wished the sun would never rise.

When it was morning, he told me I had to leave and that he did not love me anymore.

I baulked at this and wept hot tears and said I would tell everyone I was carrying his baby. He merely said no one had seen us together, so no one would believe me. I reminded him of the beautiful vow that he had pledged to me: He had called me the "soul of his life", the "heart of his heart". He had said that he would never forget me or take another mistress, not until "the water of the rivers climbed the snowy peaks", or until "wheat and barley sprout between the ocean hills", or "pine-trees take their birth from lakes and water-lilies spring from stones", or only once "the sun grows black and the moon falls on the grass". But my words fell on his deaf ears.

Distraught, with my Psyche crushed, I left his cottage and made my way through the frosty woods.

In many ways, I wish I had had then the strength of Sappho now. If only I had had her courage.

As I came across a clearing near the river, so cold it had chunks of ice floating down it, I yearned to join the naiads in their tomb. I approached the raging, azure cascades and, mustering all my resolve, meant to throw myself in, abandoning myself and my child's destiny to the naiads' mercy.

But, I could not. Would it have been different had I had a cliff to face? And perhaps had not felt the kicking in my belly, as if my baby knew she needed me to live?

Instead, with nowhere else to go, I returned to the washerwomen, who helped me deliver my child and nursed the tiny infant and myself back to strength. As soon as I was able, they bade me take the infant and return to my mother's house.

It was then that I learned that my favourite uncle had come to visit my mother. He had stopped by Pamphylia on his way to the West. It was as if Tyche had steered my uncle's ship directly to me.

On the day he was due to depart, I thanked the washerwomen for their help, and assured them I was returning to my mother. This was only a half lie. I did return to my mother's house, but only to leave my baby girl with a house slave. My mother might not have been able to love me as she loved my sisters, but she was a good woman, and I knew her home to be the only place my baby would be safe and well cared for.

Then, I made my way to the harbour and stowed myself away in the bowels of my uncle's ship, where I hid for days after we set sail, until I was quite sure he would not be tempted to turn back and return me to Pamphylia.

He was furious at my deception, but I sensed he was also proud of his young niece's bravery and cunning.

But, because of the devastation I had felt at being betrayed so young, I learnt to make denial a fine art and wore it like a shield against the world. Even years later, I would much rather write poems in which I sang of my own flesh and my life, rather than allow myself to feel the pain of compassion or empathy.

And there, sitting on that bench in Vasiliki Bay, I was again attempting to run from my pain and the pain I had inflicted. I was, at best, no better than Lycas, and at worst, more of a cold-heart than he could ever have been.

In the distance, across the bay, my eye caught the thin, winding and pale vein of the footpath across the green peninsula, leading to the clifftops—the very same path that both Anactoria took in hope and Sappho took in despair. In my mind's eye, I pictured my darling Anactoria, lying there in our room in the inn, alone, betrayed, with her heart broken. What if she pulled together the courage so many people lacked, a feat she would surely be more than capable of, to walk that same path and follow Sappho to the Styx?

Something in me broke. I could not bear the idea, not because I begrudged Sappho the company in the underworld, more because I could not imagine this world without Anactoria in it.

I got up, and as hastily as my fatigued legs could carry me, I ran back to the inn.

I was unspeakably glad to find Anactoria as I had left her, still curled on what had been, up to that moment, our bed. Morpheus had finally calmed her and claimed her.

She looked nothing like the Adonis I had met that day in the

Kallisteia. That is the problem with life and letting people into it. As you get to know them, they so often become more than what *you* need them to be. They become whole, vulnerable human beings.

Guilt constricted my chest until I found it almost impossible to breathe. If I loved her, and more importantly, truly cared about her, I needed to be a better person—I needed to be the best person I could be.

I called for the innkeeper and asked her to bring a basket of figs, bread, a krater with wine and a basin of water to the room. I also asked her to arrange for a second bed to be brought in. I was not going to make the same mistake twice. When she started to protest that eating in the room was breaking her house rules, I dropped a large gold coin into her fleshy palm, which seemed to please her enough to overlook our wrongdoing for one night.

Once it all arrived, I settled on the new camp-bed and kept watch over my love.

It was near evening when Anactoria finally stirred and I managed to coax some of the wine and bread past her lips.

We never spoke of what happened between us or about Sappho. As for talk of the future... I decided then it was not the time.

15

The material of her thin shift brushed his fingers, slipping through them. His hands grasped at the cold, thin air.

Frozen and helpless, he lay, dangerously far over the edge, threatening to fall down after her, able to do nothing more than watch as the person he loved more than a sister, more than a friend, receded, growing smaller and smaller, in surreal slow motion, plummeting towards the deep, raging seas and unforgiving rocks.

He could have caught her.

Why did she not reach out?

Then a scream burst out of his lungs as he saw her hands folded across her chest in a strangely pious pose...

Then it hit him...

She hadn't fallen.

She had leapt!

"No!" Alcaeus jolted awake from the scream.

He frantically looked around for the source. Then he realised it was him. His pulse was racing and he was drenched in sweat.

He was not on the cliff.

Where was Sappho?

It took him a few seconds to make sense of his surroundings.

Then he remembered... Sappho.

The next morning, I managed to persuade Anactoria out of bed to go and have something to eat.

The inns' gleumata were, unusually, the communal dining rooms where men and women ate together—a fact that both Anactoria and I initially found quite disconcerting. I am not sure if this was because of progressive thinking on the part of innkeepers, or whether it was simply a case of needs must, to accommodate the infrequent female traveller within the facilities provided for the men. Judging by how often the men ended up with most of their food in their beards, I could certainly understand why dining together was avoided in most respected establishments.

In any event, this arrangement made it easier for me to keep an eye on Anactoria and that morning, my focus was on getting her to actually eat something. At one point I looked up and saw Alcaeus enter. I noticed him take a deep breath before he came over to join us. It was obvious that he came over for appearance's sake and not because he wanted conversation.

"Nice of you to join us," I said quietly.

He grunted and lifted a finger to call the innkeeper. She nodded but made no effort to move.

"I think it's important to talk and for us to decide what we're going to do, in the circumstances." I continued, letting the last word linger. "I think we should probably tell the authorities here, or at the very least, send word to Mytilene to let Kerkylas, and her children, know what has happened."

Alcaeus turned with such force I flinched. "Are you mad?" he hissed. "Do you want all three of us executed?"

I frowned.

"What do you think Kerkylas is going to do?" Alcaeus continued through gritted teeth. "Do you think he's going to throw his arms around you both, and thank you for bringing him the news that you lured his wife away and caused her to leap to her death?" He scoffed. "I'm supposed to be the fanciful poet around here. But, if you believe that, then you are even more naive than Sappho was to follow you two here in the first place. No," Alcaeus shook his head, "as far as Kerkylas is concerned, I will bet my last drachma that he will have all of us stoned for murder."

"Why? We didn't kill her?" I bit back, trying to keep my voice down.

"Yes, we did," came the soft, croaky comment from Anactoria, who had not said a word since the moment Alcaeus told us what had happened.

Neither I nor Alcaeus replied. We all knew she was right. Even if we had not physically pushed her ourselves, we certainly had had a part to play in it.

After some consideration, Alcaeus shook his head. "No, it is best we don't tell anyone anything. Not unless the body —" his voice cracked, "appears." He swallowed hard. "And even then, it is best if we are not associated with it. And, even if the body washes out to sea, in a couple of days people are going to start noticing she is missing. The last thing I want is to have to start answering awkward questions." He shook his head. "I don't know about both of you, but I'm leaving here as soon as my crew have readied the boat."

"We can't travel yet." I protested. "Anactoria needs time to rest."

"I think it is best if we each make our own way back," he said.

I could see, to his credit, that he was uncomfortable about leaving us on our own. Nevertheless, he was firm.

"Believe me, the less they can connect us to each other, or to this place, the better it is for everyone," he said.

When it was clear that the innkeeper was still showing no sign of coming over, he got up abruptly. "I've got to go."

Alcaeus entered the room keeping his eyes on the floor. He turned fully towards the door as he closed it behind him, grateful for the confined space. He took a deep breath. He was not sure what he would feel going back into that little room in which he had so failed his friend.

He closed his eyes against the stinging tears. He was there for a very specific reason.

He turned and headed to the small table that stood in the corner of the room, much like in his own. He tried not to look at the bed. In the corner he found the small satchel of Sappho's things—all she had brought with her. He felt like a grave robber. He steeled his nerves. He knew it was necessary.

He picked up the satchel and upended it on the table. There wasn't very much. A few under garments, a spare chiton, a comb, a tiny leather bag of bathing and beauty accessories, a pen, a tiny vial of ink and a small roll of papyrus and another sturdier draw-string coin-purse.

Then he saw it. The shiny end stuck out from a bundle of cloth used for a strophion. It was the mother-of-pearl hairpin. He had not seen it since the day Sappho had called him to her, to ask for his help in commandeering her brother's ship. He had assumed she'd given the hairpin to Kleïs for safe-keeping. Yet here it was. His good luck charm. He picked it up. Then he stuffed the rest of her things back in to the satchel, threw it over his shoulder and left.

Alcaeus would not let either of us go with him. He was furious at the suggestion. I tried to persuade him that he should at least let Anactoria go, but he was adamant that even she had no right to pay her respects, not after everything that had happened.

All we could do was watch him head up the hill towards the

cliffs and later, at dusk, we could see the tongues of the sacrificial fire lick at the night sky, where he offered up her belongings to the gods.

After breaking our fast, Anactoria said she wanted to go for a walk. I assumed she wanted some time on her own, so I was a little taken aback when she asked me to join her.

"I don't want to be on my own," she explained.

I let her take the lead and unsurprisingly we headed out along the promontory and up the hill to the cliffs. She led us to the boulder where I had found her waiting for Sappho.

We sat down next to each other. In the distance the sea looked like a mirror. It was so calm that it was barely possible to discern where it met the horizon.

She remained silent and I didn't know what there was to say either. We just stared.

I found the silence an unspoken indictment, bearing heavily on my conscience. I turned to her, wanting to say something, anything to make me, both of us, feel better.

Whatever I was intending to say froze in my throat when I caught sight of the tears sparkling on her cheek—so beautiful yet so excruciating. Instinctively I reached over and put a hand on her shoulder. But the moment I touched her, I felt Anactoria bristle and tense.

Inwardly I chastised myself. How could she ever want solace from me again, of all people, after everything that happened?

"I can't," she said, her voice barely a whisper.

"It's okay, I know —" I started to say.

"No, I mean I can't go back to Mytilene." She took a breath to steady herself. "I don't have a life there anymore. I don't want to go back to my old ways as a slave and as Phaon, I draw too much attention there. Everyone knows my miraculous story now. If that's not enough, I'm still wanted for Tyrrhaeus's death, or at least as the last known person to see him alive."

She paused for a while. I could see her biting into her cheek.

"Besides, it will be too painful to try to make a new life in a place that constantly reminds me of her."

She leaned into me and I let her cry on my shoulder. After a while she sat back up.

"So, what will you do?" I asked.

I could see she hadn't really formulated an alternative plan. She shrugged. "I think I'll have to continue on to Sicily and try to make a new life there."

I tried hard to calm the panic that was rising in my gut. "But what will you do? How will you live?"

"Sappho gave me the name of an old trader she knew who lives there. She said he was always looking for people who know their way around a ship. I'll start there. He also has a few houses he rents out where we can live."

We... Oh, how one, such a small word, can have such a huge effect! My heart erupted with joy, but I merely nodded.

It was a clear, sunny morning—the first one in many weeks. The crew of the ship had gathered around, drinking and listening to their captain, who was leaning over a gnarled, weather-beaten, wooden table, on which lay a small, well-worn parchment map of the Greek trade routes through the Mediterranean.

"I don't know, man," the ship's first mate said, shaking his comparatively oversized head on his four-foot-tall, compact, athletic frame. He jumped up and sat himself on one end of the table, poking a stubby finger at the edge of the map. "There be Cerberus. There's a reason no map extends that far."

The captain, clearly getting agitated, shook his head. "Don't you get it? They've been deliberately lying to us. The reason it's not on the map is because they don't want us to know about it. They's scared we will take its treasures for ourselves. Word is, the land is so vast, with its inhabitants spread right across it, some of 'em live where the sun god sets and some where he rises. Just think of all those spoils that could be ours." The captain laughed and slapped his shipmate on the back. "Just imagine!"

The rest of the crew laughed, cajoled and cheered each other at the mention of the riches.

"Imagine what?" Alcaeus asked having arrived just in time to catch the end.

"Master here was just —" The first mate's words were cut short by a sharp slap to the back of his head.

"I told you not to call me that in public," growled the captain.

"Sorry, Mast— I mean Captain." He looked suitably chastised. "Captain here was just telling us where we're heading next."

Alcaeus shook his head. "I'm afraid there won't be time for any excursions. We need to ready the ship and head straight back to Mytilene without delay."

The captain chuckled.

Alcaeus paused, slightly confused and aware he might have missed something. "What?"

The captain shook his head. "Sorry, mate. I has no intention of taking any of us back to Mytilene."

"What do you mean?" Alcaeus looked around at the rest of the crew waiting for someone to help him understand. "We need to get back. *I* need to get back."

'Well," the Captain laughed, still clearly enjoying the joke, "you has better then find yourselves another vessel and crew travelling that way."

"I paid you seventy Athenian minae to take over the ship and pilot it for me."

The Captain nodded, considering his point. "Yes, you did. You paid me seventy minae to steal my own master's ship and sail you here to Lefkas." He sucked his rotting teeth. "That did not include returning you to Mytilene. That was never the deal." He waved a hand in the direction of the crew, "What do you think would be our fate, if we ever set foot back in Mytilene, or ever cross paths with Master Charaxus? How do you thinks he will react?" He made a horizontal slicing motion with his grimy finger just under his large, bony Adam's apple. "He will have our skulls pinned in place of his figureheads." He shook his head again. "No, there's no way in Tartarus that we's heading anywhere near there."

He turned away and just when Alcaeus thought he had finished his speech he started up again. "I'm the Captain and I say we's heading here."

Alcaeus didn't even see the falcata until it landed like a rattling javelin, stabbing the wooden table just beneath the small map.

A prickling sensation, a visceral memory of terror, ran up Alcaeus's spine. A long time ago, in one of his first battles, in the days when he was still fighting alongside Pittacus, a real javelin had pierced the ground between his feet, missing his manhood by a chiton's breadth. The meaning then, much as it was now, had been: Rather cut and run and live to fight another day.

Alcaeus dry swallowed. "Okay."

"Unless of course you have another, oh let's say," he sucked his teeth again, "ten-thousand drachma for us."

"Ten!" Alcaeus squawked.

The captain nodded. "Same price with a little extra danger money…. In which case we'll take you back, or near enough anyway, for you to swim to shore if you want." The Captain snorted, hacked and spat a round globule of grey gloop in the general direction of the edge of the deck. Then he turned to Alcaeus with his head cocked expectantly.

Alcaeus shook his head slowly.

"Nope? I didn't think so." He addressed his crew, "Mates, what dids I tell you? I knew it was Sappho who wore the olisbos and held the purse strings."

The crew guffawed heartily.

Alcaeus might have learnt when it was time to cut and run, but he also knew that this was his only chance of getting back to Mytilene. If he didn't manage to leave get a ride with this crew, he could be stuck in Lefkas for a very long time.

He knew he should probably assert his authority and demand that it was *his* ship and the crew belonged to him, but apart from being a poet, he was also a realist. He knew such manly endeavours were beyond him.

"How are you going to manage that?" he asked.

"How not?" The Captain shrugged. "There's enough ocean out there. We has a ship and we know what we's doing."

"How will you ever settle? You aren't free men."

"In another land who would know?" The Captain bared his rotting teeth. "Or we could roam the seas and become pirates." He laughed out loud and slapped Alcaeus on the back a little too hard, then with the other grubby hand he briskly pawed Alcaeus's bicep. "On the other hand, we could make room for a small one like you, if you would like to join my crew. What do you say boys, we's could find some use for him?" He glanced at Alcaeus's behind and winked at one of his shipmates lasciviously. This in turn, elicited a surprisingly high-pitched giggle from his first mate who was still perched on the edge of the table.

If ever, now *was* definitely time to get away, Alcaeus thought, but first he needed to take care of business.

It was late afternoon when Alcaeus finally headed back to the inn. He was feeling particularly defeated. It seemed he was stuck on the island —the one place in the world he really did not want to be. The one place in the world that would always remind him of one of the saddest times in his life.

He had spent most of the afternoon going from ship to ship in the harbour, of which there were only three, to see if he could leave with one of them. Two were heading in completely the wrong direction. Even so, he considered going with them, just to get away from Lefkas. But that meant that it would then be even harder to get back to Mytilene. The third ship was a Phoenician vessel heading to Crete. At least that was going in the right direction. However, they wanted a one-thousand drachma fare to get him to Crete—money he no longer had.

The morning we were due to depart on the next leg of our journey to Sicily, Anactoria in her Phaon disguise took charge of organising our luggage and arranged for the porters to take our chests to the harbour. I headed to the little reception to find the innkeeper to settle our bill.

"Oh, where is your young Adonis?" the innkeeper looked around eagerly. It was clear she had developed an unsavoury liking for my Phaon.

"Arranging the portage," I replied.

"So, you got to keep the spoils, I see," she said.

I was momentarily confused.

"Bet his mast was worth a climb." She chuckled and her face contorted in what I assumed was a wink.

"You got a pretty high one there. Seems a shame you want to play away." Before I could respond she nodded sagely. "I know it's none of my business but," she began, and I knew this was the start of nothing good.

"Remember the higher the masts the more wind they catch." She glanced at the scrawny, old, weather-beaten man with the kind eyes standing behind her. "Sometimes it's better to settle for a shorter mast."

I couldn't miss the slight note of resentment in her voice.

She sighed. "At least the shorter ones are often better at weathering the storms."

It was clear from the day I had met her that she was not happy with the way her life had turned out nor her choice of husband. However, the word that struck me was 'settle', combined with the lather of resentment that coated her words. I knew for sure I was not settling with Anactoria. A smile came to my face just thinking about her. She was the highest mast I could ever have aspired to—everything I ever wanted in a lover, companion and friend. And finally, she was mine.

My mind flitted over the harrowing events of the past few days. Some storm *that* had been! And yes, we had survived it and I had won her in the end, but at what cost?

Was I *her* highest mast? I faltered. Suddenly I did not want to know the answer.

"Gods' speed, and may Poseidon smile on your journey onwards" the innkeeper interrupted my thoughts, reluctantly handing me the two small coins she owed me in change.

I simply nodded, said a polite goodbye and followed the procession of porters to the harbour.

At the pier, Anactoria and I stood side by side watching the slaves load our travel chests and the ship's crew complete the final preparations for departure. It soon became clear that it was time for us to board.

"Right, that's us, Anactoria said and turned to head to the plank.

My feet would not move.

When she realised that I was not walking with her, she turned back. "Bilitis? What's wrong? We need to board? The captain has called."

I nodded slowly, still unable to make my feet move. How could I say what I needed to say? A lifetime was not long enough, let alone a few heartbeats.

I smiled weakly, nervous to speak in case my tears betrayed me.

"Have you forgotten something?" she asked.

I shook my head.

"What is it? Is this too soon? Shall we wait for the next ship? We can, if you want."

I marvelled at the fact that she was trying to make life good for me, when it should have been the other way around. I shook my head again. "Anactoria," I said softly, cautious that others couldn't hear me. "I can't."

"You can't what?"

"I can't go with you…" It suddenly struck me that she would think that I didn't want to! "I mean it would be wrong…"

A deep frown creased her brow. "How could that be wrong? We've planned it all. Gods know, we've been planning it for moons."

I took a deep breath. "You've been planning this with Sappho."

She nodded. I could see even the mention of Sappho's name caused her pain.

"It's not me you love …"

This time it was her turn to take a deep breath. She came over and took my hands squeezing them gently in her strong calloused hands. "I need you!"

I nodded. "Yes, I do believe you do… or did."

Anactoria started to protest.

"Yes," I interrupted, "I know I mean a lot to you. I do even believe on some level you care about me. But… Sappho is the one you love."

Anactoria started to shake her head.

I held up my hand. "Please let me finish. I know your sadness that she can't be here, and no matter what I do, no matter how much I regret and I wish I could turn back the days to undo what has happened, I can't. But the one thing I can do is not keep going down a path that is wrong… for both of us." My heart broke. "If nothing else, you need time to get over her. As long as I'm with you, whatever we had or could ever have will always be tainted. I will always remind you of her, of this place and the tragedy that happened here."

Anactoria dropped her gaze. She knew I was right.

I reached out to stroke a stray lock out of her eyes but stopped myself. "And, even if there were some small way in which you really do love me, I need to let you go. I would rather lose you now, than hang on to you, knowing you will grow to resent me."

Anactoria shook her head again.

"My darling Anactoria, know that I will always love you and I will always carry you in my heart, no matter where you are or where I find myself. You touched me. You have been, and probably always will be, my highest mast. When I was with you… even when I knew Sappho had your heart, you showed me how it feels not to be alone, and for that I thank you."

Anactoria stepped closer and took me gently by the chin, which was by then wet from my tears. She leant forward and kissed me.

It was the most painful kiss of my entire life.

I let Anactoria keep both our travel chests, and before the ship departed I gave her all my extra coins, keeping only enough to pay for a few more night's accommodation and my passage back to Mytilene in case I needed it. I assured her that that was all I required. Once I was home, I would have access to my usual allowance from my uncle and I really wanted her to have the best chance at starting her new life in Sicily, or wherever fate took her.

I stayed, seated on a bollard, looking out to sea, for a long time after Anactoria's ship had disappeared over the horizon. I cried silently until there was not another tear left in me. Then I got up and walked back to the inn.

The inn-keeper said nothing when she saw me. She gave me a new single room as if I was a brand-new guest she'd been expecting and offered me an early dinner of warm broth to fight away the cold, which I accepted.

While I was sitting in the dining-room dunking crisp bread crusts into my broth, I saw a male figure approach my table and sit down. I was about to tell the interloper that I did not appreciate his advances when I realised it was Alcaeus.

"Oh, it's you. Thought you would be well on your way to Mytilene on Charaxus's ship."

He rubbed his chin and cleared his throat. "No."

I waited for him to elaborate.

"What about you?" he said and scanned the surroundings. "Where is your lovely Adonis?"

I shook my head. "On his way to Sicily."

Alcaeus had either seen it coming or thought it for the better, for he didn't look surprised. Instead, he held up two fingers to the innkeeper who brought over two large skyphoi of wine for us.

As the innkeeper turned to leave, she placed a warm, tentacled hand on my shoulder and winked, cocking her head slightly in Alcaeus's direction. "Not bad either."

For the rest of the evening we sat, we drank and we shared our thoughts. He explained he had no money and no clue how he was ever going to get home.

I'm not entirely sure why; perhaps it was because I felt we had bonded in our loss and everything we had been through, or perhaps I just really needed a friend, and I suspect so did he, but by the end of the evening I had agreed to share the last of my money with him. I had enough to get me all the way to Mytilene on one of the other trade-ships, or to get two of us halfway, to Crete, where if we were lucky, we could find another of my uncle's ships on their return from Egypt to Mytilene. It was a risk, but I was willing to take it.

16

A half-moon later, Alcaeus and I landed in Crete, where we were to wait until the next of my uncle's ships destined for Mytilene passed through. We both wanted to put the horrendous experience of Lefkas behind us. I craved a return to my previous, frivolous, mundane existence, which, before all of this, I had so foolishly lamented.

Since Crete was probably the busiest supply-post in the Mediterranean, we did not anticipate being there for very long. A by-product of Crete being such a hive of activity, with so many ships docking so regularly, was that it was also a boiling-pot of information and news. That's how Alcaeus heard about what was happening in Mytilene.

It wasn't good.

Since he had left, somehow Pittacus had got word of his involvement in the disappearance of Tyrrhaeus, Pittacus's son. Both Alcaeus's brothers had been arrested and were awaiting trial, which was sure to mean the death sentence, unless Alcaeus could come up with a miracle and resurrect Tyrrhaeus.

"You are still free. No one knows who you are here," I urged. "If you go back you will be imprisoned, tried and probably put to death too. How is that going to help your brothers?"

Alcaeus shook his head. "I can't leave my brothers like that and do nothing."

"Do you love your brothers?" I asked.

Alcaeus nodded.

"And they love you?"

Alcaeus didn't respond, but the answer was obvious.

"Do you really think your brothers would want you to risk getting caught as well, and dying in a valiant but foolish attempt at heroism. Rather choose to live, be free and write about them in your poetry and thereby make them immortal."

Alcaeus shook his head. "You don't understand."

I nodded. "You're right. I don't understand why you want to die."

"It is not that. You don't have brothers, or sisters, like I do. They'd give up their lives in an instant if they thought it would save me."

I was about to argue that he really didn't know anything about me and whether I had siblings. Then I thought back to my sisters at home. Perhaps even without intending it, Alcaeus was right. None of my siblings would come to save me. In fact, I couldn't think of a single person who would risk even losing a night's sleep to help me if I was in a similar situation. Maybe Anactoria, if she were here and knew, but I was probably never going to see her again.

"I know no man braver than Antimenidas—especially when it comes to saving Cicis or me. He has done it so many times before." Alcaeus balled his fists in determination. "I need to go back."

"What are you going to do when you get there?"

Alcaeus shook his head. "I'll figure something out."

When we got to Mytilene, Pittacus's men were waiting in the harbour. They arrested Alcaeus on the spot and dragged him away in a most cruel and undignified manner. I was surprised his thin, effeminate bones did not crumble instantly, under their rough treatment. The whole time, the small object that Alcaeus had given me moments before we docked, burnt a hole in my chiton. But, considering how thorough and forceful they were with Alcaeus's arrest, I was surprised by how comparatively easily they let me off. After only a few cursory questions, in answer to which I played the ignorant female, they soon tired and dismissed me with a warning. In hindsight, I found it surprising that Kerkylas did not feel it necessary to question me himself. After years of experience as the husband of Sappho, I would have thought he'd know better than to underestimate a woman. If he had, I undoubtedly would have cracked and told him everything.

Another lunar cycle later the trial began. Alcaeus and his brothers stood before Pittacus who presided and Kerkylas who had personally stepped in as the accuser.

It was not often that a trial involved the murder of the aisymnētēs' son and involved two well-known and much-loved poet-performers. The Agora was swamped with over three hundred volunteer jurors who had come forward to serve on the case. Double that number of curious onlookers, who had travelled from all over the island and from as far away as Lydia and Athens, were crammed in to observe the most talked about spectacle of its time in Mytilene. There were rumours that Solon himself had come incognito from Athens to observe the law in action in this trial.

Additionally, from the start it was clear that it was not just going to be a murder trial. It was to be the arena for an epic personal dual between the two sides of Mytilene's controversial aisymnētēs, Pittacus —who was both the angry, vengeful father who'd lost his only son *and* the first elected ruler of Mytilene, who desperately wanted to be remembered for being just and wise. All bets were off as to which side of the man would win.

Kerkylas got up. He cleared his throat. It was obvious that the weeks since Sappho's disappearance, and the onus of the trial preparations, had taken their toll.

"He might be looking old but he's still as arrogant as ever, taking on this case as the accuser personally," a testy Antimenidas grumbled next to Alcaeus so only he could hear.

"My highly esteemed aisymnētēs and members of the jury," Kerkylas began.

The crowd grew quiet.

"I, Kerkylas of Andros, have come before you to present the case against Alcaeus, Antimenidas and Cicis of Mytilene. The charges against the defendants are of the murder of Tyrrhaeus, son of Pittacus of Mytilene... Phaon the ferryman, also of Mytilene and... our beloved Sappho, also of Mytilene."

The crowd murmured. Even Alcaeus was taken aback. He had not been told that they were trying to pin Phaon's disappearance on them as well.

"I believe Alcaeus of Mytilene will be addressing the court on behalf of himself and his brothers in their defence," Kerkylas continued.

"The case that I, as the named prosecutor, will present is as follows:

"Alcaeus of Mytilene and his brothers were seen by Xanthias, the trusted slave and servant of Phaon the ferryman, embarking on Phaon's new flagship on the day that it set sail, taking young Tyrrhaeus to Anatolia. It is the prosecution's belief that the brothers had somehow come to find out that Tyrrhaeus, the only son of their sworn political rival, Pittacus, our honourable aisymnētēs, would be on that ship. They boarded it with the intention to assassinate Tyrrhaeus, in the hope of bringing our esteemed aisymnētēs to his knees as part of their ongoing political marauding. This, despite rumours suggesting otherwise that Tyrrhaeus was alive, they accomplished, and Tyrrhaeus's body was found a few weeks later washed up on the shore of Smyrna on the coast of Ionia."

The crowd gasped and started to chatter amongst themselves.

"Silence," Pittacus commanded.

Kerkylas glanced around at the crowd assessing the impact his case was having. "When Phaon the ferryman returned to Mytilene he presented Sappho with her hairpin, which Alcaeus had taken from her previously, as proof that Alcaeus was on that ship and that they had successfully accomplished their heinous crime.

"Unfortunately," Kerkylas shook his head theatrically, getting more into the role of the bearer of bad news, "probably due to fearing for their own lives, neither Phaon nor Sappho denounced Alcaeus and his brothers at the time—a decision they would come to regret later. If they had, we might have been able to stop these villainous men, before they took more lives. If we had then our sweet, darling Sappho and Phaon, the esteemed ferryman, might still be alive today."

"I object. No bodies have been found," Antimenidas called out. "We can hardly be accused of murder if there is no evidence —"

"Instead," Kerkylas pressed on, more emphatically, "our brave, and sometimes passionate to the extent of foolhardy, Sappho decided to confront Alcaeus herself—a conversation that was overheard and reported directly to me by Sappho's personal slave. The conversation went as follows —"

"I object!" Antimenidas shouted again, "We have not witnessed the slave giving her testimony, which is our right as defendants."

The crowds murmured.

"Silence!" Pittacus shouted. "If you keep interrupting the prosecution you will forfeit half of your Klepsydra. It is not your turn to speak. As is required by proper court proceedings, your brother will have his turn to plead your case on your behalf."

Alcaeus pulled Antimenidas back down into his seat. "You are not helping, brother," he whispered.

"You are going to let him just spin lies like this?" Antimenidas spat.

"It's the way the court works. He gets to speak first for the duration of one urn of water, then it is our turn. So please be patient, brother."

"Thank you, our esteemed aisymnētēs," Kerkylas said. "As I was saying. I shall be reading Sappho's personal slave's testimony, exactly as she had told it directly to me." He proceeded to unfold a papyrus, and waited as the young slave-boy manning the water clock replaced the tiny cork at the base of the top urn from which the water was dripping into the lower urn, effectively stopping the clock for the reading of the testimony.

Kerkylas cleared his throat again.

My mistress had summoned Alcaeus to the house. Once he got there, she dismissed me, but as I was waiting outside her chamber, through the door I could hear them talk. I heard my mistress say that young Phaon the ferryman had given her the hairpin. She then asked Alcaeus how he would explain that? My mistress was very distressed. She said it is proof—proof that Alcaeus was on that ship with Tyrrhaeus and Phaon—the last time Tyrrhaeus was seen alive. She said that Alcaeus and his brothers "were up to no good" as usual. She asked Alcaeus what he thought Pittacus was going to say when he found out that Alcaeus was there? During a later visit from Alcaeus, I heard my mistress say that she was going to give me the hairpin for safekeeping. She seemed to be scared she would never see me again.

"Allow me to point out that the slave-girl never did received the hairpin for safekeeping, and that Sappho's fear that she might be in danger was well-founded."

"I object! You cannot allow that!" Antimenidas stood up and shouted.

"Silence!" Pittacus warned. "Remove one cup of water from the defence's urn!" Pittacus ordered.

Alcaeus pulled his brother back down.

"But that testimony is not admissible! We didn't witness that slave giving that testimony," Antimenidas continued.

"Right, make that two cups," Pittacus ordered again.

"Antimenidas, you aren't helping!" Alcaeus hissed.

Pittacus glanced at the audience who seemed to be waiting with bated breath. Then he addressed Alcaeus. "Is that true? Have the defendants not witnessed the slave give testimony?"

Alcaeus stood. "No, your honour, we have not."

"Well, now, we do not want to be seen to be running an unjust court, here. If you would like, we can summon the slave and have her interrogated before the court."

Alcaeus swallowed. He was aware of Antimenidas nodding profusely next to him. He also knew that the interrogation of a slave was a brutal affair and young Kleïs would suffer dearly as a result. On top of this, he had no doubt that by his proposal, Pittacus had no intention of merely serving justice. He knew Pittacus was playing to the crowd by suggesting a sensational spectacle to please the audience.

"No, that won't be necessary," he finally said.

"What are you doing?" Antimenidas hissed. "We need to get that slave in a vice and show her the truth! It is our right!"

"Violence won't solve this." Alcaeus hissed back at his brother. "I won't agree to the torture of Kleïs. She has done nothing wrong, other than be loyal to her mistress."

Antimenidas threw his hands up in disbelief. "We are facing certain death and you are worried about justice towards a slave-girl. Well, you had better find something that will save us and your other brother, or our mother will punish you for eternity in Tartarus." Antimenidas hissed menacingly and sat back with his arms folded.

Alcaeus nodded. The truth was, he had no idea how he was going to win this battle and save himself and his brothers.

"If it pleases the court, in light of the defence's objection to the slave-girl's testimony, I won't continue reading from it, but will resume my statement." Kerkylas said.

Alcaeus did not miss the smirk etched on Kerkylas's face. Alcaeus knew that arrogant son of a harpy was imagining that he could taste their blood already. If his brother went on much longer like that, he knew Kerkylas would have to do very little to sway the jury, and he'd have all three of them executed before sunset.

"Once Alcaeus and his brothers learnt that their plot to murder

Tyrrhaeus had been uncovered, and that there were at least two witnesses, they moved swiftly to make sure neither Sappho nor Phaon would ever be able to tell the truth. In order to do that, they commandeered a ship rightfully belonging to Charaxus, Sappho's brother, and abducted Sappho and the young Phaon."

Kerkylas's lip curled in palpable distaste.

"Who knows how they did it, to what force they subjected our dear Sappho or which tricks of the tongue Alcaeus employed to entice her away. Whatever it was, they managed to take them as far away from the caring eyes and ears of their friends and families as possible, to a land more morally degenerate, where they could more easily murder and dispose of them.

"In fact, I have here a statement from an innkeeper of Lefkas, who testified to having seen a woman answering to the name of Sappho, and a handsome youth accompanied by a man of Alcaeus's description at her inn. She testified that Sappho disappeared around the same time as Alcaeus was seen…" Kerkylas's voice grew shaky, "pushing her over the cliffs."

He coughed and continued, "I am sure the defence will argue that we cannot be absolutely sure that it was our self-same Sappho all the way over in Lefkas, but the point remains. I would wish for nothing more than to have our beloved poet—my beloved wife—here to testify and clear all this up." He paused and looked at the audience for a long moment. "Sadly, for us, the dead seldom testify." Then he bowed his head in a solemn gesture and sat down.

The crowd erupted in a roar. The jurors turned to each other and engaged in fervent, outraged chatter.

"Off with their heads," one man in the crowd, who was clearly too impatient to wait for a verdict, shouted. "They killed our Sappho, our revered muse." A number of others joined in. Soon they had formed a huge, angry chorus of accusers.

It became very clear that the jury was hungry for Alcaeus and his brothers' blood and a conviction seemed inevitable.

This was the moment I had been dreading. I had to make a final decision.

Should I look out for myself and not get involved? Or, should I choose, probably for the first time in my life, to come to the aid of another man—a friend. It might seem odd that I describe him as such, but in my short life I had not really had much time for friends. The world had not been kind to me, so I had resolved we must all look after ourselves. But, perhaps because of the extraordinary events that we had shared, life had somehow tied us together in some unfathomable way, creating a bond that we would carry to our graves.

I turned the small parchment parcel over in my hand. I had done my best. But, was it enough?

"Right now, our case could not be more damning if we had confessed to all three murders ourselves," Antimenidas said and shook his head. "We don't stand a chance. The best we can do is forfeit our counter-argument and use my contacts to try to escape into exile. It's not that I don't trust your oration skills, little brother. But look at them. Not even the best orators or logographer is going to sway that jury. They want blood. We would need a miracle from Zeus himself to prevent this jury from ripping our limbs from our bodies with their own hands."

Alcaeus knew Antimenidas was right! He looked at the three hundred or more jury members who were massed there, glaring contemptuously and pointing in their direction.

Honestly, if Alcaeus had heard Kerkylas's case being presented about someone else, he too would probably also have voted to push them into the pit.

He was about to concede and announce that he would not be presenting a counter-argument, but would instead move straight to a plea for a more lenient sentence, when he saw Bilitis pushing through the crowd of spectators.

She had come!

He had not allowed himself to hope.

Alcaeus watched her squeeze her way through the throng towards one of the guards standing on the perimeter. He was not sure whether the guards were there to keep the three of them in, or to keep the crowd out. Bilitis handed the guard a small parcel. The guard checked the contents of it and then brought it over to Alcaeus. These events had already caught the eyes of the more attentive members of the crowd and a suspenseful silence had begun to spread.

Alcaeus did not miss Pittacus's suspicious glare, followed by his survey of the crowd, clearly attempting to assess their reaction to the developing events. He was obviously considering whether to put a stop to this interruption.

When Alcaeus took the parcel, he found it was a folded parchment with something inside. He took it carefully and unfolded it.

"Perhaps we can thank Aphrodite," Alcaeus remarked to Antimenidas.

"Is the defence ready to counter?" Pittacus boomed over the noise, thereby inciting the crowd to roar their dissent.

Alcaeus stood up straight. "Yes, we are."

"What are you doing, brother?" Antimenidas whispered urgently.

"Now, more than ever, trust me, my brother," Alcaeus replied softly.

Antimenidas shook his head and turned to Cicis next to him, who was gawping at the proceedings, quite overwhelmed and thankfully unaware of the dire situation in which they found themselves. "I am sorry little brother," Antimenidas said under his breath. "And sorry, Mother, for letting you down," he spoke into the ether around them.

"Citizens of Mytilene and friends," Alcaeus began. "You are very fortunate today. You have just seen probably the best orator of our time, Kerkylas of Andron, in action. And, I must concur, as expected of someone with such skill and mastery, he presented a very compelling case—a feat I can't even dream to emulate. I, too, would be ready to convict, if I had just heard that speech. But…"

Alcaeus paused, and waited for the crowd to settle down and start to listen.

"Let me first remind you of something very important. You've just been presented with one possible version of events, knitted together, be it very skilfully by the prosecution, from various people's retelling of how they experienced certain occurrences, to form a list of points from which he hopes you will draw the conclusion that I and my brothers are guilty. The trouble with this is not that anyone is lying or even deliberately trying to mislead. The trouble is that from the outside, events and actions can be misleading in themselves.

So, I'm not going to do the same. What I'm going to do is simply tell you a story—a true story that I was part of—to give you not only a list of events or testimonies, but a better understanding of what really happened, so you can be better equipped to judge. Some of it will be familiar to you already, and some things will surprise you.

It started with me seeking out an old friend, my best friend in fact, for guidance in matters of the heart. That friend is our dear Sappho. She has always, ever since we were little, been a source of wisdom and insight in all matters of emotion. On that particular afternoon, unusually it was not simple matters of Eros that plagued me, but a deep pit of the sort created when Eros goes into battle with Philia. Anyway, we were interrupted, but I did tell her that I was going to go on a mission, and she gave me on loan her precious mother-of-pearl hairpin, as Tyche's charm.

So yes, I took the hairpin with me on our mission aboard Old Phaon's ship. Yes, Xanthias and those that have testified that they had seen us on the ship are correct. But, contrary to the conclusions the prosecutor has drawn, not to kill Tyrrhaeus. My brother wanted to make contact with Tyrrhaeus to talk to him. He thought that if we could find an opportunity to talk to Tyrrhaeus away from his father's watchful eye, we could persuade him to help us bring about resolution between the factions once and for all and re-establish a peaceful democracy.

One thing you have to know about my brother, Antimenidas, and I, is that we are very different. If he is Heracles, I am more one of the muses—many of my friends would say probably more like Terpsichore, on account of being more light-footed, rather than anything more profound about my art. The point is: Antimenidas wanted to sedate Tyrrhaeus so we could take him to a secure environment where we could talk. I disagreed, not because of any noble reasons. I was Tyrrhaeus's friend and a firm believer in free will, so I thought it would be best to tell Tyrrhaeus and then have him come with us willingly. I was sure he would want peace as much as we did, when he understood that is what Antimenidas was after.

In fact, I knew he did. He had told me so. He was desperate for the faction fighting to stop, but he knew his father would never let it.

"I object!" Kerkylas shouted.

"I'm only explaining what Tyrrhaeus believed. It is not Pittacus on trial." Alcaeus address Kerkylas. "Not today, anyway."

Everyone turned to see Pittacus's reaction. Eventually he nodded for Alcaeus to continue.

"He loved his father. So, the only course available to him was to get away from Mytilene, to try to find a new life somewhere else, such as in Anatolia.

"Unfortunately, I misjudged the situation.

"Once we were on the ship, despite my brother's wishes for me not to do so, I went to see Tyrrhaeus to tell him what we were planning.

"He was naturally livid. He saw me helping my brothers in this enterprise as a deliberate betrayal.

"We fought—at least he tried to fight with me. I'm a lover not a fighter. I'm useless at it. A fact that was proved countless times before. I'm sure some of you have heard the disgraceful stories of my attempts at battle. If you have you will know I'm far more likely to throw down my sword and run than draw blood, or perhaps even faint instead.

"It didn't take long before Tyrrhaeus overpowered me. Eventually he let me up and bade me to go, to leave him alone. Not wanting to fight him anymore, I did. Coward! I hear you all call me."

Alcaeus nodded.

"That I probably am…." He took a deep breath. "But murderer I am not."

He swallowed hard.

"I don't know exactly how it happened, but during that altercation I somehow lost the hairpin. I was sure I heard it clatter down the decks into the Pit. So, when he sent me away. I returned to the deck and my duties. Later, when there was another opportunity to slip away unnoticed, I returned to look for the hairpin.

"I never did find the hairpin, but when I finally gave up, I returned to Tyrrhaeus's cabin hoping to try to again talk him round, once he had calmed down a bit. That is when I found Tyrrhaeus."

Alcaeus's voice cracked and he took a deep breath before he continued.

"He had somehow got hold of Old Phaon's falcata…."

Again, Alcaeus swallowed hard and wiped away the tears that had started forming with the back of his hand.

"When I got back… there was nothing I could do. I was there and able to hold him until he breathed his last breath. So at least he was not alone. I am not sure how long I sat with him, but when I heard footsteps coming, I didn't know what else to do, I left him and ran. The usual way up to the top deck was blocked by whoever was coming, so I took the long route via the lower decks. The closest thing to a plan that I had at that point was to go to find Antimenidas and tell him what had happened."

"Excuse me, esteemed aisymnētēs." Kerkylas stood up with outstretched arms. "You cannot allow this charade to continue. The defendant wants us to believe that, by his own admission, he was the last person to see Tyrrhaeus alive, he even held him while he slipped away, but he did not murder him! Where is the logic in that? I fail to see how it could have been someone else? And even if someone else killed him before he got back to him, that doesn't mean it was not one of his brothers."

The crowd roared in agreement.

Pittacus nodded. "Order," he commanded and once the crowd had quietened down, he returned his focus on Alcaeus. "Yes, I have to agree. Alcaeus, what is your point, please?"

"Your honour," Alcaeus said more sombrely. "I can't tell you how much pain it causes me, how much pain it has caused me since that day, to bring you this news…. Your son took his own life."

"Nonsense! How dare you dishonour my son like that?" Pittacus burst out. Then he glanced around at the uproarious crowd and then seemed to remember where he was. "Order!" he shouted. Then at Alcaeus, "Explain yourself or I shall throw you in the Pit myself."

Alcaeus raised his hands, palms out. "On my honour and the honour of my family before me, that is the truth. I realised that this would be a difficult truth to bear, which is also why I did not come to bring you the news before. Who knows, given the coward that I am, if it had not come down to this trial where I and my brothers stand accused, I might never have done so. It certainly would have been much easier to allow you to believe your son died a noble death at the hands of your enemies, and allow that belief to further fuel the fire between the factions. However, your son was a better man than me. He was a thoughtful, sensitive, very intelligent young man, but over and above that, he was kind and could not hurt a fly. He could never have let your war rage on because of him, so he took precautions that would prove the truth that no-one else is responsible for his death, in case it ever came to that."

Pittacus frowned. "And what might that be?"

"He wrote you a letter before he left."

Pittacus looked perplexed. "And where might such a letter be now?"

"He told me that he had left it in a safe or a secret place that you showed him as a boy. He said it is a place only you and he know about and that he did that deliberately so you would know it could only have been him who put it there."

The crowd erupted in a sea of whispers.

"Order!" Pittacus shouted again. Then he turned his attention back to Alcaeus. "I'm going to adjourn the court proceedings while I go to see if there is such a letter. I hope for your sake what you say is true, because if I don't find the letter in question and it does not testify to your bizarre allegations, I will have you and your brothers' heads!"

With that Pittacus got up and, accompanied by two guards of the court, made his way out of the Agora.

The time that passed while they waited for the guards to return was perhaps the longest wait in Alcaeus and his brothers' entire lives.

When Pittacus eventually retook his seat, his eyes were blood shot and his hands were trembling, but his chin was firm. He formally addressed the court confirming that what Alcaeus has said was true. He had discovered a small pottery alabastron in a secret location, which he held up for the jury to see. "Inside it I found a scroll, written in my son's hand, testifying to his state of mind." His voice cracked. "However, because he wrote this letter some time before he left on that fateful voyage, it does not prove that someone did not murder him in the end. But I have to agree that it goes some way to support Alcaeus's testimony."

"Excuse me, our honourable aisymnētēs," Kerkylas interrupted. "I appreciate that this is all very tragic, but let me remind the court that Alcaeus and his brothers are standing trial for three murders. Even if there is reasonable doubt that they killed your son, the court still believes they are responsible for the disappearance and deaths of our beloved Sappho and Phaon the ferryman."

Pittacus nodded. "What say you to these other allegations?" he asked Alcaeus.

Alcaeus nodded an acknowledgement and then continued.

"By then the storm had started to rage in earnest around us. I suppose someone must have been on their way to get Tyrrhaeus out to safety. But, when I heard footsteps, I fled. I was scared people would jump to conclusions. I needed time to calm down and think what to do. The footsteps were coming down from the ladder to the top deck so I decided once again, to head the long way around, via the lower decks.

The waves and wind had started to break the ship apart and we were taking on water rapidly from cracks in the hull. Most of the galley slaves had also fled by then. I came across two slaves who were trapped by a fallen beam whom I helped."

Alcaeus was silent for a moment. Then his shook his head as if to refocus on the story.

"I made my way back to the upper deck where, luckily, I found Antimenidas and Cicis preparing to jump from the ship. By then my mind had cleared a little after discovering Tyrrhaeus and I wanted to head back to retrieve his body, but Antimenidas stopped me... As it was, we barely made it back to land ourselves.

"At some point Phaon must have found the hairpin... How or when I have no idea. Whatever else happened on that ship between Old Phaon and Aphrodite, I cannot testify to. My brothers and I had jumped from the ship by then."

Alcaeus took a breath.

"And now I address Sappho's feisty reaction to 'what I did on the ship', which was witnessed by Kleïs, her personal slave... As we know, a few weeks later Old Phaon arrived back in Mytilene, having gone through his miraculous transformation into a gorgeous Adonis of a young man, turning the heads of the old and young wherever he went. The truth that the prosecutor has not shared is that Young Phaon even turned the head of his darling Sappho, his wife."

The crowd murmured.

"In fact, she had fallen callipyge-over-cleavage in love with him and they had started spending a lot of time together after his return— a fact I am sure any husband would rather forget. During that time, he must have told her that I was on that ship with him and gave her back her hairpin as proof. As anyone who knows Sappho or who has heard her poetry and songs will know, she is passionate above all and her passion extends in all directions, into all types of temper, including being quick to jealousy and quick to rage. On hearing about me being on the ship with her Adonis, it stirred up her insecurities and she jumped to understandable but incorrect conclusions. The gods know, sophrosyne is not one of my virtues so, had circumstances been different, she probably would have been justified to be suspicious. Who knows, perhaps I would even now be serving lunch on a Phaon and Orpheus pleasure cruise under the young Phaon."

Alcaeus again paused for a few moments.

"Then finally, addressing the last of the allegations that I, again with the help of my brothers, lured Sappho to her death…

"First, I had no grounds to want my best friend dead.

"Secondly, it is my guess that after Aphrodite smiled on young Phaon and gave him his good looks and youthful virility back, he naturally felt reluctant to settle down immediately. He probably wanted to sow his wild oats a little first. Sappho being Sappho didn't take rejection very well. So, when she suspected that her darling Phaon had absconded with another, younger woman, Sappho was very upset and she called me to her. She wanted to pursue them, hence she asked me to help her commandeer a ship."

"In other words, you are admitting you stole the ship?" Kerkylas interrupted.

Alcaeus seemed to ignore the question but continued, "The ship in question was her brother's ship."

"That is still theft."

"It is not theft if you own it… Some of you might remember, a few years ago, Charaxus got himself into difficulty while trading in Naucratis where he met Rhodopis, now his wife. What you might not know is that it was Sappho who rescued him. When he got back to Mytilene, she helped him out financially so that he could start again and build up his trading business from the embers that were left.

Technically she owns at least half of his entire estate, a fact he would not have shared readily either.

We followed Young Phaon and his new lover to Lefkas where sadly, as expected, all Sappho's darkest fears were confirmed. She found Young Phaon and the girl together. As a result, driven to it by despair and a broken heart, she fled up the white cliffs and, in an attempt to rid herself of her sorrow, she leapt, at the place blessed by Zeus, hoping to find solace in death. However, Aphrodite, with her meddling ways, was not going to let her most loyal follower simply die of a broken heart, so she saved her. The mechanics of miracles I can hardly testify to. The details of that are between Sappho and Aphrodite. All that I know is she survived."

"That is an outrageous story! Where is the proof?" Kerkylas shouted.

Alcaeus nodded as if he expected Kerkylas to say that. "It might sound incredible." He addressed the crowd. "I sometimes have to remind myself it is not all fiction. But as the honourable prosecutor himself said, the ultimate, undeniable truth would come from Sappho's own testimony, which she would be sure to offer if she knew about this trial."

A wave of murmurs erupted from the crowd and they all eyed each other in disbelief.

"Sappho is not here! She is dead and you killed her!" Kerkylas shouted.

"Order!" Pittacus shouted.

Alcaeus lifted the small parchment the guard had handed him from Bilitis earlier. He unfolded it carefully.

"No, Sappho is not here in person, but she has heard about this trial and has sent a letter as her testimony."

The crowds gasped.

He began to read aloud.

I am Sappho, poet of Lesvos, writing
To you from a faraway land near Lydia.
I wanted to tell you that I am thriving,
If you had wondered.

Take this letter as proof of my intentions,
Bearing witness true at this hearing. For sure,
I left my home to elope with my darling.
That is the plain truth.

Sworn as wife to Kerkylas I was, in truth,
As a faithful spouse serving him well for years.
Breaking his heart, I regret far more than I
Can ever explain.

To a brother dear to me, O, Charaxus
Once I came to your aid despite all dangers
So, to be clear, consider your debt repaid.
Equal your ship makes us...

A hushed silence lay over the crowd like a thick morning fog.

Finally, Alcaeus refolded the parchment. "That concludes my story your honourable aisymnētēs," he said and sat down next to his brother.

As if in slow motion the jury moved to action, each man moving to cast his metal ballot.

The verdict came back with such an overwhelming vote that the usual ballot containers had to be replaced by bigger ones to catch the overflow of disks.

When it came time for the verdict to be announced, Pittacus had regained his composure after the news of his son. "You, jury of this court of Mytilene, have cast your vote, and your voice has been heard.

Therefore, by the power granted to me as your elected aisymnētēs, I declare the defendants, Alcaeus of Mytilene, Antimenidas of Mytilene and Cicis also of Mytilene... not guilty."

The crowd roared.

Pittacus held up his hand to silence them.

"Let it be known that, once again, despite the high personal stakes in this case, justice has been served in my court. Pardon is often better than punishment and forgiveness is often better than revenge. Leaving a man to the mercy of his own conscience,"[1] Pittacus paused for a moment. Then he cleared his throat, "...is often worse punishment than any a man-made legal system could issue."

*a*s Alcaeus made his way out of the court a movement caught his eye. Even though he reacted quickly he could not stop the stinging slap that landed squarely on his cheek.

It was Kleïs.

"What is it with women, thinking they can slap me about like this?" he said to no one in particular.

"I don't believe you. I heard what I heard. How could you? You murdered my mistress, I know you did." Kleïs screamed at him and started swiping at him wildly.

Alcaeus managed to catch her hands by the wrists and restrain her.

"Shh," Alcaeus said. "Stop that before someone sees you and you end up in more trouble for assaulting a citizen."

"I don't care, you killed her and now they have declared you innocent. But I know you did it. My mistress Sappho is dead because of you."

Alcaeus took a deep breath.

"Hey, stop! Just listen. I was just on my way to come and see you," Alcaeus said. "I have something for you from Sappho."

This caught Kleïs off guard. "What?" she asked defiantly still fighting him. "You are lying!"

Alcaeus looked her straight in the eye. "Kleïs, you are going to want to see what I have. If not, you can beat me up more and I promise not to fight back, if that makes you feel better."

Kleïs slowly relaxed and Alcaeus let go of her hands.

Once he was sure she was not about to take another swipe, at least not immediately, he reached into his satchel and took out the parchment he had read from earlier.

Kleïs eyed him suspiciously.

He handed it to her and she started to unfold it.

"What is this? Are you trying to be cruel?" Kleïs sneered as she held up the mother-of-pearl hairpin.

Alcaeus shook his head. "No, Sappho did want you to have it. She explains it in the last stanza."

Kleïs's eyes grew as large as clay plates while she desperately tried to devour the swirls and twirls of ink on parchment.

"Go on. Read the last stanza. I didn't think it best to read it out in the court. I suspected it was private and meant for you."

Kleïs just shook her head, growing more frantic by the second.

Finally, Alcaeus realised the problem—Kleïs couldn't read. She might have been Sappho's personal slave for over a decade but she never learnt to read.

He gently took the parchment back, leaving her to hang on to the iridescent mother-of-pearl hairpin. "Let me. This was a stanza specially written to you."

Darling Kleïs, my would-be daughter, hear me.
Give this spangled pin[1] up to Aphrodite
So that you may have your freedom now and always
As is my final wish.

When he looked up, tears were flowing down Kleïs's cheeks.

Before he could stop her, she almost dive-tackled him into a firm hug. He gently rested his arms around her.

"Thank you," she said softly.

After Kleïs had left him, Alcaeus was about to make his way over to the nearby tavern where Antimenidas and Cicis had headed to celebrate after the trial, when he heard his name being called. He turned to find the water clock slave rushing after him. "Alcaeus, the aisymnētēs would like a word."

Alcaeus nodded and, a bit bemused, headed back into the Agora. There he found Pittacus and Kerkylas still evaluating the proceedings. As he approached, he saw Kerkylas turn and stare at him with a vindictive smirk that surprised Alcaeus, before he walked away leaving Pittacus to handle the meeting.

What on earth could Pittacus have to say after all that? He was sure the aisymnētēs was not going to congratulate him on his victory.

"You wanted a word," Alcaeus said.

Pittacus nodded. "Yes, I just wanted to make something very clear in case there was any room for confusion left during the recent proceedings. You and your brothers won your case, and all three of you were given life and your freedom," Pittacus paused, "but contrary to what I said publicly, don't confuse it with a benevolent pardon and good wishes."

Alcaeus was about to assure Pittacus that he was under no such delusion when Pittacus continued.

"I hope I assume correctly that you will be leaving these shores as soon as possible, to reunite with your darling Sappho wherever she is hiding. But, just in case you had any hesitations, I wanted to make myself clear. I think you would all be best off finding somewhere off this island to call home from now on, for at least as long as I am alive. In fact, you have seven days in which to leave these shores. Next time there will be no poetic justice to save you, not even poems written by all the muses themselves."

During the weeks before the trial, my uncle had been away on business. Unlike almost everyone else in Mytilene, he wanted nothing to do with the trial. The fact that a wanted fugitive such as Alcaeus was found and arrested on one of his ships not only reflected badly on his business, but in light of the growing tensions with the Phoenicians, caused him great troubles. And my involvement in it all, the little that he knew, he was not bound to forgive soon, if at all.

After the trial, I was back home, alone, when Alcaeus came to see me.

"I have to say, that poem was perfect," he said.

I nodded sombrely. "It was the best I could do."

He smiled and his eyes softened. He understood what I meant.

"It was, after all, your idea, I just had to write it," I said.

On the way back from Crete to Mytilene, Alcaeus had come up with a plan. If all else failed, and only if all else failed, he had asked me to construct a poem, written in Sappho's characteristic style—testifying to a version of the truth that included her still being alive. It was a long shot, but if it came down to it, it could potentially be his only shot, he had said, and he was right.

Moments before he was arrested on my uncle's ship, he had handed me the hair pin to hide. We could not let the guards find it. For the weeks leading up to the trial I agonised over composing the poem and thereby perjuring myself.

Over and above that... let me tell you, writing in Sappho's meter is not an easy task. In fact, I don't think many people would even attempt it. I almost gave up trying a number of times and I'm not sure I got it quite right in the end. However, I knew Alcaeus's life, at the very least, depended on it and I was not going to let another innocent person die.

He nodded. "And you did that very well. Sappho would be proud."

I smiled ruefully. "You don't know how much I would want that to be possible." Then something occurred to me. "Speaking of genius… The other fake letter from Tyrrhaeus to his father, that was a deception worthy of the gods. How did you manage to do that? And plant it in their secret location!" I said, truly impressed.

Alcaeus's expression changed and he turned away from me. "That was not a deception," he said softly.

"What do you mean?" I was sure that he, in a similar way to how he had asked me to write Sappho's poem, had commissioned someone else to write Tyrrhaeus's suicide note and then hide it in the aisymnētes' house.

"Everything I have said in the trial was true, other than the fact that I did find the hairpin and I gave it to Anactoria. I decided no one really needed to know that. I didn't feel like I could betray her and take away her chance of a new life, not after everything else."

Finally, he cleared his throat. "Anyway, I've not come to dwell. Speaking of fresh starts, I've come with a specific purpose."

I frowned.

"As I expected to happen, Pittacus has banished me from Mytilene," he said.

"Oh," I said. A part of me was sad to hear he would be leaving. A part of me was glad, hoping that perhaps finally I could put all this behind me. "Nice of you to come say goodbye."

He shook his head. "I didn't. I've come with a proposal."

I rolled my eyes. "How many times do you want me to keep paying for my sins?"

Alcaeus looked at me with a level stare. "As many as it takes, don't you think?" He took a deep breath. "However, that is not exactly what this is. It is more of an opportunity."

I let him continue.

"I have come to ask you if you'd like to come with me."

I could not have been more shocked. I was about to argue. He held up his hand to stop me.

227

"Listen to me." He waved a hand around at the atrium where I had received him. "I hear the past few weeks have not been a warm homecoming for you either."

I nodded. There was no point denying it. My uncle's response to the recent events was not favourable.

"I believe he has plans to ship you back to Pamphylia as soon as the dust has settled."

I could feel my cheeks burn with shame. That was also a fact. How he had found it out though, was a mystery to me. As far as I knew, my uncle would not have made that common knowledge out of sheer pride.

"So, I have a proposition. Join me. Come with me to start a new life somewhere, to the East, possibly Kyprus."

I shook my head. "Why?" I could not understand why, after everything that had happened, he would be asking me to go with him. Then the penny dropped. "You want me to be your Sappho."

He looked at me with a curious look in his eyes, as if he was seeing me for the first time. Then he slowly nodded. "If you could impersonate her on paper, then in a country where no one knows what she looks like it should be easy for you to impersonate her in the flesh."

I shook my head, more incredulous than actually rejecting the idea.

"Think about it," he continued. "If you and I, I mean Sappho and I, arrived somewhere like Kyprus, somewhere far enough away that people would not have seen Sappho, even if they have heard of her or heard her poems, but near enough for word to get back to Mytilene about her settling there, it would solve all our problems."

He looked to see if I was following.

I said nothing, letting him continue.

"Don't you get it? Sappho would be 'alive' and we would no longer be thought responsible for her murder. In fact, people would stop looking and even if her body did eventually appear or wash up on the coast somewhere near Lefkas, there would be no reason to believe it was her."

I thought about this for a while.

"If people heard you were with Sappho, would that not suggest to the world that you and Sappho planned this and that you betrayed, or even worse, potentially cuckolded Kerkylas? Would it not be better to just disappear into anonymity—both of you apparently going your separate ways?"

Alcaeus shook his head. "This is better than being accused of Sappho's murder, don't you think?"

"Besides," he continued, "Kerkylas is nothing if not a very proud and astute man. The fact that he was being cuckolded is the truth. Sappho *was* plotting to leave him. On some level Kerkylas would have sensed that. His pride won't let him accept she simply left him without someone putting her up to it. He won't stop looking for her until he either knows she is dead, or he finds her and persuades her to come back to him. If he thinks it was me, that same pride would make it impossible for him to believe that a lady-boy like me could really have cuckolded him. So, he would more likely deduce that Sappho really just wanted to leave him and was using me, her hapless childhood friend, to do it."

Suddenly as he was talking, I realised something. "You loved her too," I said.

"Who?"

"Sappho."

"Yes," he said simply.

"Even though you've always loved men?"

Alcaeus shrugged. "That was different. I guess it is as Sappho said... There are many types of love and love does not bend to reason."

Within a few days, Alcaeus and I were on a ship headed for Kyprus.

It was not as if I had a reason to stay in Mytilene myself. After recent events the place had forever lost its wonder and appeal. Once again, I found myself on the brink of starting a whole new life. The gods know, I had done it seamlessly before when I came to Mytilene from Pamphylia. Only this time, I was choosing to support myself with the life of a concubine[2] as a way to make my living, rather than as the niece of a wealthy business man.

After a few false starts, we finally decided to settle in Tamassos. There, Alcaeus and I lived together as a couple. We were never lovers or married. He had his suitors and I had mine. I needed to earn my own living. So, I chose to do what I love and I lived out a life with the ladies, which, at the very least, Sappho would have been proud of, or at the most, might sometimes have even made her blush.

One could not blame someone for wondering how, in effect, two strangers managed to make a life together like that for so long. I think there is no doubt that the events of the recent past had bound us together in some intrinsic way. And, I suppose once we realised that we would probably be spending the rest of our lives in each other's company, we got to know each other a bit better.

Alcaeus turned out to be a wonderful, gentle soul and I knew my heart was safe with him, because he would never have it.

I am not sure what he saw in me. As I got to know Alcaeus, I realised I was wrong about him; he is, and probably always was, a loner in the crowd too. Maybe that is what he got from me—a kindred poet, a like-minded companion to keep the loneliness at bay, whom he also knew would never be able to hurt him either.

In time, a number of rumours[3] and sightings of Sappho living different and extraordinary lives in all sorts of place across the known world emerged to rival our own—all helping to drown out the sensationally spun tales by Xenia, the innkeeper in Lefkas, of a love sick Sappho leaping to her death, or worse being driven to that by a cuckold. It seemed that the tale of Sappho's leap had so captured the world's imagination that everyone seemed to find the need to write their own version, giving Sappho the fitting end to life that they thought she deserved. I can imagine we might not hear the last of those stories for as long as man or woman walk this earth.

A few years later, we received news that Pittacus had died. How he died was not significant. What was, was the fact that, technically, Alcaeus's exile was officially over, so he was free to return to Mytilene, as were his brothers. Contrary to my expectation that Alcaeus would rush back to his homeland the moment he had the opportunity to do so, he decided to remain with me in Tamassos. When asked why, he had said that too much time had passed and too much had changed since we left Mytilene. Secretly, I think he had grown to like the life we had made for ourselves as much as I did and, in the end, he chose to stay living in Tamassos for as long as I was alive.

18

The coughing came first. Then I started to find it hard to breathe and had little energy. Within the course of one moon I was almost half the size I used to be. I suspected my life force was fading fast.

When it was time, I called Alcaeus. He was not very willing to accept the reality of the situation. That was when I realised that I had somehow made an impact in his life too and that he would be sad to see me go.

The purpose of calling him to me was that I needed him to vow that when I died my body, as Bilitis, daughter of Damophylos, be sent back to Termessos in Pamphylia, to the place where I was born. I have wandered this earth for so many years now, since I first made that brash decision to walk away from my family all those years ago. Oh, if I had only known then as much about love, loyalty and the family you make as I do now!

It is only right that I am returned.

I had regretted never having said farewell to my mother before she died. I had always hoped we might be reunited in death and maybe then I could tell her of my life and share with her my writings—

something I couldn't do while we lived so far apart. I also regretted not knowing my daughter in this life. Again, I hoped, perhaps one day I would meet her in the hereafter and then I could ask her forgiveness for the enormous wrong I did her.

As for Phaon... my young, beautiful Phaon... and the last person ever to claim my heart. I remember that last time I saw *him*—or so I had grown accustomed to thinking of the new Anactoria—in the harbour at Vasiliki, moments before he stepped onto the ship heading for Sicily. I never did have the courage to enquire whether he reached Sicily or how he chose to lead out his life. I think, on some level, I did not want to know.

An obstinate, wilful, part of me truly regretted letting him sail away that day, and would have wanted nothing more in the world than to have followed and lived out my life with him. Still, on the whole I believe I made the right decision. I have no doubt he cared for me and he would have created a worthy, honourable new life for us and I would have been, mostly, very happy. However, it would have broken me to catch him in those silent, unguarded moments deep in thought and to wonder if he were thinking about what life might have been like with her. In truth, I know I truly did love him, because if I could, I would have done anything to rewind time and give him back his dream and his life with Sappho.

It is notable, but sad, that despite all our best efforts, together and separately, the primary object of all our affection, the one who was most wanted and desired, was to remain unclaimed, or so I thought.

"Alcaeus," I called softly. He was sitting in a nearby chair, writing, while keeping me company during a long night of pain.

"Hmm," he said.

"There is something that has always puzzled me."

"Hmm," he said again not turning his attention from the papyrus.

"What were you really doing on that ship?"

"Which ship?"

"Old Phaon's."

He stopped writing. "What do you mean?"

"Well, since then, I have got to know you quite well. By your own admission you are not a fighter, and after that time I have never seen you do much more than write a clever, witty poem in political protest. So, it has never made sense that you would follow your brothers onto that ship in the first place. Why did you go?"

He looked out of the window and from where I was lying propped against a pillow, I could see the faraway look he sometimes had, clouding his features. He thought long before he answered, with a slight question in his voice. "I went there because someone I loved needed my help?"

"I know you and your brothers were very close, but it never struck me that Antimenidas was the type of person to require help." I suppressed a little laugh that surfaced as I tried to imagine such a ridiculous prospect.

He finally turned towards me and shook his head. "I didn't go there for him. I went there for Tyrrhaeus."

He must have seen my surprised and quizzical look.

He sighed heavily. "By then Tyrrhaeus and I had been lovers for many moons. I had fallen for him and he for me. The trouble was, he was the son of my brother's enemy, who in turn was someone who could not see beyond his own obsession with power, to what that was doing to the people around him. Tyrrhaeus hated his life as the son of the aisymnētēs. He hated always being caught up in his father's life. We both knew his father would never condone our relationship, not because he found anything wrong with the prospect of his son finding a male life partner or even anything personal to me. It was simply politics. Pittacus would be uncomfortable that our agape and pragma would somehow join the two factions. He needed the fighting to continue. While there was dissent, the people looked to him to provide peace—and thus, he had power.

"Our only option was to run away and go to live somewhere like

Anatolia where we would be out from under Pittacus's control. Tyrrhaeus and I agreed that he would leave Mytilene first under the guise of wanting to travel. Then, a few weeks later, I would follow and meet him at an arranged rendezvous point. That way we would not arouse suspicion.

"When we heard about Old Phaon's new ship, it was an opportunity we could not refuse. Tyrrhaeus knew his father would relish the chance for his own flesh and blood to be one of the first special guests on such a ship.

"All went according to plan until a few days before the ship's departure, at the Kallisteia, when Antimenidas discovered that Tyrrhaeus was going to be onboard."

Alcaeus paused, staring into the middle distance.

"So why didn't you just tell Tyrrhaeus not to go?" I asked.

Alcaeus nodded. "I did try. But as the fates would have it, Pittacus, sensing this might be the last time he would see his son, decided to take him away up mount Olympus, on a father and son rite of passage expedition, which had been a tradition in their family for generations." He shook his head. "Anyway, the point is I couldn't get to him. I couldn't warn him."

"So, you volunteered to go with them?"

"As much as I love my brother, and as much as I believed he had good intentions about making peace, I know his methods sometimes require finesse. When Antimenidas insisted that he was going through with his plan I did the only thing I could think of. I had to make sure nothing went wrong and that Tyrrhaeus didn't get hurt."

"What happened? Did Tyrrhaeus really take his own life?" I asked.

It was obvious Alcaeus was struggling with the memories.

"When I got on that ship, I went along with Antimenidas's plan. He had asked me to slip a dram into Old Phaon and Tyrrhaeus's wine. I didn't like the idea much, but I figured it was the least risky plan. If Tyrrhaeus was unconscious he couldn't fight back, and then we could take him to somewhere safe once we docked at Ephesus. I resolved I would be the first person he saw when he woke and I would explain everything. However, when I saw Anactoria and she presented a means to get a message to Tyrrhaeus that would allow us to talk face to face, I abandoned the original plan."

"So, you were the person she was caught talking to below deck?"

Alcaeus nodded. "Yes, sadly. I would have owned up and got the beating instead, but that would have foiled the whole plan and put Tyrrhaeus, Antimenidas and Cicis in danger as well. Anyway, while all that was going on, I saw Tyrrhaeus excuse himself and head below deck. I followed him and found him in his cabin. Initially he was very pleased to see me. He had thought that I was there to surprise him and go to Ephesus with him. Eventually I explained why I was really there. He was furious, accusing me of siding with my brother over him. Eventually it deteriorated into a fight. Well, at least he fought with me."

"And did you drop the hairpin?"

Alcaeus nodded. "Yes, other than Tyrrhaeus and I being lovers, everything else happened as I had said in the trial, plus afterwards when I admitted to you that I had actually found the hairpin and given it to Anactoria."

I thought back to the trial, the memory of which was ingrained in my mind, as if it were only yesterday that I pushed my way to the guard to deliver the poem and the hairpin—shaking with fear and worry at the fact I was about to perjure myself. I remembered Alcaeus's telling of the final moments of Tyrrhaeus life—how he had found Tyrrhaeus. I needed to know if that was true too, but I did not know how to ask such a question. If he had... I couldn't bring myself to imagine how hard it must have been to find your lover like that.

"I am so sorry," was all I could think to say.

He smiled ruefully and after a long pause was about to turn back to his papyrus.

"There is one other thing I want you to do for me once I'm dead."

"Something else?" He asked, his voice hitting a higher register than normal.

I smiled and nodded as much as my levels of fatigue would allow.

"I am not Aphrodite," he said drolly. "You can't rattle off three hundred wishes and then expect me to just deliver."

I laughed softly.

He got up and handed me some water to drink. "What is it?"

"I want you to send word to Kerkylas explaining exactly what happened all those years ago."

He looked perplexed.

"It's important to me that Kerkylas finally knows the truth and can give Sappho a proper burial in Mytilene to lay the memory of his wife to rest, and also any hopes he might still be harbouring of her return to him someday. That is the least we could offer him and her children. It is not fair to deny them the truth and closure. We owed him and also the people of Mytilene that much."

Alcaeus stood up and turned away from me. I saw him shake his head. "I'm afraid I can't do that."

"Why? Pittacus is dead and after all these years I'm sure Kerkylas would be grateful to know what really happened and that Sappho had not in truth cuckolded him. It is not as if her body washing up is still a threat to you or me."

He turned and a sad smile crossed his features. He came and sat down near me again. "I had grappled with whether to tell you this. I was going to, as soon as we had settled here in Kyprus. Then when we got here, I couldn't find the right moment. Eventually, I stopped looking for that moment and soon days turned into years and it no longer seemed relevant."

I frowned.

He turned and stared off into the distance. Then he started to talk. He talked and talked well into the night until he had told me the whole story of how he looked out of his window, that fateful morning in Lefkas, and saw Sappho striding up the cliff path. How, without thinking he sprang into action and raced after her. How petrified he felt that he wouldn't get to her in time. How he saw her teeter on the edge of the clifftop and how he leaped and lunged for her... All of that I had pretty much imagined myself, so there was no surprise there.

However, what did surprise me was what else he had to say.

When he leapt and lunged, rather than it being a futile attempt, he did manage to grab hold of Sappho's wrist.

She was wriggling and straining against him, wanting to be let go so much so that she almost pulled him down with her. He told me of how he had shouted at her that he would not let go—he would never let go—and unless she was prepared to take him over the edge with her, she had to stop fighting him and allow him to pull her back in.

He told me how he had finally managed to drag her up and how they lay exhausted cradling each other on the rough ground afterwards. How she had cried and cried and told him she did not want to carry on her life, she couldn't, and how she couldn't bear to go back to Mytilene and the way life was before Anactoria. He had let her speak until she had got it all out and then he had dried her tears and using his best powers of poetry and persuasion he talked her round, to consider that there might be another way out.

In fact, if I think back, he didn't actually tell Anactoria and I she had died in the first place. That was our guilty assumption. It's funny how we see only what we want to see.

He explained to me how he wrapped her in his coat and before dawn carried her down the mountain to another inn on the other side of the harbour. Here he left her under another name and asked the innkeeper to keep an eye on her until he returned. He came back to where Anactoria and I were staying, collected Sappho's things and took them to her.

Over the course of the next few days he went to see her from time to time and helped her make a plan for her future. Eventually they agreed that she would depart on her brother's ship with the rogue crew who were heading to Egypt. Alcaeus had managed to persuade the captain of the ship to take her on payment of a little less than a king's ransom.

However, the part that Alcaeus was less keen to tell me was that, as the day of my and Anactoria's departure came and went and I decided not to set sail with her, he rushed back to Sappho and persuaded her that perhaps all was not lost. When she finally agreed, with most of the last coins in his coffers he had gone back to the captain of their rogue ship and had negotiated that, as a first order of business, they would take bearings and follow after my uncle's ship and rendezvous with it allowing Sappho and Anactoria one last chance at happiness together.

"Did they?" I asked. "I mean, did they find each other in the end?" I tried to keep my voice stable.

Alcaeus looked at me. Then he shrugged. "I don't know. Part of my promise to Sappho was that I would never go looking for her and I would do everything in my power to stop anyone else from doing that too."

I nodded.

I understood.

I breathed my last living sigh.

It was during this last chapter of my life, living in Tamassos that I, with Alcaeus's encouragement, wrote the majority of my songs. Those, along with this account, I now leave to you, dear reader, in the hope that they may outlive me and that, as Sappho said, "Someone will remember us even in another time[1] and so will know the truth".

NOTES

PREFACE BY JACQUIE LYON

1. Alludes to similar works: The Aesop Romance and The Alexander Romance — highly fictional biographies, which became folk books, works that belonged to no one, and the occasional writer felt free to modify as it might suit them—works of faction at best.
2. Palaiphatos "On Incredible Things"

CHAPTER 1

1. "Psappha" Part 2 *The Songs of Bilitis*
2. Sappho Fragment 31 - Ode to Anactoria
3. Alcaeus Fragment.
4. Sappho Fragment 132
5. Sappho Fragment 138
6. Sappho Fragment 165
7. Phaon thinks of Sappho as Spartan/Amazonian - thinking themselves equal to men. See later reference to Sappho being Anactoria's Spartan friend.
8. "Last Attempt" Part 2 *The Songs of Bilitis*
9. "The Wedding" Part 2 *The Songs of Bilitis*
10. "Last Attempt" Part 2 *The Songs of Bilitis*
11. Alcaeus Fragment.
12. From the Greek mōron (neuter of mōros) meaning 'foolish'

CHAPTER 2

1. Sappho Fragment 82A
2. Women of Sparta enjoyed a status, power, and respect that was unknown in the rest of the classical world.
3. "[Dreams, like]... fiction is the most effective means by which ideas are spread. Because of its non-imposing nature, fiction allows people to consider ideas without immediately becoming defensive and rejecting them as a threat …. After all, 'it's only fiction.'" Dorothy Rowland
4. Alcaeus poems Fragment 384
5. Sappho Fragment 121
6. Sappho Fragment 137

CHAPTER 4

1. Sappho Fragment 16 - Ode to an army wife of Sardis

CHAPTER 5

1. Sappho Fragment 1
2. Aphrodite is said to have been born from the white foam produced by the severed genitals of Uranus, after his son Cronus threw them into the sea.

CHAPTER 6

1. This is a type of stone masonry whereby the stonecutters created curved edges instead of straight and is known as Lesbian masonry after the island on which it originated.

CHAPTER 7

1. One of the origins of this expression is sometimes said to be the ancient Greek voting system which used white and back beans to indicate positive and negative votes respectively. The votes had to be unanimous. When the collector 'spilled the beans' and a black bean was seen amongst white, the vote was halted as void.

CHAPTER 11

1. Sappho Fragment 51

CHAPTER 16

1. There was allegedly a famous trial in which Pittacus apparently tried a man named Alcaeus as the suspected murderer, of his only son, Tyrrhaeus. At the end Pittacus let him free saying "Forgiveness is better than revenge".

CHAPTER 17

1. Sappho Fragment 98B
2. Part 3 *The Songs of Bilitis*

3. There is a theory that there were indeed two women called Sappho. One was in love with a young boatman called Phaon and leapt to her death in Lefkas, while the poet Sappho died and was buried in Mytilene.

CHAPTER 18

1. Sappho Fragment 147

GLOSSARY - GENERAL TERMS

Agora
This is the quintessential public space: a central market and place of assembly for the town's people. A setting in which ceremonies and spectacles were performed.

Aisymnētēs
A judge, umpire, a supreme ruler with unassailable power, elected by some early city-states in times of internal crisis, for life, either for a prescribed period, or until the completion of a given task.

Alabastron
A small vase to hold perfume, oil or a precious elixir. In one version of the Phaon and Aphrodite myth, Aphrodite gave him an alabastron containing the youth potion.

Amphora
A two-handled pot with a neck that is considerably narrower than the body.

Andron
The andron was a room reserved for the males of the house. Females were not allowed to enter this room as it was used for symposiums: drinking parties that were held exclusively for males. The andron was generally located on the bottom floor of a house, so that it could be easily accessed by the male guests attending the party.

Atrium
A large open air or skylight-covered space surrounded by a building. An internal courtyard.

Chiton
A form of tunic that fastens at the shoulder, worn by men and women.

Callipyge
Buttocks. Plural callipyges. Callipygian means having beautifully shaped buttocks.

Daimon
An ancient Greek word referring to lesser supernatural beings, including minor gods and the spirits of dead heroes.

Drachma
A Drachma, the equivalent of 6 Obols, is ancient Greek currency.

Falcata
A type of short sword with a distinct angle along the back.

Fibulae
A brooch or pin for fastening garments, typically at the right shoulder.

Gleumata
Common dining rooms in inns, where men and women ate together.

Gynaeceum
The women's room was called the 'gynaeceum'. In this room the females of the home could sew, spin, weave and relax. The gynaeceum was usually located on the second floor of the house in the furthest place away from the room for men, the andron. Men tended not to enter this room as it was the women's quarters.

Himation
A type of clothing, a mantle or wrap worn by ancient Greek men and women from the Archaic through the Hellenistic periods (c. 750 to 30 BCE).

Hecatoncheires
Giant creatures. Their name means "hundred - handed ones". Apart from a hundred hands of unfathomable strength, they also had fifty heads.

Kallisteia
Kallisteia, an annual festival celebrating the island of Lesvos's federation under Mytilene, held at the 'Messon', where Sappho performed publicly with female choirs.

Klepsydra
A timepiece or hour glass, by which time is measured by the regulated flow of water into or out from a vessel.

Klismos
A chair, with curved backrest and tapering, out-curved legs.

Kopis
A heavy knife with a forward-curving blade and straight or slightly curved back edge, primarily used as a tool for cutting meat or for ritual slaughter and animal sacrifice.

Krater
A large vase, particularly used for watering down wine.

Kylix
The most common type of wine-drinking cup.

Logographer
Professional authors of judicial discourse in ancient Greece
(speechwriters) hired by litigants to write their speeches.

Mastos
A drinking cup shaped like a woman's breast.

Minae
Ancient Greek currency. Seventy Athenian minae is the equivalent of
7000 Drachma.

Oikos
Three related but distinct concepts: the family, the family's property,
and the house.

Olisbos
A dildo.

Penteconter
An ancient Greek galley. They were long and sharp-keeled, versatile,
long-range ships used for sea trade, piracy and warfare, capable of
transporting freight or troops.

Phallilingus
The greek word used for this act is "arrêtopoeîn", meaning "to do
things that cannot be named". However, Old Phaon, during his
extensive travels and exposure to foreign cultures and customs had
become intimately familiar with the Latin term cunnilingus (oral sex
on a woman). In an inebriated state during the festival of Kallisteia he
coined the term phallilingus for the male equivalent. Today it is
known as to fellate, or to perform fellatio.

Philia
Represents the sincere and platonic love. The kind of love you have for your sibling or a really good friend. In ancient times this form of love was more valuable and more cherished than Eros. Philia exists when people share the same values and dispositions with another person and those feelings are reciprocated.

Psyche
Soul or spirit.

Shift
A longer version of a chiton for women and older men.

Skyphos
A deeper cup with horizontal handles.

Sophrosyne
It is an ancient Greek concept of an ideal of excellence of character and soundness of mind, which when combined in one well-balanced individual leads to other qualities, such as temperance, moderation, prudence, purity, decorum and self-control.

Strophion
The bra of the time, which women wore under their garments and around the mid-portion of their body. It was a wide band of wool or linen wrapped across the breasts and tied between the shoulder blades.

Symposium
Part of a banquet that took place after the meal, when drinking together for pleasure was accompanied by music, dancing, recitals and conversation.

MORTALS

Anactoria
A young androgynous slave girl belonging to Phaon the ferryman and also the object of Sappho's undying love.

Sappho
Known to some as the 'mortal Muse', Sappho was a lyrical poet who lived on the island of Lesvos around 630 BCE.

Bilitis
The narrator, a fellow poet and contemporary of Sappho and Alcaeus, and the author of *The Songs of Bilitis*.

Mnasidika
Bilitis's young former lover.

Lycas
A young man from Pamphylia, responsible for Bilitis's first heartbreak.

Selenis
She is the woman, originally a friend and confidant, who Bilitis writes about in *The Songs of Bilitis* as being the person responsible for stealing Lycas, her first love's heart away from her.

Kleïs
Sappho's young personal slave, whom she cherished like the daughter she never had.

Alcaeus
Poet, musician and orator, contemporary of Sappho, rumoured to also have been her lover.

Antimenidas
Alcaeus's oldest brother, well known as a formidable warrior.

Cicis
Alcaeus's older brother, whom he and his oldest brother cared for.

Kerkylas of Andros
Sappho's husband and right-hand man to Pittacus.

Pittacus
First elected ruler of Mytilene (see Aisymnētēs).

Tyrrhaeus
Pittacus's beloved and only son.

Old Phaon
The ferryman of Mytilene, who ran a ferry service across the straits to Lydia, which is now modern-day Turkey.

Xanthias
Old Phaon's faithful main slave, a good mariner, who operated the ferry boats for Phaon.

Syros
Skilled mariner and ship's captain for hire, with expertise in penteconters.

Myrsilus
The previous tyrant of Mytilene, overthrown by Pittacus with the help of Alcaeus and his brothers.

Charaxus
Sappho's older brother who was a merchant mariner.

Rhodopis
She was a fellow-slave of the fable teller Aesop, with whom, in one version of her story, she had a secret love affair while they both belonged to Iadmon of Samos. Later, as property of Xanthes, she was taken to Naucratis in Egypt where she met Charaxus, Sappho's brother, who had gone to Naucratis as a merchant. Charaxus fell in love with her, and ransomed her from slavery with a large sum of money—a big bone of contention between him and his sister, Sappho.

GODS & MYTHICAL CHARACTERS

Adonis
A young man loved by Aphrodite whose cult was popular with women and, to quote Anne Carson's humorous explanation. "had something to do with being covered in lettuce".

Adrestia
She is the daughter of Ares and Aphrodite. She was venerated as a goddess of revolt, just retribution and sublime balance between good and evil.

Anemoi
The winds: Boreas from the north, Notus from the south, Eurus from the east and Zephyrus from the west.

Anternos
He is one of the Erotes. The god of returned love—the avenger of unrequited love.

Aphrodite
She is the goddess of love, sex and desire.

Apollo

He is the god of archery, music and dance, truth and prophecy, healing and diseases, the sun and light and poetry, amongst other things. He is the son of Zeus and Leto and the twin brother to Artemis.

Artemis

She is the daughter of Zeus and Leto and the goddess of animals, hunting, wild places and female freedom. One of the most important of the Greek deities. Twin sister to Apollo.

Cerberus

The hound of Hades. A multi-headed dog that guards the gates of the Underworld to prevent the dead from leaving.

Dionysus

He is the god of the grape-harvest, winemaking and wine, of fertility, orchards and fruit, vegetation, insanity, ritual madness, religious ecstasy, festivity and theatre.

Eros

He is the god of everything erotic. Eros also signifies sexual passion in contrast to Philia or any of the eight other types of love.

Eurus

The east wind that blows towards the west.

Hades

He is the god of the Underworld.

Harpy

Agents of punishment who abducted people and tortured them on their way to Tartarus. They were vicious, cruel and violent.

Heracles
He was the greatest of the Greek heroes, the epitome of masculinity and a champion of the Olympian order against chthonic monsters. Also known as Hercules.

Hestia
She is the virgin goddess of the hearth or fireplace, domesticity, the family, the home and the state. She is the firstborn child of the Titans, Cronus and Rhea.

Hymenaeus
One of the Erotes, he is the god of marriage, weddings, receptions and bridal-hymn.

Himeros
One of the Erotes, he is god of pressing desire or impetuous love.

Morpheus
He is the god of sleep and dreams.

Orpheus
A legendary musician, poet, and prophet in ancient Greek religion.

Pothos
One of the Erotes, he is god of longing and desire.

Poseidon
He is the god of the sea, earthquakes, storms, and horses and is considered one of the most bad-tempered, moody and greedy of the Olympian gods.

Silenus
A companion and tutor to the wine god Dionysus.

Tantalus

He is a figure from Greek mythology who was the rich, but wicked, King of Sipylus. For attempting to serve up his own son at a feast with the gods, he was punished by Zeus to forever go thirsty and hungry in Hades, despite standing in a pool of water and within reach of a fruit tree.

Terpsichore

The light-footed muse of dance.

Tyche

She is the goddess of fortune, daughter of Aphrodite and Zeus (or possibly Hermes).

Zeus

He is the god of the sky, thunder and lightning. He is the sixth child of Cronos and Rhea, King and Queen of the Titans and the ruler of all the gods on Mount Olympus.

PLACES

Anatolia
Also known as Asia Minor or most of modern Turkey.

Elysian fields
Also called Elysium, is the final resting place of the souls of those deemed heroic and the virtuous in life.

Ephesus
The most important Greek city in Ionian Asia Minor.

Kyme
The largest of the Aeolian cities. According to legend, it was founded by the Amazon (a mythical tribe of warrior woman), Kyme.

Kyprus
Today know as Cyprus.

Lefkas
Today known as Lefkas, Lefkas or even more colloquially Leucadia (not to be confused with the town in California). It is a Greek island in the Ionian Sea on the west coast of Greece, connected to the mainland by a long causeway and floating bridge and it features spectacular white cliffs on the southern edge that can be seen across the sea for miles.

The mount Olympus
A mountain in the south of the island of Lesvos. Not to be confused with the home of the Gods, Mount Olympus.

Pamphylia
A region in the south of Asia Minor, between Lycia and Cilicia, extending from the Mediterranean to Mount Taurus.

Phlegethon
The river Phlegethon translated from the ancient Greek as "flaming" was one of the five rivers in the infernal regions of the underworld, along with the rivers Styx, Lethe, Cocytus, and Acheron. Plato described it as "a stream of fire, which coils round the earth and flows into the depths of Tartarus".

Styx
The river that forms the boundary between Earth and the Underworld.

Tamassos**
Town in Kyprus near where Bilitis spent the last part of her life, living with Alcaeus and working as a courtesan.

Tartarus
The deep abyss that is used as a dungeon of torment and suffering for the wicked and as the prison for the Titans. Tartarus is the place where souls are judged after death and where the wicked received divine punishment.
In the Iliad (c. 8th century BCE), Zeus describes Tartarus as being "as far beneath Hades as heaven is above earth."

Termessos**
A town in Pamphylia, Asia Minor, in the region where Bilitis grew up.

**In my view, reader, this may well explain why the location of Bilitis's tomb was never authenticated as being near Tamassos. Although she had lived near Tamassos in Cyprus for the latter part of her life, after her death, in accordance with her wishes, her remains were returned to her homeland for internment, to a place near Termessos in Pamphylia.

AFTERWORD BY SAM SKYBORNE

As a wise person once told me …

"Don't believe everything you read!"

This is a work of fiction, based on wild hypotheses at the very best and manipulated conjecture, quoted and misquoted, to suit the story purpose, at the very worst.

A number of sources, fiction and non-fiction, both online and in print were drawn on purely as inspiration for this novel. No copyright infringement is intended.

I have thoroughly enjoyed weaving the tapestry of tales of Jacquie Lyon and Dorothy Rowland, and The Sappho Romance.

IF YOU ENJOYED THIS…

1) Reviews are one of the most important ways for authors to gain visibility and bring their books to the attention of interested readers.

If you've enjoyed this book, please leave a review on your favourite reader platforms. It can be as short as you like and need only take a few minutes but would really mean a lot.

PLEASE NO SPOILERS! It ruins the reading experience for other readers.

Jump to your favourite reader platform now >>

Alternatively, send me feedback here:

mail@SamSkyborne.com

Thank you very much!

---

2) To be notified of future releases and receive writing related news, please

JOIN MY VIP READER CLUB

http://SamSkyborne.com/Signup

This is a spam free zone, used exclusively to keep in touch with VIP readers.

---

3) Turn the page to see other books you might also like…

BY SAM SKYBORNE

LESVOS ISLAND COLLECTION (ROMANCE)

Sealed with a Kiss

The Sappho Romance (*Alt. Hist. spinoff*)

A Change of Heart

Eye of the Storm

Sugar and Spice

Amenah Awakens*

SHORT STORIES

Unbroken* (Steampunk Romance)

Milton Meets Her Match

The Yellow Tandem

Stakeout

Love in the Time of COVID

LESBIAN EROTIC SHORTS (L.E.S) STORY & FILM

Cat Sitting: Lesbian Cat Custody Complications

Saying Sorry: A Queer & Complex Process

* Free to VIP Reader Club.

See back of book for details >>

BY S.M. SKYBORNE

TONI MENDEZ SERIES (LESBIAN PI THRILLER)

RISK: Three Crime-fighting Women Risk All for Love, Lust and Justice

Project ALICE

Starting Over*

———————

Free to VIP Reader Club.
See back of book for details >>

BY JACQUIE LYON

ALT HISTORY FICTION

The Sappho Romance

The Songs of Bilitis (Translated by)

ABOUT

"The sky is merely the start..."

Sam Skyborne is the proud author of a number of award winning novels and currently lives & loves in London (UK) while happily going on writing adventures across the globe ... or as far as the mind will travel.

Connect with Sam:

Join Sam's Reader Club: http://SamSkyborne.com/Signup

Private Facebook Reader Group:
Facebook.com/groups/SamSkyborneGroup

Facebook Page: @SamSkybornePage

Instagram: @SamSkyborne

YouTube: @SamSkyborneAuthor

Sam's online home: SamSkyborne.com

Or drop Sam an email: mail@SamSkyborne.com

ACKNOWLEDGEMENTS

I'd like to thank everyone who has helped and been involved both directly and indirectly with this very special project.

In particular, I'd like to thank my editorial team for your time and effort in helping me bring out the best in this book. Very special mentions go to Alison Crowe, Jude Dempsey, Barbara B, Rob and Adri Heller, Anny Knight, and last but not least Lily Wolf. Without you this book would not have been possible.

To my wonderful ARC team. Your feedback, reviews and promotion of my work is essential to its success. Thank you!

I would also like to say a big thank you to my family and friends (you know who you are), for your endless encouragement and support every step of the way, and for helping me get through the highs and lows of these past few months so I could focus on finishing this book.

I could not have done this without all of you!

A very big commendation and thanks to the very talented Jane Ramsay for creating the fantastic linoprint used in the cover of this novel.

Last but not least, I would like to thank my readers, both new and old. If it was not for you, I wouldn't be doing this.

Printed in Great Britain
by Amazon

19692980R00171